She was complete [D1454878]

Maggie teetered on black stiletto heels, and prayed she'd make it through the evening without falling off them. Her black silk dress itched at the waist. She wondered fleetingly if men were worth all this discomfort.

Then Jack asked her to dance.

"Jack, I haven't danced in years. I don't think I remember how."

"Just hang on, Princess. I'll do all the work. Now, tell me where I'm supposed to put my hand so I won't get slapped."

"Here." She moved his hand to the curve of her waist.

"We look like we should be dancing the minuet. I can't lead very well like this."

"Then, here," she said, and moved closer. The space between them ceased to exist. Jack didn't move. He stood there on the dance floor, stiff as a board, his reaction to her closeness obvious.

"Maggie?" Jack whispered coarsely into her hair.

Maggie looked up. She was eye-level with Jack's entirely-too-sensual mouth. Her throat went dry. Her pulse scrambled. "Yes, Jack?"

"If I hold you this close, every man in this place is going to think we're shacking up."

She thought over her answer carefully. "I can handle that, if you can," she said. "My feet hurt."

"Then take your shoes off."

"It wouldn't be ladylike. The shoes stay on until the dress comes off."

Jack tightened his hold on her. "I'd be careful who I said that to, if I were you."

. . . And loving every minute of it!

FOR THE VERY BEST IN ROMANCE— DENISE LITTLE PRESENTS!

AMBER, SING SOFTLY   (0038, $4.99)
by Joan Elliott Pickart

Astonished to find a wounded gun-slinger on her doorstep, Amber Prescott can't decide whether to take him in or put him out of his misery. Since this lonely frontierswoman can't deny her longing to have a man of her own, who nurses him back to health, while savoring the glorious possibilities of the situation. But what Amber doesn't realize is that this strong, handsome man is full of surprises!

A DEEPER MAGIC   (0039, $4.99)
by Jillian Hunter

From the moment wealthy Margaret Rose and struggling physician Ian MacNeill meet, they are swept away in an adventure that takes them from the haunted land of Aberdeen to a primitive, faraway island—and into a world of danger and irresistible desire. Amid the clash of ancient magic and new science Margaret and Ian find themselves falling helplessly in love.

SWEET AMY JANE   (0050, $4.99)
by Anna Eberhardt

Her horoscope warned her she'd be dealing with the wrong sort of man. And private eye Amy Jane Chadwick was used to dealing with the wrong kind of man, due to her profession. But nothing prepared her for the gorgeously handsome Max, a former professional athlete who is being stalked by an obsessive fan. And from the moment they meet, sparks fly and danger follows!

MORE THAN MAGIC   (0049, $4.99)
by Olga Bicos

This classic romance is a thrilling tale of two adventurers who set out for the wilds of the Arizona territory in the year 1878. Seeking treasure, an archaeologist and an astronomer find the greatest prize of all—love.

GLASS SLIPPERS

NANCY BERLAND

PINNACLE BOOKS
KENSINGTON PUBLISHING CORP.

PINNACLE BOOKS are published by

Kensington Publishing Corp.
850 Third Avenue
New York, NY 10022

Pinnacle and the P logo Reg. U.S. Pat. & TM Off.

First Printing: April, 1996
10 9 8 7 6 5 4 3 2 1

Printed in the United States of America

For Mike—

Remembering the terrific things you did for combat boots, although, I admit, I wasn't looking at your feet. Happy 25th Anniversary!

One

"If that's the same girl in both pictures, I'll buy lunch."

"Great. I skipped breakfast, and I'm broke."

"How can you be so sure you're right?"

"In both pictures the girl has that mole right there on her cheek."

"And the same dimples."

The morning break-time chitchat of the three other seamstresses at Miss Caroline's Couturier niggled at Maggie Kincaid's concentration. She pressed her thumb and forefinger to the strained muscles around her eyes, then anchored the slippery satin debutante gown on her Singer and gave her attention license to stray.

Across the room on the break couch the opened newspaper still obscured the faces of Kayla, Desiree, and Juliana. By Maggie's watch the three had frittered away almost an hour. They were right in the middle of August, the month when all of Austin's debutante parties were held. Didn't the girls realize there were party dresses to sew, bodices to bead, alterations to make? Or didn't they care?

Maggie wondered if she was cursed or blessed by the work ethic that kept her at her machine.

Lord knows the aroma of freshly brewed coffee had her longing for a cup. But the gown she was working on was due for an afternoon fitting. Refocusing her attention on the slippery ivory satin before her, she ignored her desire for creature comforts, and only listened as the debate over two pictures continued.

Kayla spoke from behind the newspaper with her usual voice of authority. "I still say it's not the same girl. Look at her 'before' picture. My word, she's as plain as . . ."

The newsprint rustled. The sentence went unfinished. Maggie glanced up and found Kayla, Desiree, and Juliana staring at her over the top of the lowered newspaper.

"As plain as what?" Maggie asked them suspiciously.

Kayla cleared her throat and ducked behind the newspaper. "A brown paper bag."

Or me, Maggie thought in a flash of resentment. But not even Kayla, who frequently made cutting remarks about Maggie that were as sharp as her dressmaker's shears, possessed the nerve to voice the observation out loud.

Maggie wouldn't give Kayla the satisfaction of knowing she'd scored a hit with her latest jab. Ignoring the unspoken insult, she pressed the reverse feed button on her Singer, then released it. Her machine had stitched ball gowns for eight years of Austin's debutantes; it responded to her touch as if it were a lover. With a whir of well-oiled gears, she executed a tidy end knot. Her feeling of accomplishment was salve for the hurt. She could mark off another task on her list for the day. This newest drape of fabric would give an artful flourish to her best design to date.

Maggie might be plain, but the gowns she designed and sewed so expertly had earned the respect of Miss Caroline and the Couturier's affluent clients. For the resulting praise her skill brought her, though, Maggie had to endure the resentful barbs of the other seamstresses. Kayla was the ringleader, the queen of put-downs.

Maggie kept telling herself that one day she would marshall enough nerve to tell them exactly what she thought of their antics. Kayla, Desiree, and Juliana could give up their free evenings to study design at night school, as she had done. If they did, they, too, could improve their skills so that clients would ask for them.

The injustice of their taunts, coupled with Kayla's latest insinuation about Maggie's plainness, had her more determined to succeed than ever. She would get that degree and hang up her own designer's shingle one day. She only wished she could do it sooner.

Regardless of her goals and aspirations, Maggie couldn't pretend away the deeply felt hurt at her continuing isolation at Miss Caroline's. She couldn't help wondering what was wrong with her to make the others continually exclude her. Just once, she wished Kayla, Desiree, and Juliana would invite her along on one of their group outings. Not that she would agree to go. But being asked would give her the feeling of belonging she had missed since leaving home and her sisters, whom she was so close to.

"In the 'after' picture, that girl looks like a movie star," Desiree said. She lowered the newspaper and gazed at the picture wistfully.

"Think about it," Kayla said with a gleam in her eyes that almost matched the rich sheen of her hair. "If Beauty Pix can make someone that plain look that good, imagine what they could do for us."

Maggie didn't need to look in the mirror to know she defined *plain*. In her spare time, she taught swim lessons three days a week to pre-schoolers at the Westwood Country Club. As a result, her chlorine-damaged hair was the color of walnut dulled by years of yellowed furniture wax. Then there was her wide forehead. A sign of intelligence, her mother assured her. Even if it was, it merely emphasized Maggie's light eyebrows and fair skin. She was the kind of woman men could walk by and not notice, unless her cocker-spaniel eyes caught their attention.

That was a situation she had recently decided to remedy. Last weekend, on her twenty-ninth birthday, one by one, the women in Maggie's family had called her from their far-flung residences across the country. Her older and younger sisters, both married and mothers by now; her mother, even her Aunt Barbara in Charleston, South Carolina—all of them had expressed concern over Maggie's single status. Her mother had even prevailed upon Maggie to consider a relationship, if not marriage. Maggie had hung up with her head spinning. Her very proper, very Catholic mother had just told her she wouldn't disapprove if Maggie shacked up with a guy.

That evening Maggie had sipped a rare margarita with Jack, her downstairs neighbor, before retreating to her apartment. Her family's words haunted her as she slipped into her bed alone. They were right. If Maggie was ever to have those precious children she longed to nurture, she needed to meet and marry the man of her dreams.

But how, when she blended into the fabric of life like a piece of unbleached muslin?

An idea kindled in Maggie's mind, one that set her heart to fluttering, her hopes soaring as high as the recent bolt price of hand-beaded silk. What if she made an appointment for a make over at that place in the newspaper? What if she told their makeup artists and hair designers to pull out all the stops? Could they work magic on her dowdy hair and unmemorable features so she could make men's heads turn? Could she inspire men to notice her? To send her bouquets of roses for no particular reason except to see her smile? Get them to think in terms of marriage? Children?

Maggie could almost hear the nuns from her schooldays clucking at her with disapproving tongues. Vanity they'd say. She would remind them that her attack of vanity was inspired by her yearning to bear children. Even nuns would approve of that.

* * *

Kayla pitched the newspaper on the coffee table. The most vocal of Miss Caroline's seamstresses paced the cramped alcove they used as a lunch room. Kayla paused, took a sip from her foam coffee cup and stared straight at Maggie as if studying her features intently.

Maggie pretended not to notice, but she felt Kayla's disapproving scrutiny pass over her. The sudden attention had Maggie wondering if she should throw up a shield to deflect the next attack.

"Why don't we call Beauty Pix," Kayla said, snapping her attention back to her two ardent followers, "and make appointments for all of us?"

All of us? Maggie's hands stilled on the gown. She held her breath, sure she had misunderstood the comment tossed out by the undisputed social leader at Miss Caroline's. But Kayla was smiling at her as if she understood the hope for a miracle that still percolated in Maggie's mind.

Desiree, who, like Maggie, had been recruited from local high school sewing classes, popped up from the couch. "That's a great idea!" She scooted around the cutting table to the production calendar on the work room's back wall.

Frowning, she skimmed her finger over the rest of August's calendar. "Aha!" She tapped the square of what looked like a lightly scheduled day in an otherwise packed month of consultations, fittings and deliveries. "Miss Caroline's coming in for an hour next Monday. Then she's driving to San Antonio for a bridal fair. She'd never know if we took a long lunch."

Juliana's Oriental eyes turned dreamy, her expression wistful. Chin propped in one hand, she stared out the side window of the Victorian Queen Anne house in Austin's chic West End.

Maggie followed the direction of her gaze. Outside, the unrelenting August sun had live oak leaves turning yellow and periwinkles losing their wink.

"I got a letter from Jeff yesterday," Juliana announced. "His ship sets sail for the Mediterranean next week. He wants me to send him a picture. He hinted he might ask me to marry him when they dock in San Diego in a couple of months. Maybe, if he had that picture, he wouldn't forget me when he was at liberty in all those exotic places."

"With all those exotic women," Desiree added.

"That does it!" Kayla reached over the back of the couch to the thread supply cabinet for the telephone. "We're going. All of us. And nobody chickens out."

The thrill of being included, for the first time, in one of the girls' frequent outings, had Maggie's lips lifting in a smile. She could already picture the four of them sitting having their makeup done—helping each other with garment and accessory selections from the extensive wardrobe she had heard that Beauty Pix maintained for its customers. Jack, her downstairs neighbor and resident cynic, would never believe it.

Still, while Kayla phoned Beauty Pix, Maggie considered their plan. Leaving the shop unattended, for at least two hours, violated one of Miss Caroline's hard and fast rules. If she found out, she would rant and rave and threaten to fire them all. Yet Maggie knew Miss Caroline couldn't afford to lose all her experienced seamstresses and designers. Not now, in the midst of Austin's annual debutante season.

Maggie's sense of justice stirred, demanding equal consideration. Didn't the haughty Miss Caroline deserve the deception? Always stretching the workday without paying overtime? Never giving compensatory time off? Presenting Maggie's designs as her own with the couturier's best customers?

Two wrongs don't make a right, her well-schooled conscience recited. Maggie thought of an alternative. Maybe one of them could find someone to answer the phone during their make over appointments. Then everyone would be happy.

"Hello? Beauty Pix? I'd like to make an appointment for a week from Monday. During the lunch hour." Kayla covered the mouthpiece and whispered, "She's getting her appointment book. Keep your fingers crossed she's got time for all of us at once."

Maggie lifted a vague hand to her thick, mousy hair and fingered the dry, brittle ends. She wore the stubborn mass pulled back and tied at the base of her neck so it wouldn't get in her face when she sewed. Problem hair, her mother had called it. As straight and coarse as a horse's tail.

Could the Beauty Pix stylists temper its stubborn qualities? Could they make it wave and shine like the models' hair on television shampoo commercials?

"Eleven-thirty? Terrific. No, no, not just me. This is a group project. A discount? Great!" Kayla covered the mouthpiece again. "Because we're going in together, she's giving us fifty percent off our sitting fees."

"I wonder how much the pictures will cost?" Desiree said, twining her finger in her silky, blond hair and frowning.

"Lots, I hear," Juliana provided. "But it'll be worth it."

Kayla waved her hand to quiet them. "How many?" She beamed a smile around the work room. "There'll be three of us."

Maggie lifted a finger to correct Kayla. "Actually, there'll be four."

Kayla frowned and held up one finger each time she recited a name. "Desiree, Juliana, me. I count three."

Desiree lowered her gaze. Juliana looked to Maggie, then Kayla. "But what about Maggie?"

Kayla gave Maggie a thousand-watt smile. "Someone has to sit on the phones. You won't mind, will you, dear?"

Jack Lewis extracted a *Photography* magazine and a handful of bills from his mailbox. The outside door to his apartment building in the least desirable section of Austin's West End whipped open and whacked him in the butt.

"What the . . . ?"

His second-floor neighbor, Maggie Kincaid, swept past him in a blast of breath-robbing August heat. She stomped up the stairs. No "Hello, how are you?" No "Sorry for the blow to the buns." What the hell? "Hey, Margaret, hold up."

Without turning to look at him, Maggie froze on the stairs. Her spine stiffened straight as a board. When she spoke, her voice, normally sweet and friendly, sounded as brittle as the scorched Johnson grass outside. "How many times do I have to tell you? My name's Maggie. You can call me Mag. Mags. Maggie. But don't *ever* call me Margaret."

"Ex-cuse me, *Maggie,*" Jack shot back, in no mood for her rare outburst. He had just finished a tricky outdoor ad shoot with a temperamental model. She was ticked off royally because the award-winning photographer originally scheduled for the job had canceled at the last minute. To make matters worse, the model was so skinny she didn't fill out the designer jeans the client had sent over for the shoot. Jack had to sit in the shade, swatting flies and polishing his lenses while they waited for a size three to be delivered. His shirt was still plastered to his back. His temper bore a hair trigger Maggie had just tripped.

Mild-mannered Maggie, of all people. He lounged against the door frame of his apartment while Maggie stomped up the stairs. With each step she kicked up a puff of dust in the thin, commercial-grade carpet. Jack gave his quirky, designer friend's retreating backside his photographer's brutally frank assessment.

Laura Ashley in combat boots. That's what Maggie looked like since she'd taken to wearing the

trendy Doc Martens boots. Jack didn't care if they
were favored by the coeds at the University of
Texas where Maggie took night courses toward
her master's. They squelched any desire a guy had
rolling around in his libido. Especially when worn
with Maggie's drop-waisted dresses that neutral-
ized any curves her body might possess. The boots
and baggy dresses made Maggie as visually appeal-
ing as a sack of potatoes.

Still, occasionally Jack noticed a subtle shifting
of fabric over her chest, and he realized she actually had breasts there. Once, when she must
have forgotten her slip, the sun had outlined the
graceful shape of her legs through a thin cotton
skirt.

During these times he saw the spark of potential in Mags. And thought about it. If she ditched
the boots, hiked her hem a foot, cinched her
dresses at the waist, she might not spend so many
nights alone in that perfectly ordered apartment
of hers.

Which reminded him why he wanted to talk to
her. "Maggie, wait up."

"I'm in no mood for conversation," she snapped
from the top of the stairs.

Jack watched her wriggle her key into the lock.
Even at a distance, he could see the rare hot flush
on her cheeks, the tight pursing of her lips, the
heaving of breasts of indeterminate size and shape.
With those tight-to-the-neck, pristine blouses of
starched cotton she wore, even in the dregs of summer, she reminded him of the nuns she spoke of
so affectionately.

She had spent years under their watchful eyes and those of the priests, while her mother served as a parish secretary. It had done a number on Maggie. Hell, she might as well have taken a vow of chastity. Her cat, Homer, showed more skin than she did. And the rascal had a more active social life, for sure.

Then Jack realized something strange. For the first time in months, Maggie was home early. Five-thirty. And in a rotten mood. Something must have happened at work.

He took the carpeted steps two at a time and palmed her door open as it was about to close in his face. He followed Maggie into her homey apartment that smelled of furniture wax and a potpourri of cleansers. Homer clumped off his perch on the back of the Early American couch and threaded his feline tabby body between Jack's legs.

"By all means, come in," Maggie grumbled on her way to the kitchen. "Make yourself at home, why don't you? Let good old Maggie get you a drink."

"What's the matter? Did one of those bowheads you sew for demand you remake her dress?"

"No, and why must you be so condescending? Just because the women I sew for have money doesn't mean they're not nice. Actually, they treat me a lot better than other people I know."

She yanked open her cupboard and drummed her fingers on the immaculate formica counter. "Tea or coffee? Decaffeinated or regular?"

"My, aren't we testy today. Make it a beer."

"I don't have beer."

"Why?"

"Because I don't drink it. It makes me burp."

"No, I mean *why* are you spitting sewing needles in my face?"

"Your imagination is working overtime." She opened the cabinet under her sink, fetched the window cleaner and a disposable polishing rag and disappeared around the corner.

Jack followed her into the living room where she spritzed the already-gleaming, sliding glass door that led to the balcony. Her body jerked rhythmically as she buffed the hell out of a teeny-weeny smudge where Homer had probably pressed his button nose.

In the year Jack had lived in the apartment building, he'd never seen Maggie so agitated. A real pleaser, she took things too easily, let people walk over her. Until now he'd thought her incapable of getting pissed off about something. Maybe with his constant goading he'd accomplished the impossible—instilled in her the makings of a backbone.

"Ah, come on, Maggie," he said with a chuckle, "tell me what happened."

She arched one brow and shot him a haughty look over her shoulder. "It isn't a laughing matter."

"So I gather. Did Miss Caroline take credit for one of your designs again?"

"No."

"Did your machine break down? Did you run a needle through your finger?"

She whirled around, lips pursed, window cleaner trigger gun aimed at his face. "I'll give you five seconds to get out."

"Fine." He threw up his hands. "You want to be miserable all by yourself? Be my guest." He scooped the fat, orange cat into his arms. "When you feel like being civil, you know where to find us. Homer and I'll be watching the Cowboys slaughter the Redskins."

Maggie's shoulders sagged. She uttered an un-Maggie-like sigh. One side of her mouth lifted in a weak attempt to smile. "I'm sorry, Jack."

"For what?"

"For being ugly. You were only trying to be nice, I suppose."

The despondent tone of Maggie's voice pricked Jack's jaded heart. "Ah, Margaret, you could never be ugly."

She slanted him an icy look. "Why must you insist on calling me Margaret?"

"Jesus, Maggie, what is it? The heat? You never complained before."

"I'm complaining now."

"Okay, okay. From now on, I won't call you Margaret." He stroked his hand over Homer's silky fur and thought for a moment. He hated the name Maggie. By the time Jack was two, his mother had tired of the mommy routine. That's when she had dumped him on his dad and returned to her pampered, Highland Park Dallas lifestyle. One of the string of women who had flitted in and out of the Tulsa apartment Jack and his dad shared was a woman named Maggie.

Ah, yes, Jack remembered her well. Maggie with the bright shiny nails. When his dad wasn't looking, she used to dig them into Jack's tender flesh until the skin broke, and he bled. Fortunately, like all the others, she'd decided sleeping with Jack's dad wasn't worth taking care of little Jack, the Brat.

"You don't like the name Margaret? Okay, I'll call you Princess," he announced. He lifted Homer in both hands so they stood, man to cat, face to face. "You think that'll suit Her Highness?"

Sparks fairly flew from Maggie's huge brown eyes. Her finger twitched on the window polish spritzer.

Give me a shot, Jack wanted to yell. *Show me you've got some backbone beneath all that sweetness.*

But Maggie merely lifted her chin and said between gritted teeth, "You won't mind if Her Highness doesn't walk you to the door?"

"I wasn't quite ready to leave," he taunted her.

"You want to bet?"

"Okay, have it your way." Jack tucked Homer under his arm and turned on his heel, hoping for an angry spritz but getting none. "I'll ask somebody else over for dinner."

"Dinner? That's what you wanted to talk about?"

Jack paused in the doorway, letting the subtle invitation sink in before he clarified himself. "Well, it'll be dinner if you throw together some of those great sub sandwiches. I'll furnish the beer and the chips. And tea for Her Highness," he told Homer.

"Your generosity is exceeded only by your impeccable manners and gentlemanly deportment."

Jack flashed his most charming grin. "Are you coming, or aren't you?"

Something flickered in Maggie's eyes—a hunger for companionship, he thought—that seasoned Jack's gut with guilt. That, coupled with the fact that she'd come home early from that sweat box of sequins and silk, all churned up about something, raised the protective hackles on Jack's back. What could possibly have transpired in the carefully ordered life of his rock-steady neighbor to put that pitiful look in her eyes?

She averted her gaze. "I'll need a few minutes to freshen up."

Jack took her chin in his hand. When she lifted her gaze, he saw that her eyes had misted over. Aw, hell. He hadn't meant to make her cry. He was a sucker for a woman when she turned the faucet on. "Hey, Maggie, I was only kidding about the subs. We can order pizza in."

Her lower lip trembled. Yet she straightened her shoulders and appeared to stuff whatever troubled her into some mental box. "I'd appreciate that."

Jack had the sudden urge to pull Maggie into his arms and give her a brotherly hug. Instead, he put a hand on the curve of her shoulder and gave her a light, massaging squeeze.

Her shoulder felt like a sock crammed full of film canisters. "No wonder you're testy. You're got kinks in your shoulders as big as golf balls." He turned her around and dug massaging thumbs into tensed back muscles. "There, how does that feel?"

Maggie stiffened beneath his touch. Jack was

almost sure she had also stopped breathing. If he hadn't known better, he'd have guessed that no man had ever come close enough to do what he was doing. Yet he distinctly remembered Maggie telling him one night when she got tipsy over a margarita that there had been one man in her life. A jerk named Melvin. The delivery man had pursued her unmercifully until he'd worn down her resistance and claimed her virginity.

One day, after confessing her sins of the flesh to the parish priest and saying a rosary of Hail Marys, Maggie walked into the boutique next door to the Couturier. There she found Melvin boy driving himself into the shop's panting owner. For once Maggie's boss showed some sensitivity. She told the delivery folks if Melvin ever darkened her door again, she would personally slash his truck's tires.

Maggie whirled around, her eyes wide, her fingers pressed to her lips. She swallowed thickly. "You'd—uh—better hurry up if you don't want to miss the kickoff," she advised and bumped her slender backside into the foyer wall.

Two

The Cowboys' quarterback hauled off and sent the football sailing down the sideline. The wide receiver leaped into the air and curled his fingers about the pigskin. Both of his feet came down in the end zone with one second to spare in the last quarter.

Jack howled, knocking Homer off his lap. The orange tabby landed on his feet, lifted his chin haughtily, then headed for Jack's bedroom, tail twitching.

Maggie wiped the residue of pepperoni pizza from her mouth delicately, precisely with a paper napkin. "Lucky catch."

"That'll be a buck, which brings your total debt to . . ."

"Five dollars. I'll have to owe you."

"I keep telling you, Princess, you're rooting for the wrong team."

"Maybe that's the problem," she grumbled and, gathering up their plates, stalked off toward the kitchen.

Jack grabbed his beer can. Stepping around the month's stack of newspapers, he followed her.

Beneath her refined manners and quiet demeanor Maggie had been simmering all evening. Now the pot of her patience was finally boiling over. Jack propped his hips against the counter and watched her slam cabinets and scrub counters viciously. She washed silverware until it squeaked, while the story of what had transpired that morning at Miss Caroline's spewed out.

Those damned seamstresses! When would Maggie get her fill of their condescending attitudes and tell them to go suck an egg? Jack wished he could wrap his hands around the necks of the inconsiderate bitches for her.

"The trouble with you is you sit there and take it."

"What was I supposed to say? Excuse me, girls? Silly me. I made the mistake of assuming you were including me in your plans, for a change? Stick it and answer the phones yourselves?"

"That'd do for starters."

"You know me better than that. Jack, this kitchen is a pig sty."

"You're changing the subject."

"There's nothing more to say," she pointed out with a dismissive lift of her shoulder. "Even if they asked me now, I wouldn't want to go with them." She pulled the door to the dishwasher down and frowned. "How long since you've run this thing?"

"I don't know. A week maybe."

"What are you waiting for? The health inspector?"

Accustomed to her lectures about his lack of concern for such mundane things as housekeeping when he had film to process and prints to make, Jack ignored her sarcastic comment. "For once I'd like to see you stand up for yourself."

"I try, Jack. Honestly I do. This morning I was so furious I thought, okay, this is it. I'm going to tell them what I think of their little plan. But when I opened my mouth to speak, I was still so taken back by Kayla's audacity, instead of telling them to stick it, I found myself saying I'd stick around and answer the phones."

"The Sisters of Mercy strike again. Until you put some starch in your resolve, Princess, people are going to keep taking advantage of you."

"Forget I told you anything. I'll find a way to deal with it in my own way." She opened the refrigerator to stow away the leftover pizza. "There's something disgusting growing in here. It's black and fuzzy."

Jack peered around her shoulder. "Oh, that. It's a tomato. I think."

"Every tomato I've ever see was red or green. This one's black. And it looks like it needs a shave."

"You should have seen the one I threw away last month."

"Bring the garbage can over here," Maggie muttered on a sigh.

"Will you stop it!" Taking her arm, Jack pulled Maggie away from the refrigerator and closed the door. "I didn't ask you down to clean my kitchen."

"But—"

"Maybe what happened to you at work today is your fault. Maybe you ask to be used."

"You make me sound like a masochist."

"If the shoe fits . . ." He folded his arms over his chest. "Case in point. If I hadn't stopped you, you would have cleaned out my refrigerator."

"I don't mind cleaning refrigerators. And I've never seen one that needed it more."

"Do you mind being stuck answering phones while the sisters of swing run out to do something fun and exciting? Something they should have included you in?"

"I don't see how one has anything to do with the other."

"Come on, Maggie. Admit it. You let people treat you like a doormat. We've got to put a stop to that." He looped a brotherly arm around her shoulders and guided her back into his living room. "For starters, I know a way you can get back at those sanctimonious bitches at work."

She slanted him a withering glance. "Watch your language."

"Maybe if you used the vernacular occasionally you could paint people as they are, not as you prefer to see them."

"They aren't *bitches*," she responded testily. "They're just inconsiderate."

He gestured her to the couch and settled back in his green plaid recliner. "Then let's discuss how you can get your *just inconsiderate* acquaintances to treat you better."

"What I want is common courtesy. Respect for the extra hours I put in at work and at school. And is it too much to expect an occasional 'Hey, Maggie, how about joining us for a cup of coffee or a movie?' "

"Sometimes you have to demand respect."

"I thought you were supposed to earn it."

Ignoring Maggie's well-ordered logic, Jack leaned forward, propping his elbows on his knees. "You're due some vacation time, aren't you?"

"A week."

"So, take it beginning a week from Monday. Don't tell those sweethearts you won't be there. Ask the boss lady to keep your vacation a secret. Day comes for the gals to go to Beauty Pix—" He spread his arms wide. "—Ta da! You're gone. I guarantee after they have to reschedule their precious appointments they'll think twice before treating you like their personal servant again."

"It would be incredibly rude of me to intentionally sabotage their outing."

"Yeah." Jack grinned. "Poetic justice, don't you think?"

"Blame it on the Sisters of Mercy, but I can't do it. Besides, where would I go all week?"

"Weren't you planning to drive out to see your sister in Arizona?"

"I was. She and her husband wanted me to take care of the kids while they got away for a few days, but I had to buy a new refrigerator last month. Money's a bit too tight."

If Maggie hadn't been so down, Jack would have pointed out that her sister should be the one paying for the gas. Instead, he said, "I could loan you twenty, thirty bucks."

"Which might get me to the Texas border."

"What's your sister like anyway?" Jack asked out of curiosity.

"Which one?"

"You have two?"

"An older sister in D.C. and a younger one in Phoenix."

"So what are they both like?"

Maggie appeared to think for a minute, glancing down into her lap, where her thumbs twiddled nervous circles around one another. "I guess I can tell you this. It pretty well describes my sisters, as other people saw them anyway."

"Tell me what?"

"When I went to my tenth-year high-school reunion last year, I learned the nuns had nicknames for us."

"You and your sisters?"

"Yes."

"This ought to be good. What were they?"

"Sheridan, the older one? She's your age, thirty-three." Frowning, she shook her head in distinct disapproval. "They called her Sister Slut. Can you believe it?"

"Obviously you didn't take after her," Jack commented dryly. "I don't suppose you have a picture of her."

Maggie shot him a murderous glance. "Men!"

Jack gave an innocent shrug. "What did they call your younger sister?"

"Alyssa was a cheerleader. She has a wonderful voice and performed in all the school musicals. They called her Sister Star."

"And she probably tap danced."

"How did you know?" Maggie asked with a straight face.

"Just a lucky guess. What did the nuns call you?"

Maggie made a face. "Sister Sweet."

"I'm surprised they didn't call you Sister Saint. Or Sister Sucker."

"So I enjoy doing things for people. What's wrong with that?"

"You get stepped on, that's what. Tell me something. How did you all turn out so different?"

Maggie shrugged. "Maybe sibling order in the family. And, too, we were all adopted."

"Well, even if you can't afford to drive out to see Sister Star, surely you could find something to do here on your time off. Take in a free concert, go to the zoo. Hit the Neiman-Marcus outlet to finger fabrics, get ideas."

"I guess I could clean my miniblinds." Maggie glanced around the room and sighed. "And yours."

"Maggie, my girl, you've got to get a life. Think. What else could you do with a week off?"

"I do have that gift certificate my Aunt Barbara sent me for Christmas."

"A certificate for what?"

"Two free nights at a hotel."

"Here in town?"

Maggie nodded. "The one that just opened on Town Lake a couple months ago. The Grand Perimeter."

Jack whistled. "That's not a hotel. It's a palace. Five star. First class all the way. I spent the afternoon wandering around there shortly after it opened."

"What would a person like me do in a place like that?"

"Lie around the pool. Flirt with the lifeguard. Pick up rich guys in the bar."

Maggie rolled her eyes. "Right." But a telltale flush spread over her cheeks, a tip to Jack that the desire to meet men probably wasn't as foreign to Maggie as she pretended.

"As long as we're giving your attitude a make over, I've got to tell you, Princess. That's something else you need to work on."

"What?" she asked cautiously.

"Learning how to get a guy to give you a second look. You know, if you'd put on a little makeup, do something with your hair, ditch those ugly boots, make some new clothes—something besides those tent things you wear—you'd be downright . . . attractive."

"Attractive," she repeated flatly. "Your choice of adjectives is so flattering I'm positively overwhelmed."

"I didn't mean . . ."

She held up her hand. "Don't patronize me, Jack. I know very well in my current state if a man decided he was interested in me, he'd be attracted to my mind, not . . . the rest of me. But don't worry. I intend to do something about that."

At that last declaration of Maggie's, Jack almost fell out of his chair. He tried not to look surprised, or pleased, afraid she might change her mind about trying to fix herself up a little. "Good.

Go on. Call the hotel. Make your reservation for a week from Monday."

"I can't."

"You want to give me one good reason why not?"

"Disappointing the girls might be a good way to get revenge, but that's not for me. Besides, you wouldn't be the one who'd have to endure their dirty looks and cutting remarks when you got back."

"Okay, forget getting even. Just be good to yourself, for a change. Pack up and go to the hotel for a weekend of R and R."

She tilted her head. The angle showed off high, regal cheekbones that hinted at Indian heritage somewhere in Maggie's genetic background. "What would I do with Homer?"

"Leave him with me."

Homer sauntered around the corner, the tip of his tail twitching, and shot Jack a go-to-hell look.

"I don't know, Jack. Homer doesn't like it when I'm gone."

"Screw Homer." Jack leaned back in his recliner and rested his head on folded arms. "Admit it. You want to go."

The hint of a smile played on her lips. "The certificate expires in a month. I would hate to see it go to waste."

"That's my girl!"

"I have an idea," she offered shyly. "You could come down and visit me. Use the swimming pool, maybe. And eat. It wouldn't cost you anything. The certificate includes three meals for two in the hotel. According to the brochure, the Grand Perimeter has three restaurants, one with a nightclub."

Meals for two, huh? Why that crafty Aunt Barbara! Jack grinned, figuring he and Maggie's aunt shared the desire to see his sweet, accommodating neighbor break out of her impossibly dull mold and live a little. "I just might take you up on your offer, Princess."

"That is, if you don't have a date," she tacked on awkwardly and lowered her gaze.

Jack would make sure he didn't have plans so he could help Maggie enjoy her adventure. Besides, maybe he could give her a few tips on meeting guys. "I'll make sure I don't have a date."

Somewhere in the apartment, Jack's phone rang. He scrambled out of the recliner and found the phone under the couch on the fourth ring. "Lewis Commercial Photography. Jack speaking."

Maggie fluttered her hand and disappeared into the kitchen. The female voice on the line purred into Jack's ears. Her words faded as he imagined how Maggie would look in a swimsuit. *Maggie* didn't starve herself like the models he photographed. She swam regularly. *She* would have long, lanky legs—he'd caught a hint of them occasionally, despite Maggie's nun-like clothing. Nicely contoured hips, real breasts—soft, not metal cones like those silicone jobs so many of the models had.

Too long, he decided with a mind-clearing shake of his head. He focused on the none-too-subtle invitation extended to him carried by the miracle of fiber optics. When Laura Ashley in combat boots inspired his libido, he'd been working too long, too hard and staying away from the ladies too much.

Three

Maggie endured the humiliation of watching the phones while Kayla, Desiree, and Juliana fulfilled their fantasies of becoming glamorous at Beauty Pix.

Determined not to dwell on depressing thoughts, though, Maggie put her extended lunch hour to good use. She sketched an elegant evening gown with an Oriental neckline and clinging lines.

Alone in the shop for once, she stood before the three-way mirror in the spacious bridal dressing room with the rose-colored carpet. She draped an end bolt remnant of beaded chiffon over her body to test its suitability for her design.

The fabric provided an interesting emphasis to her breasts. It draped alluringly over her hips and thighs. The brilliant emerald green gown drifting through her mind would make some lucky lady the glittering center of attention.

If Maggie could talk Miss Caroline out of the remnant.

Maggie carefully refolded the fabric and tucked it away in an empty drawer. The job shouldn't be too difficult. Miss Caroline wouldn't use such end bolt goods in the gowns for her affluent clients. They usually contained fabric flaws. However, Maggie had checked the piece three times and found only a tiny snag. She could camouflage the flaw with artful sewing.

She figured if she didn't have to admit what she wanted to do with the fabric, she could barter overtime for the remnant. That morning Austin's most harebrained social maven had phoned in a panic. She had overlooked, on her debutante daughter's social schedule, a Sunday brunch in only two weeks at one of the posh estates on Scenic Drive overlooking Lake Austin.

Maggie knew if she sewed through the coming Labor Day weekend, the maven's daughter could have the original dress in floating organza that she wanted for the occasion. Tomorrow, when Miss Caroline returned, Maggie would offer to sacrifice her weekend to create a masterpiece for a spoiled socialite in exchange for the green, beaded remnant. She could then transform the fabric into the dress of her dreams, just as soon as she could find the time.

Maggie's stomach fluttered with excitement. That green gown could launch her career as a designer. At her Aunt Barbara's insistence, Maggie had recently sent her some of her sketches. Barbara, a sales representative for a clothing showroom in Atlanta, had raved about the designs. She had assured Maggie she could sell the finished garments to any number of boutiques in her South Carolina territory.

Her Aunt Barbara's encouragement was what

Maggie desperately needed. In addition to the much-appreciated vote of confidence, her aunt would provide her with the means to finance the other night courses in fashion design required for Maggie's advanced degree at the University of Texas. Her swim lesson money dried up each year at summer's end.

One day, with her degree nailed to the wall of her own design studio, Maggie would openly solicit boutique business with garments bearing the Maggie Kincaid Designer Original label.

The thought that she was taking steps toward succeeding as a legitimate designer bolstered her confidence as she took the Metro bus over the river to her weekend at the Grand Perimeter. At the Riverside Drive stop, she disembarked and reached into her tote bag for a tissue. Even at five-thirty in the evening, the scorching heat of a ninety-five degree day had perspiration popping out on her forehead.

Maggie took her time walking the two blocks north to Town Lake. There the Grand Perimeter snuggled up to the south shore. When she caught sight of the hotel's marble and glass facade gleaming against the backdrop of glistening water, Maggie couldn't breathe. She projected herself into her dream. Many of the women who frequented this grandest of Austin's many fine hotels were probably the type who didn't buy their clothing off the rack. If she worked hard, saved her money and established herself, those same women might someday clamor to buy her designer originals.

Thinking how that would shock her sister seamstresses and Miss Caroline, Maggie headed for the hotel entrance with a smile.

She had barely set foot on the sidewalk when a doorman in a burgundy and gold uniform hastened to help her with her bag. The tapestry tote contained little more than a library book on the history of design and one of the serviceable one-piece swimsuits she wore to teach. If she carried the bag herself, she could save what Jack had told her was a customary doorman's tip.

"I can manage by myself, thank you," she said politely and wandered through the revolving door into the spacious lobby.

The rush of bubbling fountains, the cry of un-caged birds soaring overhead in a domed atrium had her mouth gaping open. Broad-leafed plants, lush and emerald green, filtered the light from the beveled glass canopy dome overhead. The air smelled of freshly cut flowers and expensive Parisian perfume. From an elevated platform of cream-colored marble, a Victorian vision dressed in ecru tulle and lace plucked the tune, "New York, New York," on an ornate, gilded harp.

Maggie's wandering path through the lobby ended abruptly when she bumped into a marble registration desk. She set her tote on the Oriental carpet and wondered if she looked as out of place as she felt.

The clerk, an attractive man in his late twenties, gave her a cultured smile. "Welcome to the Grand Perimeter, Miss . . . ?"

"Kincaid. Maggie Kincaid. I have a reservation."

The clerk's nimble fingers flew over a computer keyboard. "Is this your first stay at the Grand Perimeter, Miss Kincaid?"

She nodded, not admitting that the only other hotel she had ever stayed in was a Motel 6. She extracted the gift certificate from her bag and handed it to the clerk, feeling as if she would be more at home cleaning a room at the opulent hotel than checking into one.

She was admiring the expertly matched seams of the draperies on the lobby's front windows when bells reminiscent of High Mass on a holy day chimed. Maggie glanced around and saw hotel employees scurrying to the registration desk. Each drew a long-stemmed red rose from a crystal vase on the marble counter.

"Is some celebrity checking in?" she couldn't help asking the smiling clerk.

"I guess you could say that."

"Can you tell me who it is?" she whispered, so the employees crowding behind her wouldn't hear.

"I'd be glad to."

"Who is it then?"

"You, Miss Kincaid."

"Me?"

"If you'll turn around . . ." he said with a tilt of his head and a gesture of his hand ". . . our manager wishes to greet you personally."

Feeling as if she'd walked into a dream, Maggie dared a glance over her shoulder. Her knees all but buckled. Her lungs ceased working. She pressed a hand to her chest and grabbed the registration counter for support.

Like footmen for the royalty of England, all those hotel employees—at least two dozen of them—stood in two precise lines that converged at a gleaming ice sculpture in the shape of the hotel. Each wore the hotel's richly appointed burgundy and gold uniform. Each held a velvety American Beauty rose. Each smiled at her.

Lights flashed. Voices murmured. The reservations clerk passed a white card down one line of employees while the harpist executed a hand-blurring fanfare.

The hairs on Maggie's arms stood up. She felt all eyes in the hotel's lobby turn her way. She remembered Jack encouraging her to wear something besides her dress and boots when she checked in. She had told him no one would notice her anyway. Now she wished she had listened to Jack and worn something more fashionable. Maybe one of her own designs.

A distinguished-looking gentleman Maggie took to be the manager lifted her hand, the one with the chipped nail. He bowed at the waist, kissed the tips of her fingers and handed her the linen card.

"Congratulations," he said. "You're the one millionth guest of the Grand Perimeter's world-wide chain." He offered her his arm and gestured to the bank of elevators. "If you'll step this way, a party awaits you in my offices. I'm sure you'll be pleased with the prizes we have selected to commemorate the occasion."

* * *

Maggie gripped the gleaming brass rail to steady her trembling legs as the door to the glass bullet elevator whispered shut. She was sure any moment she would blink and wake up. Find Homer snuggled at her feet in her double bed while she clung to the wispy fragments of an incredible dream.

The elevator lifted smoothly to the third floor. When the doors slid open, a photographer was waiting, his camera ready.

"Smile," he said and before she could tuck the wind-whipped strands of her hair behind her ear, he snapped a picture of her bleary-eyed attempt to comply with his wishes.

Black dots danced before her eyes. She was still trying to regain her equilibrium when she stepped into a luxuriously appointed office.

A uniformed waiter appeared at her elbow, with two exquisitely cut crystal flutes of champagne on his silver tray. A tuxedoed gentleman who identified himself as the manager handed Maggie one of the slender stems. The beams of light from a whirring video camera were refracted by the intricately cut crystal. Specks of rainbow luminance flickered around the room in a whirl that matched the dizzy feeling in her stomach.

"To you, Miss Kincaid," the manager murmured, and lifted his glass. "And to your fairy-tale weekend at the Grand Perimeter."

Maggie took a sip of the bubbly champagne

and managed a weak smile as it fizzed in her throat. "Fairy-tale weekend?"

"For the duration of your stay, all the hotel fa-cilities and the entire hotel staff are at your dis-posal." He handed her a program bound in burgundy velveteen that matched the bellhops' uniforms, the thick carpet beneath her feet, and the manager's cummerbund and bow tie. "I trust you'll find the weekend to your liking."

Maggie opened the program and skimmed the first page. "Oh, my," she uttered on a cry. "I'm staying in the Presidential Suite?"

"And you may ask the guest of your choice to join you."

Guest? Maggie's heart plunged, all the way to the Docs supporting her unsteady feet. Who could she ask to share her fairy-tale weekend?

She *wouldn't* ask any of the girls at the shop. She'd rather spend the weekend alone. Could her Aunt Barbara fly in? No, when Maggie had phoned to ask if her aunt wanted to join her in taking ad-vantage of the gift certificate, Barbara had said she was committed to an apparel show in the Atlanta market that weekend.

There was her sewing circle at the church, some of whom were among the original dozen ladies who had introduced her to the joys of dressmaking when she was barely five. Although she considered them friends, she didn't know any of them well enough to ask them to share a hotel room with her.

Maggie twisted the satin cord of the program between her fingers, embarrassed to admit there wasn't a single soul with whom she could share her excitement.

Wait a minute. Jack had said he would join her for dinner, hadn't he? But dinner did not a weekend make.

"There won't be anyone joining me," she answered demurely. "Except maybe for dinner."

"In that event, may I introduce Armand Foster, the chain's vice president of public relations, who shall be honored to accompany you should you wish an escort during the weekend."

The manager crooked his finger. From behind Maggie stepped a strikingly attractive man, also in a tuxedo. Possessing an athletically built body, expertly clipped black hair and crystal blue eyes, Armand Foster was more than physically qualified to be cast as the male lead of Prince Charming in any woman's fairy tale. He bowed slightly and inclined his head, but Maggie didn't miss the flicker of aloofness in his eyes. "Miss Kincaid."

Tilting her head, she lifted her champagne glass in a silent toast, then took a solid swig. If she possessed the courage Jack was constantly badgering her to show, she would tell the hotel manager she could find her own escort, thank you.

Feeling a flush of angry heat steal over her cheeks, she lifted her chin instead and said oh-so-politely, "Thank you, Mr. Foster. I'm a lucky woman."

"There's more, Miss Kincaid," the manager told her.

She hoped there weren't more PR guys masquerading as condescending escorts. She sipped from her glass, flipped through her program, and choked over what she read. In addition to her posh suite, the hotel chain was granting her a thousand dollars' credit at the Grand Perimeter's boutique, unlimited use of the beauty salon, and the services of the masseuse for the weekend. The hotel was awarding her, as a permanent memento, a dozen hand-blown, hand-cut French champagne flutes identical to the one she held in her hand.

She tried to think of something appropriate to say. With her head a bit woozy from the champagne, all she could think to murmur was, "Well, this ought to keep me off the streets."

She handed her glass to the manager and stood. She couldn't wait to get to her room and phone Jack. She had promised to call him before seven. That's when he and his buddies went behind closed doors in the apartment across from hers for their monthly poker game.

"Ah, Miss Kincaid, there's one more thing," the manager said with a smooth smile. He handed her another linen envelope. "Since your weekend was already paid for by gift certificate, I thought it only appropriate to present you with this."

Maggie broke the gold seal and found inside an engraved card granting her a free room at any of the chain's properties. She pressed a hand to her chest. "Anywhere in the world?"

"Including Paris," the manager responded and passed her a gleaming black Mont Blanc pen and a sheaf of papers. "All we ask in return is your permission to take your picture this weekend and use the prints in our advertising . . ." He glanced briefly at his PR man. "That is, if we so decide." He pointed with manicured nails to a red check mark on the third page. "If you'll just sign here."

"Sure. Why not?" Maggie responded and penned her signature to the page, then handed the expensive writing instrument to the manager.

He was exchanging glances with that Armand guy again—strange glances.

While Maggie wondered what thoughts were going through their minds, the manager took the proffered pen and pressed it insistently into her palm. "Oh, no, Miss Kincaid. The pen is from the Grand Perimeter's boutique. It's another gift from us."

Maggie rolled the expertly balanced writing instrument between her fingers. She knew immediately what she would do with the pen. She would send it to her Aunt Barbara, in appreciation for the weekend. "Thank you."

"We've scheduled a press conference for tomorrow morning at ten in the lobby. Our international president, Raleigh Cordell, will be present. You should plan on, say, an hour, at the most. Then you'll be free to enjoy the hotel the rest of the weekend."

"I'll be ready," Maggie replied.

The manager exchanged another glance with the escort she wouldn't use. "I'm sure you will be, Miss Kincaid."

* * *

The Presidential Suite occupied a good portion of the hotel's top floor and offered an expansive, glittering view of Austin's Town Lake.

While the bellhops positioned crystal vases of fragrant roses about the suite, Maggie counted the telephones. There were seven. One in each of the two bathrooms, two in the living room, one on either side of the monstrous king-sized bed. The last rested on the lip of the tub.

And what a tub! Streaked with what looked like real gold, the jetted tub in cream-colored marble was contoured for two. It sat atop an elevated platform bordered on two sides by walls of windows with the sheerest of burgundy privacy curtains. Floor-to-ceiling mirrors covered most of the other two walls.

"What a waste," Maggie murmured at the thought she had no one with whom to share the tub. Then a vision of the President and First Lady swatting bubbles in the hot tub while playing underwater footsie brought a smile to her lips.

The last bellhop politely refused Maggie's offer of a tip and slipped out the door. Alone, Maggie plucked a rose from one of the vases, flopped onto one of three cushy couches in the living room and dialed Jack's number on the French-style telephone.

"Please, please, please, be in," she murmured and gazed about the opulent suite. She would pop if she couldn't share the news of her weekend with someone. When she'd made the reservation, Jack had told her he would meet her there for dinner one night, probably Saturday. Maybe when he wound up his poker game, he could join her in the suite for a drink.

Jack's answering machine kicked in on the fourth ring. "Oh, darn," she murmured into the receiver and left him a message. "I have good news. Call me at the hotel when you get in. No matter how late it is. Bye. Maggie."

She placed a quick call to her Aunt Barbara, found her also gone and left a message on her machine. Then she busied herself for a few minutes unpacking what little she'd brought to wear, playing with the suite's sound system and checking out the bed's mattress for firmness.

While she tested the bed, she thought of Kayla, Juliana, and Desiree. If they hadn't treated her like a servant, she would phone them all, invite them up, and share the suite with them for an all-girls weekend.

Not even she could be that forgiving of their insensitivity to her feelings. This morning they had ground salt into the wound. Having just received the prints from their make overs in the mail the day before, they'd had the audacity to bring them to work and show them to every client who came in.

Maggie's favorite client had asked to see her picture. Kayla had boldly explained that *dear Maggie* had volunteered to watch the phones so they could have their pictures taken. During the ensuing discussion about what a sweet woman she was, Maggie had felt like stuffing a pin cushion in Kayla's mouth.

She was forcing remnants of hurt feelings from

her mind when the telephones rang. All seven of them. Figuring Jack must have gotten her message, she hurried to the extension on one side of the bed and answered the ring. "Hello."

"Miss Kincaid?"

The voice wasn't Jack's but it sounded friendly. A woman's. Maggie heaved a sigh, her disappointment showing in the drop in her voice. "Yes?"

"This is the Grand Perimeter beauty salon. Congratulations."

"Thank you."

"I understand there's to be a press conference in the morning. I was wondering if you'd like to avail yourself of our services?"

Maggie met her gaze in the mirrored wall opposite the bed. A bedraggled-looking, grown-up urchin with drooping shoulders stared back at her.

"Oh, dear," she murmured. She had been unaware that during her walk from the bus the wind off the lake had whipped strands of hair from the clip at the nape of her neck. Those strands now stuck straight out from her head. She looked like a mature Pippi Longstocking. She thought of the way the hotel manager and the chain's PR vice president had exchanged strange glances during the official presentation. No wonder.

Well, she wouldn't embarrass them at the press conference. She would make sure she was suitably groomed when she faced the cameras. "How early do you open in the morning?"

"For you, we're here around the clock this weekend."

"We?"

"Your hair stylist, your manicurist, and your makeup artist."

What irony! Kayla, Desiree, and Juliana had to pay for their make overs, and she, Maggie, was getting one for free. "Which one are you?"

"My specialty is makeup," the woman responded.

"Makeup," Maggie repeated, wondering if the woman could work magic. "I'll take your first appointment in the morning. I'd like the works. Hair. Nails."

"Pedicure?"

Maggie stuck out her feet and angled her head at her comfy boots. She had always wanted a pedicure but could never justify the expense. Pampering herself was going to be such fun. "That would be terrific. When do you want me there?"

"Oh, Miss Kincaid. We don't expect you to come down here. We'll be there anytime you wish."

"Here? In my room?"

"Unless you'd prefer coming down . . ."

"No, that's terrific," Maggie replied, hitching her shoulders in pleased surprise. "Have you all had dinner?"

"I can only speak for myself, but no, I haven't. However—"

"Great. Come on up. We'll order room service. Pass the word."

"Miss Kincaid, the manager would never approve of us—"

"Pooh on the manager! We're ordering room

service, and that's that. We'll order as soon as you get here. Come on up," Maggie said. "We'll put this suite to good use. Invite anybody else you like."

"How would you like a massage?"

"I don't know. I've never had one."

"Then you're in for a treat. Why don't you take time for a shower or a leisurely bath. I'll send up the masseuse in thirty minutes. We'll give her forty-five minutes, then join you."

"Something tells me," Maggie mumbled before hanging up, "this is going to be an evening I won't soon forget."

Four

In the apartment above his, Jack knocked back a long swallow of Celis Golden, his favorite local brew, and studied his cards. The four, six and eight of hearts, the jack of diamonds, the king of spades.

Garbage.

But what the hell? It was eleven o'clock. He had more money in his winnings pocket than he'd drawn from his poker stash. Might as well commit poker suicide. Try to draw to an inside straight flush.

If he lost, he'd fold. Check to see if Mags had called. If he got lucky and drew the two magical cards, he'd fold anyway and give her room a buzz. He had to run down to the hotel or she'd probably pass the entire first evening of her weekend holed up in her room, reading a damned textbook. He'd take her down to the trendy club on the first floor, spend his winnings on a couple of drinks. There he'd teach his shy friend the finer points of meeting the opposite sex.

He pitched the jack and king face down on the table. "Gimme two."

Face impassive, the neighbor in whose apartment they were playing clamped his teeth around his putrid-smelling cigar. He dealt two well-worn cards across the scratched and marred table.

Jack crammed a handful of Spanish peanuts into his mouth, knocked back another swig of beer, then retrieved the cards one at a time.

Cripes! He should have known better. His neighbor buddy had dealt him the friggin' deuce of clubs and a five of diamonds. He added them to his still worthless four, six, and eight of hearts and steeled himself not to sweat.

After watching all those women drift in and out of his dad's life when he was a kid, he was an expert at hiding his emotions. He could conjure up a face of granite when needed and finesse a bluff when desired.

Knowing his only hope was to convince his poker buddies he held a hand of gold, he let the barest hint of a grin quiver his lips, then frowned. Milking the moment, he knocked back a considerable swallow of Celis, bumped the hand a whole damned buck and waited for the fun.

"Jesus, Jack. You got a winnin' hand again?"

Jack shrugged and shot his host a level glance. "You going to meet me?"

"Hell, no." The systems engineer pitched his hand on the table. The three other grim-faced players followed suit. "You sure you didn't stack the deck?"

"You dealt, buddy," Jack reminded his friend, and spread his nothing hand across the table.

"Shit."

"Watch your language, boy," Jack said and

raked the hand's pot to his edge of the table, thinking how Maggie would boil over at the use of the expletive.

Wilson Jamison, his childhood buddy who religiously drove over from Lake Travis for the poker game, slanted him a disbelieving look. "Who washed your mouth out with soap?"

"I'll tell you who," interjected Buck, the young, soon-to-be divorced attorney who worked for the district attorney's office. "Our resident bootlegger, Maggie Kincaid."

At Buck's deprecating tone of voice and the resulting raucous chuckles, Jack's hands stilled on the table. "You guys got any complaints about Maggie?"

"Ah, come on, Jack. I thought we agreed. She's so straitlaced, she probably starches her underwear, which is most likely plain white cotton."

"Talk like that is probably what got you your walkin' papers from Beth," Jack tossed back at Buck. "I'm out of here, boys."

"It's only eleven o'clock."

"I got plans," Jack alibied, figuring he'd taken in at least twenty bucks for the evening. He bent to scoop up Homer from the couch.

"Who with?" his neighbor shot back. "Maggie?"

"Maybe," Jack responded.

The four men sitting around the table howled. "Lost your touch with the models, huh?" Buck goaded him.

"At least I'm not prosecuting pimps and hookers."

"I should be so lucky," Buck lamented.

"The trouble with you guys is, you don't know a lady when you see one," Jack maintained.

Wilson looked mad enough to punch Jack's lights out.

"Except you, Wilson. Sorry. You know Polly's like a sister to me. How's she doing?"

"Not good."

"What do you mean?" Jack asked with concern.

"I can't put my finger on it, but she hasn't been herself lately."

"Let me know if I can do anything to help," Jack offered his childhood friend. "See you guys next month. My place," he reminded the disparate group and made for the door.

"Call for you, Miss Kincaid," said the manicurist and held the receiver to Maggie's ear. "Watch your nails."

Maggie's cheeks and forehead were caked with a mud pack. She wondered if she could speak without her face cracking and falling into her lap. "Hi," she managed to utter.

"Hey, Mags."

Hearing Jack's familiar voice resonate over the line, Maggie's natural inclination was to smile. Because of the mud pack, she had to settle for letting her pleasure find expression in her eyes. "Jack. Did you win?"

"Twenty bucks. You sound funny."

"Just a minute." She motioned to her cheeks. The makeup artist pressed a hot, white towel to her face for a few seconds. The towel came away smeared with the brown residue of her masque, freeing the tingling muscles around her mouth to move freely. "There, is that better?"

"Yeah. Did I catch you eating dinner?"

"Yes and no."

"That's as clear as mud."

Maggie chuckled. "If you only knew how funny that was." She moved the receiver to the other ear so more of the masque could be steamed from her face.

"What's the good news?"

"It's so exciting, I can't believe it. When I checked in, all these bells rang, and the bellhops ran over and lined up behind me next to an ice sculpture. It seems I was the millionth guest to check into a Grand Perimeter Hotel."

"What did they do? Give you a free drink?"

"Try the Presidential Suite for the weekend."

"You've got to be kidding!" Jack boomed.

"And I have a gift certificate for the boutique and some other freebies."

"Congratulations, Princess. About time Lady Luck came your way. What's the trade-off?"

"Trade-off?"

"The hotel's not doing this out of the goodness of their hearts. They expect something in return."

"Oh, Jack, you're such a skeptic."

"Then tell me I'm wrong."

"Well . . ."

"I knew it," he said with typical Jack smugness.

"It isn't much. Not when you consider what I'm getting in return."

"Let me guess. All you have to do is appear in their advertisements and gush about the hotel."

"No, all I have to do is agree to let them take my picture and give them permission to use it in their ads."

"Same difference."

"What's wrong with that?"

"Nothing, if you enjoy your stay."

"I'm sure I will. Wait until you see this room. It has seven phones, three televisions and a bar stocked with liquor."

"Don't drink any if you don't want to pay through the nose for it."

"The manager said everything's on the house this weekend, including the liquor."

"Maybe you ought to have a party then."

"Just a minute." She covered the receiver and looked to the makeup artist, who was stippling rich, soothing cream over her face with her fingertips. "How long until I'm through?"

"I'd like thirty minutes. By then the hot oil treatment on your hair can be rinsed out. If we rush, we can have you ready in an hour-fifteen. But I've taken the liberty of having the boutique manager bring up some things for you to look at."

It had been ages since Maggie had bought anything from a store other than her undergarments and shoes. She would need something appropriate for the press conference in the morning, though.

"I'm not sure I feel like a party," she told Jack. "But how would you like to meet me for a drink? Say, twelve-thirty?"

"Lucky for you I'm a night owl. I'll see you at twelve-thirty. Where should I meet you?"

"Just have the desk ring me when you arrive."

"Tell him to wear a tie," the hair stylist mouthed and pointed at her neck with a conspiratorial wink.

"I'm supposed to tell you to wear a tie."

"Now you're pushing your luck, Princess, but okay. You'll owe me one, though. Who's with you anyway?"

"Oh, just some people I've met since I got here," Maggie said and smiled at the manicurist.

"Sounds like you're doing all right for yourself. See you in an hour and a half."

Only for Maggie would Jack truss up in a jacket and tie on his free Friday night.

Too many other weekends he had to wear his monkey suit while he photographed Austin's beautiful people at some mucky-muck society affair.

Brushing strands of Homer's orange hair from his navy blazer, he rode the private elevator up to the Grand Perimeter's penthouse level. There a classy-looking chick with collagen-enhanced lips gave him a pouty smile. She insisted on seeing identification before ringing Maggie's room.

"Miss Kincaid said to show you in," she finally announced and led him down a lushly carpeted hallway. She pressed a series of numbers into a security pad beside massive double doors of carved teakwood. A red light blinked. She inserted a plastic card into a slot in the door, then opened it with an ornate brass handle and gestured inside. "Enjoy your evening, Mr. Lewis," she said and sauntered back down the hall.

Jack's first reaction was that he'd seen bowling alleys smaller than the hotel's Presidential Suite. He looked around the spacious living room but didn't see Maggie at any of the intimate groupings of furniture.

By the light of what were probably genuine Oriental lamps, he did see a bottle of wine chilling in a champagne bucket beside a hunter green couch. Sitting on the cream-colored marble coffee table was a gleaming silver tray. There radishes cut to look like birds garnished an assortment of hors d'oeuvres. Two crystal wineglasses stood at the ready.

Even though it was early September, a wood fire hissed and crackled in the fireplace. The flames flickering on the wall created a cozy illusion of intimacy.

For anyone else in Jack's economic bracket, the poshness might have provided a welcome change in surroundings. For Jack, though, the silver, crystal and ridiculous number of phone extensions were grating reminders of his mother's family and a time in his life he associated with painful rejection. Thankfully, Jack sensed a hint of Maggie's well-grounded presence in the air. That natural freshness Jack found comforting.

But where was she?

"Maggie?" he called out. "Where the hell are you?"

"Here," came her demure voice from an alcove to the side.

Jack turned in the direction of Maggie's voice, and his mouth dropped open. "Maggie?" He gulped at the sudden tightness in the knot of his tie.

The woman standing before him in a simple cream-colored dress bore no resemblance to the Maggie he knew. His Maggie was plain. Her eyes weren't mysterious and exotic, the deep brown of her irises shimmering with joy. Her hair didn't tumble about her face in a riot of auburn waves. Her mouth was never painted a sassy red.

His Maggie would never wear a dress like that. Not that it wasn't stunning. But the dress draped the curves of a body with more allure than any model he had ever photographed. All those curves and hollows Jack had speculated about—well, he was speechless.

Maggie did, after all, have nice breasts, as he had suspected. High and well-rounded. And a waistline. Narrow enough so he could probably clamp his hands around it, and his fingers would meet.

She'd taken his advice and ditched the combat boots. She now wore high, narrow heels that emphasized her shapely swimmer's legs. He let his gaze drift up from her ankles, over her calves, and his male imagination thrummed wild.

He stuck a finger in the practically nonexistent

space between his Adam's apple and his shirt collar. "Maggie," he croaked. "Is that really you?"

She pivoted, the fullness of her skirt flaring at the base of her hips. Her spinning motion gave him an even better look at her shapely legs. "You like it? My new dress?"

"Dress? What dress?" He reined in his wandering imagination and forced himself to focus on her face. "It's you I'm looking at, Princess. It's like I told you. A little makeup, a good hair style, and you're downright beautiful."

"I believe the word you used was attractive. Yes, that's it. You said if I fixed myself up, I'd be downright attractive."

Jack let his gaze take in the total package. He ran his palm over the nape of his neck and gave a wry grin. "So I underestimated."

Smiling radiantly, Maggie caught his hand and pulled him to the couch. He sat down beside her, not sure how to act around the new Maggie. In a strange way, he missed the boots.

"I ordered up wine. I hope you like white."

"White. Wine. Oh, fine. Fine. That's great, Margaret. That is, Maggie. Here, let me pour."

She sat primly beside him, her hands folded in her lap while he sloshed wine into the stemmed glasses. He handed her one, their fingers touching briefly in the exchange. Her hand was warm, her fingernails long and tapered. They glimmered red in the reflected light. Red hot.

Something that had nothing to do with a guy-and-gal friendship flickered in his belly. He was pretty sure it wasn't the beer or Spanish peanuts.

Not sure how to deal with it, Jack held Maggie's gaze for an awkward moment. He had the strangest feeling Maggie had zipped herself into a new outer covering, like a glamour flight suit or something. He liked it, and he didn't. Either way he was uncharacteristically all hands, all feet.

He took a fortifying gulp of his wine and blinked. "What did you do to yourself?"

Maggie's face crumbled. She lifted a tentative hand to her mass of thick, shiny waves. "You don't like my hair."

"The hell I don't. I'm nuts about it."

The corners of her mouth shot up. "You are?"

"Maggie, you're . . ." he sipped his wine again, searching for the appropriate words to describe her fresh, new appeal. He could say if she wasn't his good old friend, Maggie, he might think about hauling her off to the bedroom. But friends didn't haul each other off to the bedroom.

Did they?

"I'm what?" she prompted him, a flicker of hurt in her luminous eyes.

"A knockout."

She expelled a deeply drawn breath, her breasts rising enticingly beneath the knit fabric as she subsequently inhaled. "No one's ever said I'm a knockout."

"You've never dressed like that. Or, or fixed your hair, or . . ."

"Then you don't think it looks false?"

"Kiddo," Jack admitted, "you've only enhanced what God's given you. What the hell's wrong with that?"

"Nothing, I guess. Are you hungry?"

"Depends. What have you got?"

"Not much. Since it's so late, I just ordered hors d'oeuvres. I thought you might have forgotten to eat."

Maggie knew Jack so well. Oftentimes on his poker nights he munched out on peanuts and beer and complained of a bad stomach the next morning. To show his appreciation, he popped a miniature quesadilla into his mouth. Austin's best goat cheese. Yum.

Maggie passed a hand over the tray. "If you like, you can take those home with you. Homer would really like the marinated chicken."

"Homer, hell. He can eat Nine Lives. What we don't eat, we can save for Monday night."

Maggie cocked her head. Fine strands of woven gold chain shifted at her ears, drawing Jack's attention to the slender slope of her neck. Funny, he had never noticed how creamy her skin was. He thought about reaching out to test its texture with his fingers.

Better not.

"Monday night?" Maggie asked.

"Hmm?"

"Monday night. You said we could save the leftover hors d'oeuvres for Monday night. I wasn't aware we were doing anything together then. You need help with a shoot, or something?"

"Well, I, uh, that is, I just figured we could get together and you could tell me all about your weekend. Yes, that's it. And watch football, if the

Cowboys play. Better let me check my schedule, though. I'll call and let you know."

Maggie dropped her gaze to her wineglass. She ran her fingertip around the smoothly cut rim. The resulting squeak pierced the awkward silence. "You could share the weekend with me, if you like."

At Maggie's spoken invitation, the air in the cavernous suite thickened. The flames in the fireplace flickered low, yet Jack sensed a decided increase in his body temperature. A drop of perspiration trickled down his armpit.

Share the weekend? Exactly what did Maggie have in mind?

He blotted the perspiration from above his upper lip with his napkin and tried to clear his mind. If any other woman had made Maggie's offer, the implications would have been as crystal clear as their wineglasses. Jack wouldn't waste time getting to the bedroom. He'd take the stemware from her hand, set it on the table and ravage first her mouth, then her voluptuous body.

Coming from Maggie, though, the invitation sounded innocent and sweet, devoid of blatant, sexual overtones. Still, Jack couldn't help imagining taking this new Maggie's hand, drawing her from the couch into his arms, carrying her to the bedroom.

His mouth went dry.

"I'm sorry. I didn't think. I'm sure you already have plans," Maggie said with forced cheerfulness and a trace of disappointment in her voice.

Jack opened his mouth to say he didn't have a

damned thing planned for the weekend, and if he did, he'd weasel his way out of it to be with her. But before he could utter a word, she grabbed his hand and popped up from the couch. "You've got to see the rest of the suite. Just think. The President and First Lady slept here. In the same bed where I'm going to sleep."

Alone, Jack thought regretfully.

She led him on a brisk tour of the Presidential Suite. While she chattered and pointed out the expertly sewn seams of the drapes, he catalogued at least ten places where a guy could make love to a woman—if he had a mind to. The chaise on the balcony, with a view of Town Lake. The hot tub. The monstrous bed. The surface of the bar. The very floor beneath their feet—his and Maggie's.

The last stop on her narrated tour was the bedroom. Plopping into a chair, she slipped her high, narrow heels off her feet. "These things are killing me." She laughed, the lyrical sound of her voice bouncing around the room. "But the owner of the boutique insisted I couldn't wear my Docs with this dress."

She glanced up and caught him staring at her legs. Furrows lined the smooth skin of her forehead. "Oh, my, Jack. You don't look so good."

She popped up, Maggie fashion, and pressed the back of her fingers to his forehead. "You're perspiring."

Damned if he wasn't.

"You must have a fever." Her bottom lip protruded in a pout he could imagine taking gently

between his teeth. "Oh, dear. You don't suppose
the goat cheese was bad?"

"I'd better be going," he announced flatly, or
as flatly as any guy could whose pulse was thun-
dering in his ears.

Maggie rose to her tiptoes and pressed a kiss
to his cheek. "Thanks for sharing tonight with
me, Jack."

He lifted a hand to cup the back of her neck,
then let it fall awkwardly to his side. "Ah, Maggie-
girl . . ."

Her lips quivered, just a little, then spread in a
hesitant smile. "I'm looking forward to Monday
night."

"Monday?"

"You know, leftover hors d'oeuvres. Talk about
this weekend. Football."

"Oh, yeah. Monday."

"My place or yours?"

"Mine. I mean, whichever you like."

"I could make those subs you wanted."

"Maggie?"

Her pretense of a smile faded. She straightened
her dress, tossed the loose waves of her auburn
hair over her shoulder. "If you were teasing about
Monday, just say so."

The only teasing done since Jack had walked
into the suite was the womanly scent of Maggie
driving him nuts. "You know me better than
that."

"Well, you were acting kind of funny."

"That's because I was thinking."

"About what?"

Phew! How much should he tell her? "Mainly that if you really were serious about wanting me to share the weekend with you, I could probably break away—"

"Oh, Jack! I love you!" Maggie threw her arms around his neck and gave him a jumpy little hug that had her breasts jiggling against his chest and him wondering what the heck he should do with his hands. "I'm so lucky to have you for a friend."

"Friend," he repeated. "Right."

She hooked her arm through his and walked him to the suite's door. "I have to be at a press conference at ten. It shouldn't last too long. Why don't you show up oh, say, eleven? We can have an early lunch, then swim."

"Swim," he repeated numbly, trying to give himself time to reassemble his scattered brains.

"That's right. You teach swimming. To kids."

"Five- and six-year-olds." Her eyes turned dreamy. "They're so cute. They look like little tadpoles. You swim, don't you?"

Jack lifted a hand to her cheek and let his gaze roam affectionately over her face. She looked up at him, her skin radiant, her eyes glowing. She was happier than he'd ever seen her.

It occurred to him at that moment that she was still just his Maggie. Totally unaffected by the beauty that had been hiding beneath her plain facade. She didn't know that he could hardly swallow for looking at her, marveling at the transformation.

Can I swim? If I don't drown, soaking up your beauty, Princess. "You bet. Backstroke. Four-forty.

Seventy-seven Class Five A district high school champion."

A challenge glinted in her eyes. "Two-twenty. Breast stroke. St. Mary's High School Swim Team, nineteen-eighty."

Breast stroke? Jack stifled a groan. "Think you're up to a little race?"

"I am if you are. The outdoor pool's Olympic size."

"Care to place a little wager?"

"I don't know. District champ, huh?" She let her gaze drift down to assess his shoulders and his chest, as if to determine if he was still in shape. Jack hauled in enough air to expand his chest and wondered if he measured up. "Depends on the event," she answered him.

"Seeing as how you're a woman, I'll give you a break. Say, a couple of seconds' head start."

"Maybe I won't need those seconds," she tossed back. "I am in shape."

"I noticed," he said dryly.

"Well?"

"Well what?"

"What event?"

"Breast stroke," Jack announced.

Maggie beamed. "You're on!"

He had to get the hell out of there, and soon. Acting on impulse, Jack tilted Maggie's chin with his knuckle and bent to give her a chaste good-bye peck on the cheek. His lips strayed to hers and forgot the chaste part. The kiss was brief but by no stretch of the imagination brotherly. "See you in the morning, Princess," he said gruffly.

Then he saluted her with a hand he hoped she couldn't tell was trembling and beat it to the door of her suite.

Five

Maggie didn't walk to the door to see Jack off; she floated. Halfway down the hall, he turned and caught her leaning against the door frame, her cheek pressed to the wooden molding, her fingertips touching her lips. Before she could collect herself, he gave a lopsided grin and disappeared around the corner.

Safely removed from Jack's magnetic field, she closed the door and collapsed against it. She fanned her face with her hand to cool her burning cheeks and tried to catch her breath. Her bones felt like mush.

Jack had kissed her! On the lips!

Okay, so it was only a casual peck, a parting courtesy from one friend to another. But since Jack's warm, sure lips had pressed against Maggie's mouth, her pulse had been racing like high gear in Jack's five-year-old Mustang. Her stomach had been flip-flopping like her young swim students in their first attempts to dive.

The scent of his breath, a heady combination of dry wine and spicy salsa, still lingered in her nostrils. She ran her tongue over her lips and tasted the tart residue of Chardonnay.

And Jack. My, how she liked the taste of him.

"Too long," she uttered on a cry. When she reacted this turbulently to a simple, friendly kiss—from Jack, no less—it had been too long since she'd experienced the pleasure of a man.

Melvin had never affected her this way. Still a virgin at twenty-two, she had been wildly curious about the deflowering process. She later reasoned that's why she had welcomed Melvin's smooth advances in the back room of Miss Caroline's when he made deliveries.

Going to bed with Melvin, though, had made her wish she hadn't satisfied her curiosity. There had been whispered words of passion—two, maybe three—and Melvin's hot sweaty body. He had entered her too soon, thrust too hard. He'd hurt her, then humiliated her later by saying he guessed quiet types like her were made for the domestic arts, but not for the art of loving.

There had been few kisses since then, little revving up of her female hormones, unless she counted her secret fantasies that Jack would one day be attracted to her. The fantasies hovered on realization that evening after work, on the day Kayla, Desiree, and Juliana had pulled their Beauty Pix trick. The moment Jack's strong, massaging hand had closed over her shoulder, the equation between them had subtly changed. She had told herself she was foolish to think so, but tonight proved it.

"The man just gave you a friendly good-night kiss," she lectured herself out loud and headed for the bedroom. "Don't go jumping to conclusions."

Yet, after she scrubbed the makeup off her face and crawled between the crisp sheets of the huge, king-sized bed, thoughts of Jack produced a telltale quiver down there, in the most private part of her body.

By morning the old Maggie was in control again. During her flip-flop night of attempted sleep, she had hammered some good sense into her flighty head. Jack, she had assured herself, had reacted to the made-up, fluffed-up version of her. That was a three-hour production she could scarcely hope to duplicate.

Still, when her makeup artist popped open her case of jars, tubes and pencils and set about working her wizardry on Maggie's plain face, Maggie paid close attention this time. She studied the way she applied foundation. She noted the techniques of subtle highlighting, the just-so flick of this brush and that.

At precisely ten o'clock she stepped off the elevator in a jaunty red gabardine jumpsuit from the boutique. She smoothed her hands down the row of star-shaped brass buttons and glanced around the lobby. The harpist had been replaced by an accomplished flutist. The clear, crisp notes sounding from her silver flute blended with the muted rush of the fountain. Sunlight slanted through the overhead canopy of beveled glass. The smell of pastries spiced with cinnamon wafted into the lobby from the Riverwalk Cafe.

Maggie spotted the hotel manager waiting for

her by the registration desk with several people, a couple with camera bags. She recognized one woman as her favorite Austin newscaster, a woman she had always wanted to meet. Maybe she could get her autograph for her swim students.

"Miss Kincaid," the lovely journalist addressed her and extended her hand. "I understand you got lucky."

"I'll say!"

"How did it feel when they told you what you'd won?"

"Like Cinderella," Maggie responded and smiled at the hotel manager. "All that's missing is the glass slipper."

The manager didn't smile. He just stood there, staring at her as if she had two heads.

She pressed a hand to her chest and felt the nervous thumping of her heart. His gaze swept over her, from her hair to the tips of her gleaming black shoes, and back again. She glanced briefly at the front of her jumpsuit, wondering if she'd missed a spot of makeup or coffee when she'd checked herself in the mirror. She saw nothing amiss, not even a stray thread. "Did I say something wrong?"

The manager blinked and gave his head a brisk little shake. "No, no. You're doing fine, Miss Kincaid." He slanted a disbelieving glance at the distinguished-looking man beside him. But the man didn't appear to notice. He held Maggie's gaze with his eyes—black, like his hair— while he gallantly dipped his head and kissed her hand.

"Mademoiselle Kincaid, you look lovely this morning." He gave her hand a barely perceptible squeeze, then released it. His gaze flitted over her hair. "Perhaps striking would be a more accurate description."

"Why, thank you." She looked to the hotel manager questioningly, then back to the gentleman who spoke with a French accent and wore a crimson rosebud in his lapel. Maggie couldn't help noticing the expensive cut of the man's impeccable, gray silk suit. Custom-made, Maggie decided, with admiration for the tailor's skills.

"Forgive me," the manager said. "Raleigh, this is the winner of our free weekend, Maggie Kincaid. Miss Kincaid, Raleigh Cordell, the president of Grand Perimeter Hotels International."

Which explained the expensive suit. "I just love your hotel," Maggie gushed as the president kissed her hand. "Everyone's so nice."

"You flatter us, mademoiselle."

"I understand you're a seamstress," a second reporter cut in as if impatient to pose his questions.

"Yes, at Miss Caroline's Couturier. I make most of my clothes, too."

"That jumpsuit you're wearing is delightful," piped in Maggie's favorite newscaster. "Did you make it?"

"Oh, my, no. I bought it at the hotel's boutique." She slanted a grateful smile at the president. "That is, I got it with my gift certificate. You might want to take a look before you leave. They have some exquisitely made garments. Their prices aren't bad for the quality."

"What do you plan to do with the rest of your prize weekend?"

"Swim. Eat." Maggie glanced around the posh lobby, still not believing this was happening to her. "Pinch myself. Eat again."

"Have you ever stayed at the Grand Perimeter before?"

"Oh, my no. But isn't it lovely? I can't imagine a better place to go to feel like you're being treated like a queen."

The television personality slanted her a dubious look. "Are you sure this isn't a setup? These hotel guys didn't feed you lines, did they?"

"I suppose I am gushing," Maggie said with an embarrassed grin. "But I think you'd feel the same way if you were me."

Apparently satisfied, the reporter said, "Do you mind if we shoot some footage of you walking around the hotel?"

"Of course not," Maggie responded and hoped she wouldn't fall off her high heels on camera.

"We'll tour the hotel while you ask your questions," the president explained and gestured to the manager for the tour to begin. He moved beside her, tucked her hand into the crook of his arm and gave it a reassuring pat. "Relax, mademoiselle. You're doing beautifully."

Encouraged by the president's confidence in her, Maggie did relax. She answered questions about her job, her background and her family during the tour. Then came a flurry of pictures, most of them with Mr. Cordell.

When the last reporter left and the manager disappeared to answer a page, the president took Maggie's hands and kissed her cheek. That's when she noticed the graying at his temples, the softness in his smile, the twinkle in his eyes so much like her father's.

"Thanks for helping me relax," she told him, then glanced over his shoulder and saw Jack strolling into the lobby.

At the sight of him, Maggie's pulse tripped. He wore baggy sweat shorts, sandals made from tire treads and a faded orange T-shirt. Emblazoned on the front was the menacing-looking head of Bevo, the longhorn steer mascot of the University of Texas. The slogan above Bevo's head read, "Turn around, and I'll give you some pointers."

The classic Jack attire helped Maggie tamp down the insistent fluttering in her chest. She lifted her hand high over her head and waved until he saw her.

"Someone special?" the president asked and draped an arm loosely about her shoulders.

"My neighbor," Maggie replied and was reminded how nervous her sisters' boyfriends were when her father checked them out for the first time.

"Only a neighbor?" Cordell asked.

"Unfortunately, yes," Maggie admitted on a sigh.

Cordell chuckled. "I see."

By the time Jack crossed the lobby to where she and the president were chatting, her neighbor's smile had faded to a frown. Maggie was wondering if Jack had ambivalent feelings about the night before. But then, why should he? The kiss had been only a gesture of friendship on his part. *She* was the one who was overreacting.

"I'd like you to meet Jack Lewis," she said to the fatherly president. "He's a very good friend of mine and a fantastic commercial photographer. You ought to call him sometime to do some work for you. Jack, this is Raleigh Cordell, president of the hotel chain."

The two men gave each other measuring looks, shook hands and exchanged formal pleasantries. Jack placed a proprietary hand at the back of Maggie's waist. "Ready for that swim, Princess?"

"Princess," Cordell repeated and smiled broadly. "The name fits."

Maggie cocked her head. "Thank you, Mr. Cordell. I think."

"It's most definitely a compliment," the president responded smoothly and kissed her hand again. "You were quite a spokesman for Grand Perimeter with the reporters, mademoiselle."

"It was easy. I just told the truth."

"Indeed. Enjoy your stay," he said, lingering over her hand. He slanted a sideways glance at Jack. Jack was glowering. Cordell released Maggie's hand and winked at her. "Do call me if you're ever in San Francisco."

Jack moved his hand to the curve of Maggie's waist. The heat, the weight of his hand over that sensitive area, the brush of his chest against her back made her system go ten kinds of haywire.

She felt like someone had pumped the breath out
of her lungs. "I—I will, Mr. Cordell," she responded shakily. "Again, thank you for this weekend."

"It's been my pleasure," he murmured and was
still smiling at her when she turned to leave with
Jack.

"I don't like that guy," Jack grumbled on the
way to the pool. He let his hand drop from her
waist.

"Mr. Cordell? Why not?"

"I don't like the way he was looking at you."

"What way?"

"You know what way." Jack's gaze swept the full
length of her. "Like he'd like to peel you out of
that damned jumpsuit."

"You're imagining things. Mr. Cordell is a very
nice man. What's the matter with my jumpsuit?"

"It's . . . not you."

"I don't know," Maggie said and caught her
reflection in a mirror they were passing. She
could still hardly believe she was the woman who
stared back at her. "I think it goes with the new
me. And the makeup artist insisted it was perfect
for the occasion."

Three men in tennis shorts stood talking jovi-
ally at the bank of elevators. When Maggie and
Jack walked past them, their conversation came
to an abrupt halt. Their gazes locked on Maggie.
As inexperienced as she was at dealing with the
attention of men, she felt their fixed looks follow
her as she and Jack walked toward the glass doors
to the outdoor pool.

An unaccustomed pleasure skipped through
Maggie. Men were looking at her, and not as if
she weren't there. Maybe that's what Jack meant
about the jumpsuit not being her. She supposed
the new her would take some getting used to—on
her friends' part, as well as her own.

Maggie briefly wondered how women who drew
the constant, admiring glances of men dealt with
the attention. Was a woman supposed to acknowledge the looks with a demure smile? Ignore
them? Say hello? Dip her head? Or pretend she
didn't notice?

"Jack?" she said, as they walked through a maze
of closely cropped hedges to the Olympic-size
pool.

"Yeah, Princess?"

"What's a woman supposed to do when a man
looks at her? Smile? Ignore him? Say hello?"

"Depends on how he looks at her."

"Like those men were just looking at me."

Jack drove a hand through his thick shock of
hair. The noon sun glinted in the red highlights.
"Depends on what you want him to do."

"Could you be a bit more specific on my
choices?"

"Jesus, Maggie! How can you be so naive? Okay,
I'll tell you. If you want him to get lost, look away.
Pretend he doesn't exist. If you want him to know
you're interested, when he looks at you, make eye
contact. If you want to encourage him to come
over, say hi, whatever, don't glance away until you
see a twinkle in his eyes."

"A twinkle?" she asked, remembering her father's and Raleigh Cordell's. "What kind of twin-kle?"

"One that says, okay, baby. I got the message. Here I come."

"Then looking at a guy's an invitation?"

"If you look long enough. If you smile coyly." He batted his eyes outrageously. "If you flutter your lashes. Flip your hair over your shoulder. Preen."

Maggie sat on one of the chaise longues that formed two white rectangles around the pool. "Show me preen."

"Come on, Maggie. I'll look like a damned fool."

"Then tell me how to do it."

Shaking his head, he sat sideways on the lounge next to hers. "I can't believe I'm doing this. Didn't you learn this from Sister Slut?"

Maggie bristled, not expecting her sister's crude nickname to fly back and hit her with the force of a slap to her face. "Her name's Sheridan. I'd appreciate it if you'd call her that."

"Sheridan," Jack repeated. "Got it. Anyway, I'd have thought you would have learned this kind of thing from her."

"She was four years older than me."

"So?"

"So we didn't run around together."

"But surely you noticed the way she—"

"I'll tell you what I noticed," Maggie shot back, a temper she didn't know she had firing her retort. "I noticed all my friends talking about her, saying embarrassing things. I saw the looks people gave her wherever we went. I saw red faces whenever she seared them with words I never would have dared to say. You can understand why I didn't make it a habit to imitate what she did and how she did it."

"Hey, I'm sorry. You don't have to jump all over me. I didn't know you were so sensitive about her."

"She isn't a slut anymore. She's a wife and a mother. A good one. And I'd appreciate it if you didn't make fun of me when I ask you to teach me how to meet men. It isn't something I've concerned myself with. I've been . . . busy concentrating on other things."

"But now you think you're ready."

"I know I am," she announced.

"Good, because the way you look now, you're going to meet a lot of men, whether you want to or not."

A hot flush crept up Maggie's neck and heated her cheeks. "I know I look better. The hair. The makeup." She shifted her focus to the swimming pool and sighed. "But . . ."

"But what?"

"This," she said, pointing to her face, "was a construction job that rivaled the building of the Taj Mahal. A miracle of modern makeup."

Jack took her chin in his hand and angled her face to the left, then the right. "Who did it? Cherry? Rachel? Mary Beth?"

"Rachel. How did you know?"

"There are only a few good makeup artists in

Austin. I've worked with all of them. I can spot
their work. Rachel's one of the best."

"I'll say! If she can make me look this good,
think what she could do with the girls at work."

"No amount of makeup could give them your
brand of beauty."

Maggie opened her mouth, then shut it. "Exactly what do you mean?"

He poked her lightly in the neck opening of
her jumpsuit. "That."

Maggie's pulse stuttered. She pressed her fingertips over the spot of skin Jack had touched all
too briefly and tried to pretend he hadn't affected
her. "What about it?"

"I'm talking about inside you. You're beautiful
there, too. You said it yourself. It gives you pleasure doing things for people. Unlike your *just inconsiderate* sister seamstresses at work."

Maggie threw back her head and laughed.

"I wasn't aware I said anything amusing. What's
so funny?"

"Men!"

"What about us?" he asked defensively.

"You're—that is, *they're* so shallow."

"I beg your pardon."

"With this inner beauty you claim I possess,
how many of the men sitting around this pool do
you think would give me a second look if I hadn't
had that make over?"

"Well . . ."

"Case closed. All this—" she swept her hand
over her face and batted her freshly tinted hair,
"—is superficial. It takes forever to make me look

this way. I'm not sure I want to go to the trouble just so I can attract men."

"That isn't the only reason women wear makeup and color their hair."

"Name one other reason."

"Business."

Maggie snorted. "Right. Look, I'm going to go change and wipe off the makeup so when I swim it doesn't streak down my face. I don't want to look like some creature from a horror movie." She twisted a finger in her hair. "Once I dive in that water, this'll be a mess. I'll look like the same old me, Jack. Just plain Maggie." Her determination to reinvent herself so she could attract a man who would return her love and give her babies slipped not one notch, but a whole ladderful.

"Once I'm me again, the men will treat me as if I don't exist."

"Somehow I doubt it, Princess. But go slip into your suit, and we'll see."

Despite Maggie's common-sense attitude about her appearance, Jack couldn't stop his blood from simmering as he watched her walk across the courtyard.

She drew enough admiring gazes to make any woman envious and any man feel threatened.

He didn't like guys looking at her that way. He knew what was going through their hormone-hazed minds. He knew because similar thoughts had been rolling around in his head since he

walked in and saw her in that knockout dress last
night.

He didn't care if Raleigh Cordell was president
of Grand Perimeter Hotels or President of the
United States. Jack had taken one look at the
smooth-looking character with the French accent
and been tempted to ask him for his handkerchief. Jack would have tied the linen square
around Cordell's skinny neck to catch the jerk's
drool.

Although Maggie had some inclination of the
stir she was creating, she really had no idea how
powerfully a man could react to a woman who
looked the way she looked. That naivete could get
her in trouble someday when Jack wasn't around.

Determined to cool his simmering ardor, he
yanked off his Bevo T-shirt, stretched his kinked
muscles, then plunged into the cool water of the
pool's deep end. Testing the capacity of his lungs
to divert his line of thinking, he swam underwater
for a lap, then surfaced in a gasp for air.

His lungs had barely recovered from the test
when Maggie emerged from the cabana housing
the women's facilities. He took one look at her
and hoped to hell his lungs would survive the onslaught to his heightened visual sense.

Maggie wore a simple swimsuit of royal blue. A
one-piece. A knit tank. The fabric clung to awe-
inspiring curves he had only begun to imagine
belonged to Maggie after he'd walked into the
hotel suite and seen her the night before.

She wasn't voluptuous. That suited him fine.
He'd never been a huge boob man. Her breasts

were high and firm. *Natural.* Beneath the surface of the water his hands curved around the imagined softness of the sweet mounds of Maggie's flesh.

Her legs were long, a fashion photographer's dream. He pictured them slicked with water while she ran down a sandy beach, the glow of sunset on her cheeks while foamy waves licked at her bare feet. He pictured her legs stretched out on a bed of slippery satin while she scooped her hair high on her head and pouted for a Victoria's Secret layout. He pictured them wrapped around his hips while he plunged into her with the need that right now was bunching in his groin.

He blinked away the vision and the momentary madness. Maggie dumped her bag on the lounge, spied him in the pool and waved. He waved back, then splashed a handful of water over his blazing chest.

Maggie removed her sunglasses, slid them into a case with her customary tidiness, then headed for the pool. Walking toward him with an easy smile and a relaxed gait, she was Bo Derek in the movie *10;* he, as equally dumbstruck as Dudley Moore had been. With each step she took, a bass drumbeat sounded in Jack's head. Boom-ba-da-boom, ba-da-boom.

Before she covered five feet, a body builder type lounging in the row nearest the pool swung his feet around and stood, blocking her path. The interception dispelled Jack's *10*-ish fantasy and silenced the booming in his head.

Seeing that Mr. Muscle Bound was detaining

Maggie, Jack started to bolt from the pool. By God, she might need his protection. But something stopped him. He had no right to treat Maggie as if she were an innocent ingenue. True, she was innocent, but at twenty-nine she was old enough to learn to deal with her newfound attractiveness.

He watched smiles spread and lips exchange words and wished to hell he could read lips. Facing the pool, Maggie tilted her head and glanced up into Mr. Muscle Bound's admiring eyes.

Too long.

Jack thought her gaze darted his way for the hint of a second. He was puzzling over that development when he saw her lift her chin a saucy measure and flip that glorious auburn hair over her shoulder.

Hell, Maggie, ask him to bed, why don't you?

Jack reached the side of the pool in two quick strokes and shot out of the water like a grounded porpoise. Water streaked down his chest and his waterlogged boxer-style swimsuit.

What now? he thought. He didn't want to make an ass of himself, or Maggie. Then he spied the bar. Yeah, that's it. He'd buy her a drink. Take it to her. Interrupt the action.

He arrived, plastic cup in hand, just in time. Her admirer was saying, "So how about dinner tonight?"

"Dinner?" Jack looped his arm around Maggie's firm shoulders. He gave her a lot-more-than-friendly kiss on the lips. She was looking at him as if he'd walked off an alien space ship when he added, "I'm afraid she's got plans for the evening."

The interfering muscle man flexed his oversized pecs and gave Maggie a dazzling smile. "Maybe breakfast then."

"That would be very—"

"Impossible," Jack interjected. "Our court time's at eight."

"But you know I don't—"

"That still leaves lunch," the silver-tongued workout king told Maggie, but he wasn't looking at her. He was staring at Jack with steely eyes. His fingers were curling into the beginnings of fists.

Jack glanced down into Maggie's wide, astonished eyes. "How about lunch, Princess? Think we can make it?"

Maggie gave him a look that would have seared leather and said through a poorly pretended smile, "May I speak with you a minute?"

"My time's your time, babe."

"Excuse us for a minute, will you?" she asked her newest admirer and taking Jack's hand yanked him toward the pool.

Jack followed Maggie to the far side of the shallow end. She crossed her arms over her chest and glared at him.

With much difficulty, Jack diverted his gaze from the cleavage that formed between her firm, high breasts. "You wanted to speak with me?"

She tilted her head in the direction of flexing male muscles. "What was all that about back there?"

"I was merely running interference for you."

"Who asked you to?"

"Maggie, you don't know guys like I do. What did he say to you when you started for the pool?"

" 'Well, hi.' "

"And you said?"

"Hi back."

"What did he say then?"

" 'Nice day.' "

Jack snorted. "Brilliant conversationalist! What did you say?"

" 'It's positively beautiful.' "

"Well, go on," Jack told her, wishing he could shake her and say, *Listen, babe, the guy was putting the make on you. Wise up!*

"That's about it," Maggie said curtly.

"Oh, yeah. You say, it's positively beautiful, and he says, how about dinner? Who are you kidding? I wasn't born yesterday. I *saw* you hold his gaze and flip your hair over your shoulder."

"Okay, Mr. Nosy," Maggie tossed back and propped her hands on her hips. "He said, 'Are you here alone?' and I said, 'No.' He said, 'Too bad, because I'd like to ask you to dinner tonight.' It struck me, like a ton of bricks, I want you to know, that he was actually asking me for a date. Me! So I explained I was here with you, and we were just friends. So, he said, 'How about dinner tonight?' That's when you walked up and made a fool of yourself. And me, I might add."

"Maggie, you don't know that guy."

"I might have if you hadn't interrupted."

"You can't go around talking to every guy you meet."

"Why not?"

"There are a lot of weirdos walking around. They aren't all as nice as me."

"How am I going to find out if I don't talk to them?"

"Hell, Mags, I don't have all the answers!"

"All I know is, you've been telling me I need to get a life. I need to break out of my boring routine and meet people. You said yourself I could lie around the pool, flirt with the lifeguard, pick up guys in the bar."

"That was before," Jack said through clenched teeth.

"Before what?"

"Before you looked like—like that."

"Let me get this straight," Maggie said, cocking her head as if listening to a strange sound. "When I looked plain, I was supposed to meet guys, get a life. Now that I'm not so plain-looking, I'm supposed to keep to myself. What kind of logic is that? Logic according to Lewis?"

"It makes perfectly good sense to me. Do you want to race, or don't you?"

"You bet I do, and I'm going to beat the pants off you."

A vision of that bareness knocked the breath out of Jack as Maggie sliced the water in front of her with a perfect racing dive. Before he could gather his wits, she had eaten up ten feet of lane.

Six

Not surprisingly, Maggie's fingers touched the pool's tiled wall several seconds before Jack's. He managed to recover from his slow start, but his downfall came because he swam with his eyes open.

During the second half of the lap, Jack turned to see Maggie's svelte body undulating in the water in the lane next to him. Totally focused, she pulled her arms down and power-kicked, her muscles tensed in the determined effort of champions.

How, Jack wondered, with a slip in his concentration that cost him precious seconds, could the sleek woman driving herself to best him in the pool be his Laura Ashley in combat boots?

When he hauled himself out of the water, he found the omnipresent photographer snapping Maggie's picture as she shook the tenseness out of her thigh muscles. Jack bent at the waist and gripped his knees, hauling air into his depleted lungs.

Before he could catch his breath, Mr. Muscles sauntered over to chat with Maggie, a thick, white hotel towel slung over his shoulder. The photographer motioned for him to stand next to Maggie so he could take a picture of them. Declining smoothly, the guy with the flexing pecs and audacious grin stepped back. He watched while Maggie wrung the water from her hair and smiled shyly into the camera.

As soon as the photographer made himself scarce, Maggie's admirer moved in again. He handed her what looked like a business card. When she took it from his hand, the guy put a classic move on her. Stepping behind her nonchalantly so he was looking over her shoulder, he put a casual hand at her waist while pointing at something on the card. He was close enough to bury his nose in Maggie's hair.

Time for action. Jack shot from zero to sixty in a split second. He had to help Maggie rid herself of the handsy jerk.

Intent on eating up the ground between him and Maggie, Jack didn't notice the protruding leg of a deck chair until he connected smartly with the tubular metal. The next few seconds were a blur of throbbing shin, flailing arms and uncontrolled forward motion.

A startled cry from an onlooker alerted Maggie and her admirer. They stepped apart in time for Jack to sail between them. He landed in a horizontal sprawl across the oil-slicked legs of two women sunning themselves on deck chairs.

Jack was apologizing profusely and attempting to extricate himself from the startled ladies when Mr. Muscles took his arm and pulled Jack to his feet.

"I don't need your help," Jack sputtered and yanked out of his grasp.

"You're right about that," the interloper retorted with an amused grin. "You can make a perfectly good ass of yourself without me."

"Oh, dear," Maggie cried and pointed to Jack's shin. "You're going to have a terrible bruise."

"The only thing here that's bruised is your friend's ego," the guy muttered, then turned his seductive smile on Maggie. "Call me if you have second thoughts about breakfast. You have my room number."

He saluted her with a finger to his forehead. On parting, he slanted Jack a cocky, victorious look.

"Now look what you've done," Maggie grumbled under her breath and stalked past Jack to her lounge chair.

Jack was sorely tempted to tackle the smart-mouthed guy and shove him into the pool where they could duke it out. But Jack was already in the proverbial doghouse with Maggie. The best thing he could do was give her time to cool down.

Collecting what was left of his dignity, he grabbed his gym bag off the chaise and jammed his baseball cap on his head. "I'm out of here."

Maggie caught up with him at the door to the hotel lobby. "Where do you think you're going?"

"Home."

"But it's only one-thirty."

"So? I've got film to develop."

"Can't you do it tomorrow?"

"Excuse me, Mags, but the way I see it, you're better off without me interfering in your affairs."

Maggie opened her mouth to say something more, then snapped it shut. "Fine. Go print your pictures. Maybe I'll call Franklin and see if he wants to play tennis."

" 'I think I'll call Franklin,' " Jack mimicked, then barked, "You do that!" He could almost feel the steam pouring from his ears, the blood pounding through his veins. "But don't blame me if *Franklin* makes a move on you."

"I can handle myself," Maggie insisted, then softened her manner when she added, "You are coming back, aren't you?"

"That depends."

"On what?"

"On whether or not you think I'll get in the way while you're trolling for men."

"I am *not* trolling for men," she answered hotly.

"Oh, no? What do you call it then?"

"The guy who talked me into this called it something like, 'lying around the pool, flirting with the lifeguard and meeting guys.' Now are you going to join me for dinner, or aren't you?"

"Are you sure you wouldn't rather go with *Franklin?*"

"You want a bruise on the other shin?"

"I hate it when you answer a question with a question. I'll be here at eight."

Maggie lifted her chin haughtily, sending her thick mass of wind-dried auburn waves bouncing over her shoulders. "Fine."

Jack palmed open the door, then paused, think-

ing how easy it might be for Franklin to sweet talk
Maggie into his room. "Hey, listen, kid, do me a
favor, will you?"

"What is it now?" Maggie asked impatiently.

"Watch yourself in the clinches, okay?"

Alone in his darkroom that afternoon, Jack ab-
sently poked at a piece of photosensitive paper in
the acrid-smelling developing solution with his
tongs. He'd finished processing the film for his
Friday shoot and had decided to tackle a roll he'd
shot for the hell of it.

Most of the roll were pictures of Maggie he'd
taken from his balcony with a telephoto lens before she underwent her head-turning transformation. In the diffused yellow light of the darkroom,
little by little, the first image of Maggie walking
home from work sprang to life on paper.

Wearing a loosely fitting dress and her clodhop-
per boots, she was strolling down the sidewalk, into
the wind. The breeze molded her skirt to her legs
and the bodice to her breasts. There were hints of
the alluring figure Maggie had kept hidden beneath her uninspiring attire. The rays of late afternoon sun streaked across her shoulders through
the foliage of a live oak. She was looking to her left,
her face in profile, her expression wistful.

Jack remembered following the direction of her
gaze and seeing a toddler sniff the tissue-paper-
textured pink blossoms of a crape myrtle. Jack
had caught Maggie's smile of delight in a second
frame as the toddler decided tasting was a much

preferable method of examination than sniffing the odorless flowers.

Having preserved Maggie on film was reassuring to Jack. Like so many women he'd known—his mother, and all those who had subsequently drifted in and out of his and his father's life—Maggie was proving to be elusive. Her emotions, as well as her appearance and her demeanor, were shifting and changing. But for his camera, he might wonder if the Maggie he remembered ever existed.

Perhaps that's why he had turned to photography, first as a hobby, then as a career. Peoples' emotions might change, they might walk out of his life, but with his camera he could capture the essence of them—something to hold and touch and prove to himself he hadn't imagined things he'd felt.

He lifted the print of Maggie from the developing solution and carried it to the dryer. He was in big-time trouble. Since kissing her the night before, he'd come to realize he couldn't settle, this time, for an image on a piece of paper.

He wanted more.

A lot more.

One of Maggie's endearing qualities that made Jack appreciate their casual friendship was her short memory when it came to holding grudges.

Judging from her sunny smile when she opened the door to her suite at eight that evening, she'd already forgiven Jack for interfering in her efforts to launch herself into the singles dating scene.

Jack handed her a gardenia wristlet he'd picked up on a whim from the hotel florist, then willed his eyes back into their sockets.

Maggie wore silk.

Black silk.

The dress had a calf-length, slender skirt slit provocatively up one thigh to—holy cow—a couple of inches above her knee. Jack slid his arms around her waist for a platonic forgive-me hug and discovered two things. Her arms were covered. Her back wasn't.

Jack's mind fell into the trap sprung by the dress's crafty designer. He figured there was no way in hell Maggie could be wearing a bra beneath that thin, seductive layer of silk and thought-destroying cloud of perfume.

Maggie sniffed the gardenia and smiled at Jack over the fragrant bloom. "Thank you. This will match my pearls."

And very possibly your breasts, his rampaging hormones whispered in his ears. "Ready for your night of magic, Princess?"

She hitched her shoulders. In her glittering eyes he saw a hint of the old Maggie—the undisguised excitement, the unsophistication that contrasted with auburn waves caught up on top her head with a comb of seed pearls.

Jack found himself wishing he had his camera so he could catch her like this—the deadliest threat to a man's bachelorhood. A combination of ingenue and vamp.

Maybe later, he mused as he prepared to do battle for her attention with every man in the hotel who had good eyes and half a libido.

Maggie's last thought as Jack escorted her from her suite was that she never should have let the boutique owner and the beauty salon contingent talk her into the black dress.

The hotel's impossibly frigid air-conditioning sent a continuing wave of goose bumps across her bare back. She teetered on the black peau de soie stiletto heels and prayed she would make it through the evening without falling off them and spraining her ankle. Because some seamstress had been too lazy to tuck the waist seam into the lining, Maggie's dress itched at her waist.

She wondered if men were worth all this discomfort. That morning she had let the concierge talk her into giving the bellhop her boots and dress to polish and dry clean. Otherwise, she might have been tempted to change clothes at the last minute.

Reverting to her old clothes, though, would be tantamount to pulling her baby blanket out of her hope chest and rubbing the slick satin border between her fingers. If she intended to attract men, she needed to take the plunge. Wear clothes that complimented her. Learn to style her hair, and apply makeup to highlight her facial features. She pressed a palm to her stomach and blew out a short breath.

Maalox, she thought. That's what I need.

After a candlelight dinner on a rose-colored damask tablecloth in the Grand Perimeter's Marseilles Room, Jack gallantly helped her from her chair and guided her to the dance floor.

"Oh, Jack, I haven't danced in years," she confessed as he took her awkwardly in his arms. "I don't think I remember how."

"Just hang on, Princess. I'll do all the work." He stood motionless on the dance floor, frowning. One hand held hers in a prelude to a dance. The other stayed suspended in air several inches from her waist. "Just tell me where I'm supposed to put my hand so I won't get slapped."

"Here," she said and moved his palm to the left curve of her waist.

"We look like we should be dancing the minuet. I can't lead you very well like this."

"Then put your hand here," she suggested, and moved it around her back to settle on the right curve of her waist.

The space between them ceased to exist. Maggie's breasts pressed softly against Jack's chest, her abdomen to the flat plane of his stomach. The band launched into a tune with a decided Latin beat. Jack didn't move. He stood there on the dance floor, as stiff as a fabric cutting board, his reaction to her closeness as obvious as the flesh swollen hard against her abdomen.

"Maggie?" Jack whispered coarsely through her hair.

She looked up and found she was eye-level with Jack's lips. Her throat went dry. Her pulse scrambled. "Yes, Jack?" she all but croaked.

"You said you want to meet guys here. Right?"

Until Jack had kissed her, that's what she'd wanted. But something told her to watch what she told him. She remembered her sister, Alyssa, commenting one time that guys got scared off when girls got serious too soon. "That's what I *said*," she answered Jack, with enough emphasis on the *said* to imply she might have changed her mind.

"Then I got to tell you something. If I hold you close like this, the guys in this joint are going to think you and I are, well . . ."

"Are what, Jack?"

"They'll think we're shacking up," he finished succinctly.

She thought over her answer carefully. Her pulse beat strongly against her vocal cords. "I can handle that, if you can."

"I don't have any problem with it. But since you are looking to meet guys, you got to know, with most of us, if we think a man and a woman are . . . well, you know, *involved*, we won't even bother to strike up a conversation with her."

The thought of what *involved* meant had Maggie's body thrumming. She wanted to ask Jack, *Are we involved? Do you want to be?* Instead, she swallowed with great difficulty and focused on the black stud in Jack's tuxedo shirt. "I see."

"So maybe we'd better dance farther apart."

"All right," Maggie agreed and prepared to put a bit more space between her and Jack.

He didn't move, though. He merely looked down into her eyes, frown lines creasing his forehead. "There's just one problem."

Maggie's patience snapped. Caution over her choice of words vanished. "Jack, you're making too big a production out of this. What is it?"

"I'll have to put my hand somewhere else."

"Then do it."

"There aren't many choices."

"For Pete's sake, pick one," Maggie insisted, all too aware that the air between them was growing thicker and more difficult to breathe by the second.

Jack cleared his throat and loosened his hold on Maggie at the same time he released his tenuous grip on her waist. Suddenly Maggie felt Jack's warm, moist hand rest lightly on the bare skin of her back, just above her waist. She sucked in a quick breath. Jack's touch had her pulse leaping.

She snuggled closer to Jack's chest and let the air trapped in her throat come out in a sigh.

"You realize if you let any other guy touch your back like this when you're dancing, he'll have mush for brains before the song's over."

"But not you."

"Uh—right." Jack craned his neck as if his tie were too tight, then swept Maggie in a full turn that left her dizzy.

"Jack, I almost fell off my heels," Maggie complained.

"Then kick them off."

"I couldn't. It wouldn't be ladylike."

Jack glanced quickly around the nightclub, then bent his head and murmured in her ear, "I wouldn't worry about it. It appears it's way past the nuns' bedtime."

If the teasing tenor of Jack's voice hadn't sent a chill tingling over Maggie's shoulders and down her arms, she would have boxed him in the chest for his comment. Instead she put a steadying hand on his shoulder and moved awkwardly to his lead. "The shoes stay on until the dress comes off."

"Maggie, my girl, I'd be careful who I said that to, if I were you," he commented dryly and tightened his hold on her. "Which reminds me. Did you and Franklin-boy play tennis this afternoon?"

Fragments of long-ago conversations between Maggie's older and younger sisters and their boyfriends wafted through her mind. She faintly remembered her sisters talking about the importance of making guys feel jealous of their competition. She contemplated giving Jack the impression that in his absence she had seen Franklin, both on and off the court. But it wasn't in her to perpetuate such a lie. "No, I didn't."

Jack pressed his lips to her forehead and drew her closer. "Good. What did you do?"

"Lounged around the pool, flirted with the lifeguard and tried to pick up rich guys," she returned and batted her eyelashes outrageously.

"If you did, I'd have had to stand in line to get to your room tonight."

"Don't be silly."

"You think I'm kidding? Take a look around. See how many guys are looking at you. And the women."

"Oh, Jack, I don't need that right now. I'm self-conscious enough as it is."

"I thought you wanted the attention."

"I do, and I don't."

"The dilemma of being beautiful," he murmured and swung her in another dizzying circle. "I'll bet every woman in this place would like to know where you bought that dress."

"I almost didn't buy it."

"Why not?"

"I wasn't sure I'd have the nerve to wear it. Jack, did you really mean it?"

"Mean what?"

"The part about women looking at what I'm wearing? Wanting to know where I bought it?"

Jack glanced into Maggie's uplifted face. Her lips were moist and slightly parted. She held herself in anticipation of his answer.

He didn't want to answer. He wanted to close his mouth over hers and pull the comb from her hair—to let that glorious hair tumble around her shoulders so he could thread his fingers through it. But Maggie didn't want him. She wanted other guys. She'd made that clear. Logically, he knew that was best for her, to meet and date many men. To learn things about herself in the process and figure what she wanted in the long term. But damned if he had to like it.

What was it she had wanted to know? Oh, yeah. If women would want to know where she got what she was wearing. "Sure I meant it. Why?"

Maggie said nothing for a moment, then meekly asked, "Do you mean by wearing a dress, I might induce women to buy it?"

"I'd bet my best lens on it. Why?"

"You know I design dresses when I have the time."

Jack shook the cobwebs of desire from his addled brain and forced himself to concentrate on the conversation. "Which your crafty boss takes credit for."

"Well, I've been keeping some designs to myself."

"Good for you. What are you going to do with them?"

"I'd like to open my own design studio someday."

"You never told me you wanted to do that."

"You never asked."

"True."

"How about you?"

"I've never been good at the designing thing."

Maggie poked his chest playfully. "You know what I mean. What do you want to do someday?"

Jack moved his hand so his thumb barely skimmed the curve of her cheek. What did he want to do someday? Take his time peeling off Maggie's clothes. Find out if her skin all over was as soft and smooth as that on her cheek. Move his thumbs, *his tongue,* to trace the undersides of her breasts, then watch her nipples tighten with need.

"Jack?"

"Hmm?"

"I asked you a question."

"You did?"

"Uh-huh."

Maggie's breath was hot and sweet against his

chin. The softness of her breasts was yielding to
the pressure of his chest. Her eyes were staring
up at him, luminous and trusting. Muscles in
Jack's nether regions flexed and swelled, not at
all like a good-old-buddy neighbor's ought to react.

Jack swallowed over a monster wad in his throat.
"I didn't answer you, did I?"

Maggie shook her head slightly. Her auburn
bangs brushed over his chin, smelling overtly of
perfume designed to make a man lose his mind
in need. "Mags?"

"Yes, Jack?"

"I don't want to dance anymore."

"Okay. What do you want to do?"

He clamped his jaw over the words that would
tell her exactly what was running through his
mind.

Maggie's expectant smile faded. "I'm sorry,"
she said and backed away, touching only his hand,
holding it hesitantly as if she expected him to
sever the connection if she hung on to him too
tightly. "It's late. I know you want to leave. You
have an assignment tomorrow?"

"Princess?"

"Yes, Jack?"

"I don't have to work tomorrow, and I'll tell
you something else. I don't want to leave."

Maggie's face bloomed in a smile. "I was hoping you'd say that. How about a nightcap then?"

If Jack had anything else to drink, his inhibi-
tions would drain right out his fingertips. "Milk,"
he stammered. "Do you have milk?"

"No, but I'm sure room service will bring some up. I didn't know you drank milk."

"Neither did I," he grumbled.

Grabbing her cocktail bag off the table, he touched the hot, bare flesh of her back and escorted her from the nightclub.

Maggie ordered Jack's milk from room service, then excused herself to slip into something that didn't itch. She found her old dress in the closet, cleaned and pressed.

When she returned in the baggy, low-waisted dress, Jack sat on the couch, holding his head in his hands.

"Jack?"

He lowered his hands and lifted his head. When he saw her, a jaunty, lopsided smile creased his face. "I'm glad you put that on."

"I thought you hated these dresses."

"I did."

"But you don't now?"

"They're okay for certain things, I guess."

"Like what?" Maggie asked and sat beside him on the couch.

"Hiding that body of yours from the guys."

"Oh, for Pete's sake!" she groaned and left Jack and his protective attitude to test the night air on the balcony.

Below and beyond, the ribbon of river that Austinites called Town Lake murmured by the hotel. At this late hour, only a few shore lights from restaurants reflected in the inky water. Down river, music from a blues band spilled through an open doorway to echo across the water. Nearby a night bird gave its plaintive cry.

Maggie ran her hands up and down her arms. The balmy air whispering off the lake softened the stiffness of the starched fabric of her sleeves.

Jack's arms came around her, crossed over her breasts and pulled her against the solid thickness of his chest. Maggie closed her eyes to the bitter-sweet agony of wanting Jack to feel what she felt. The desire to feel his lips nipping at her neck. His breath raising goose bumps on her flesh.

Jack pressed a kiss to the side of her head, his breath soughing through her hair. A traitorous whimper of desire escaped Maggie's lips.

Mortified that she had betrayed herself, she bit down on her lower lip. She wasn't good at this man-woman thing. She had too little experience. Why didn't Jack drink his milk and go home? Leave her to treasure her secret desire to be more to him than a dependable friend.

Jack inhaled a deep breath through her hair. "I like the way you smell. Like flowers."

"Thank you. I bought some new perfume downstairs, in the boutique."

"They really know how to fix a lady up, don't they?"

Maggie bristled, as much at Jack's sarcastic tone of voice as his offhanded compliment. "What did you mean by that?"

"Dress. Jumpsuit. After-five outfit. Shoes. Jewelry. Hose. Purse. Perfume. They're a regular department store."

Maggie turned in his arms. She thought he would release her. He didn't. She splayed her hands over his chest, testing her newly found initiative. She expected Jack to take her hands in his, kiss the backs of them, then the tip of her nose.

He didn't. He merely stood there, staring into her uplifted face while she felt the strong, steady beat of his heart beneath her fingertips. "I'm confused," she admitted.

Amusement flickered for the briefest of seconds in his eyes. "So am I, Mags."

"First I got the feeling you liked my new clothes. Now I get the impression you wish I'd never bought anything from the boutique."

"That's what I'm confused about."

Before Maggie could question his logic, he angled his head and claimed her lips.

The kiss—oh, yes, this time there was no mistake. It was a kiss. A full-fledged, lips on lips, lingering kiss. It robbed Maggie of her breath and churned her blood. It turned her knees to rubber and her willpower to ashes.

Willpower? What willpower! She didn't even try to back away from the deliriously pleasant sensations that swirled through her body.

Jack's tongue teased her lips apart; Maggie's knees buckled. He caught her with his strong, reassuring arms and bound her to him. A ribbon of heat licked through her abdomen, resensitizing dormant nerve endings.

Her head was woozy with arousal when Jack

broke the kiss and pressed his forehead against
hers. "The nuns were wrong about you, Princess."

"Hmm?" she asked in a haze.

"There's an S word they missed when they nick-
named you. They should have called you Sister
Sensuous. I've got to go now, before I'm tempted
to figure out some more S words they missed."

"Like?"

Giving that lopsided grin, Jack chucked her on
the chin. "Don't tempt me, Princess."

They strolled arm-in-arm toward the suite's
front door, saying nothing more, each apparently
thinking how the evening had changed things for
them.

On the credenza in the entryway, Maggie spotted a white envelope propped up by the lamp.
She must have missed it when she walked in with
Jack. No wonder, she thought, with a smile. "I
wonder what that is."

"Probably a message. You might want to open
it. It could be from your aunt. She knows you're
here, doesn't she?"

Maggie nodded and followed his advice.
Scrawled on the hotel message card was a two-
sentence note in a bold, masculine hand. "The
offer's still open for breakfast. I'll be in the Riverwalk Cafe at eight. Yours, Franklin."

"Franklin," Jack snarled over her shoulder.

Maggie slipped the card back into the envelope.
She could hardly believe that one man had just
kissed her, and another was asking her to breakfast. Is this how her sisters had felt all those years?

"Yes. Franklin," she said and dropped the note on the credenza.

Jack took her shoulders and turned her to face him. "You do realize you can't go."

"Why?"

"Because you're having breakfast with me."

"But—"

"I'll be here at seven-thirty."

Maggie smiled, sure she was dreaming. "But that's only five hours from now."

"So. You didn't come here to sleep, did you?" Jack traced the curve of her cheek with his thumb. His gaze lingered on her lips then lifted to meet her eyes.

He wasn't looking at her like the old Jack. The blue of his eyes was deeper, more intense. The heat in them had that ribbon in her stomach uncurling again. She fixed her gaze on the fullness of his lower lip and remembered how he had coaxed her mouth open and done incredible things with his tongue. She wished he would do them again.

What was it he had asked her? If she came there to sleep? She started to tell him that she wasn't sure she would sleep at all tonight. But the Maggie who had always been able to tell Jack anything stammered. "N-no."

"See you at seven-thirty then."

Jack was halfway across Congress Street Bridge before his head stopped spinning and he realized what a selfish bastard he'd been.

For the first time in years a man had asked Maggie for a date, and he, Jack, had ruined it for her. He'd acted like an ass at the pool and had no intention of meeting her for breakfast until "Yours, Franklin" extended the invitation.

Jack's finely honed instinct told him Franklin was sleaze. Something wasn't right the way the guy had stepped out of camera range when the photographer showed up at the pool. Jack was willing to bet Franklin had something to hide, which meant he wasn't for Maggie.

But who was Jack to judge? Maggie was a twenty-nine-year-old woman, capable of making her own decisions.

Still, the thought of that guy sitting across the breakfast table from Maggie, maybe talking his way into her suite—her bed—had Jack clenching his jaw.

He didn't want another man in her room, running his thumb over the smoothness of her cheek. He didn't want him pulling her against his chest until her breasts yielded against him. He sure as hell didn't want Franklin tasting the sweetness of her near-virginal mouth, sensing her hover on the verge of surrender as she had with Jack on that balcony tonight. Another man might not be so damned honorable.

By the time he got home, Jack was so riled he couldn't sleep. Across the courtyard Buck's apartment was dark. He was either out or asleep. Jack thought about calling Wilson, but nixed that idea. Wilson and Polly went to bed early, and Wilson had been concerned lately about Polly's health.

Not bothering to turn on the light, Jack pitched

his tuxedo jacket, then his cummerbund and
pants in a heap on the couch. A muffled screech
sounded from the heap.

"Hey, cat, that you?" He lifted his jacket to find
Homer batting at the dark fabric. The cat gave
him a haughty look and arched a bristled tail.
"Sorry, fella." Jack scooped him up, carried him
to his recliner and turned Homer on his lap to
face him for a man-to-cat talk. "You got a minute?"

Homer blinked and swept his tail from side to
side.

"Good. I need a guy to talk to. Buck's either
asleep or out. Wilson's probably in bed, with his
wife, lucky guy. So you're it, buddy. What I want
to know is, what am I going to do about Maggie?"

Jack smoothed his palm over Homer's head and
down his back. The orange tabby arched his back
against Jack's stroking hand, then gave him several swipes with his sandpaper tongue.

"That's what I want to do." Jack gazed out the
window, thinking of Maggie alone in that huge
hotel bed. "Run my hands all over Maggie's body.
Taste her skin."

Homer stretched again, this time unsheathing
his front claws. The needle-sharp points pressed
into the flesh of Jack's bare thighs.

"Yeow! Jesus!" Jack grabbed Homer under the
front legs and brought him to his face. "I said
that's what I want to do. I didn't say I was going
to do it. Hell, you old alley cat. You ought to know
what I mean. How do you feel when you see a

lady cat who makes your blood pump like you've chased a rat four miles?"

Homer gave a plaintive cry.

"My point exactly." Jack set Homer against his chest and stroked his silky fur. "She kissed me tonight. Boy, did she! She may be inexperienced, but she isn't frigid."

At the memory, Jack's libido stirred. "No, sir. Far from it. I didn't want to leave. I wanted to stay all night and . . ." He gave Homer a measuring look. "Never mind.

"Anyway, you won't believe the new Maggie. She's beautiful. She wants to date, do all the things she's missed. The way I figure it, she responded to me because I was the first guy who gave her a whirl since Melvin. She wants to meet other men. She even had me teach her how to flirt."

Jack smoothed his cheek over Homer's fur, wishing he were holding Maggie in his arms instead of her damned cat. "So I got to do the right thing. I got to step back and keep my hands to myself. If she wants me after she's dated a while, we'll see. Meanwhile, I guess I'll do what I've been doing. Be like a brother to her. Yeah, that's it," Jack announced with a determination he didn't really feel.

"But I'll tell you what, Homer, if any bastard tries to take advantage of Maggie, he'll get a good taste of my fist."

Maggie was in the master bathroom applying her mascara the next morning when the suite's seven phones rang.

She snapped up the closest receiver and cradled it between her shoulder and her chin. Her caller was Jack. His voice sounded husky, as if he were still in bed.

Maggie smiled, thinking of the few occasions she'd seen Jack vertical at the hour she left for Miss Caroline's. Each time he hadn't bothered to comb his hair or put on a shirt before he leaned out of his apartment to scoop his newspaper off the doormat. The morning sun had filtered through the entryway's glass panels to highlight the reddish cast in the triangular pelt of blond hair on his broad chest. His sweat shorts had hung low on his narrow hips. Maggie remembered thinking how nice it would be to wake up to him.

She blinked, leaving a black imprint of her eyelashes below her eyebrow. She wiped at the mascara with her finger and smeared it across her brow line. "Oh, darn."

"What's the matter?" Jack asked.

"I can't seem to get the hang of putting on all this makeup." Reaching for a tissue, she checked the crystal clock on the vanity. Seven-fifteen. "Are you downstairs?"

"Yes, but I'd like to talk to you about—"

She looked positively ghoulish. "Could you give me a few minutes before you come up?"

"Actually, I was thinking maybe us having breakfast wasn't such a good idea."

"Nonsense. We're both up and dressed, and don't forget, we're eating free."

"Hey, Mags, I mean it. Let's forget breakfast."

"You want to do something else instead?"

"No."

"The food didn't make you sick, did it?" Maggie's own stomach was a bit queasy, but not because the food hadn't been good. Every time she thought about Jack kissing her, holding her, making her body tingle with desire, her stomach turned into a mass of quivers.

"Nope. Feeling fine."

"Then why . . . ?"

Jack said nothing for a moment. Maggie heard a telltale exhaling of breath over the line, as if her question had produced a sigh of exasperation in her neighbor. A sickening dread spread in the pit of her stomach, eating away at the euphoria from the night before.

"I just think it'd be better if I gave you some space to do your own thing here," Jack finally stated.

Her own thing. What did that mean? If she couldn't see Jack today, she'd didn't care about sticking around the hotel. The thought of being with Jack again had inspired wildly romantic fantasies through the night. Sharing breakfast with Jack. The sounds of other diners swirling around them as they stared at each other over untouched omelets. Walking hand-in-hand along the jogging path that bordered Town Lake. Jack stopping to kiss her beside the sheltering arms of an ancient live oak. Sitting on the grass, shoulder to shoulder, hip to hip, knee to knee. Watching the rowers glide smoothly over the quiet waters as Jack would glide into her in the privacy of her suite during a glorious sunset at the end of the day.

Apparently she was the only one inspired by the events of the night before. Obviously, to Jack, the kiss, their touching, had meant nothing. Or worse still, maybe they were an embarrassment to him.

"I see," she replied coolly. "Well, thank you very much for taking the time to come down and break our date in person." She paused to press a fist against her mouth to keep from crying. "Don't forget to give Homer his vitamin."

"I won't. Hey, Maggie. You sound funny. You do understand what I'm getting at, don't you?"

"Of course," she replied, trying to sound nonchalant.

"Good. I'm glad that's settled. When will you be home?"

What do you care? she wanted to cry. "I don't know. My award card said I can check out as late as six."

"Oh," he said flatly.

Oh, what? And then it occurred to her. Jack probably had plans. A date. How could she be so dense? "If you have plans for the evening, don't worry about sticking around until I get home. Homer will do fine by himself. Take him up when you leave. I really must be going now."

She was about to hang up when she heard Jack say, "Maggie?"

Hesitantly, hopefully, she lifted the receiver to her ear. "Yes?"

"Are you going to meet that Franklin guy for breakfast?"

Maggie's cheeks were flaming, whether from anger or embarrassment, or a combination of both, she wasn't sure. "I might. It appears I'm up and dressed with nowhere to go."

"Be careful, Princess. There's something about him that doesn't sit right with me. Frankly, I don't trust the guy."

"How can you make such a judgment? You don't know him."

"Let's just say, I'm big on instinct."

"I'm a grown woman, Jack. I can take care of myself."

"That's what I was thinking," Jack replied with what Maggie could have sworn was a tinge of regret. "Have a good time."

$\mathcal{S}even$

By the time Maggie met Franklin for breakfast an hour later, her pulse was still wildly erratic. She tried her best to be bright and conversational. But how could she smile and make small talk when anger and disappointment over Jack's phone call sabotaged her conversation and demeanor?

The hotel's beauty wizards might have worked miracles on her appearance, but inside she was the same Maggie. She was sensitive to a fault and not sophisticated enough to hide her feelings.

Until midway through huevos rancheros, Franklin asked polite questions about her job and her family. About her winning the free weekend at the hotel. The questions had her wondering what her sisters would do if Jack had broken a date with them. She heard Franklin clear his throat and realized her attention had strayed.

"I'm sorry," she said and managed a thin smile.

"Your mind was somewhere else? On the guy at the pool maybe?"

"Jack?"

Franklin nodded.

Maggie lifted her chin and shook off lingering

thoughts of Jack. "Actually I was thinking about my sisters."

"Anything wrong?"

"No."

"About this Jack fellow, are you two dating?"

"No."

"Really just friends then?"

Maggie tried to feign indifference, although she knew her feelings for Jack had taken on a new dimension—a one-sided dimension, unfortunately. "Jack and I have known each other for over a year. He's been like a—a brother to me."

"A protective brother," Franklin said with a broad smile. "That explains why he looked like he'd like to deck me yesterday at the pool."

"I suppose."

"Where is he now?"

"I don't know," Maggie replied, yet she wished she knew. Did he have other plans? Was he with one of his model acquaintances?

Franklin leaned forward. "Your free weekend and all the excitement ends today—right?"

Maggie nodded, but as far as she was concerned, Jack's phone call had already signaled the end of her weekend's euphoria.

"You know, there's no need for the fun to end today. I'll be here until Wednesday on business. You could move into my suite with me. After work, you could show me the Texas Hill Country I've heard so much about."

Maggie's mouth dropped open. Appearing not to notice, Franklin looked around for the waiter.

Maggie was still trying to get her mouth to form

a refusal to Franklin's brazen invitation when he reached into his pocket and pulled out a calfskin wallet. To retrieve his credit card, she realized in a blur of disbelief. While he was wresting the rectangular piece of plastic from its snug compartment, a wallet-size picture tumbled out.

Maggie's gaze followed the photo to the tablecloth. The picture appeared to be a group shot—a family portrait to be more precise. Franklin with three little girls and a lovely-looking brunette woman.

A sick feeling stirred in her stomach, souring her breakfast. She had to put this man in his place. Let him know she wasn't the kind of woman who dated, much less *slept* with a married man. But how?

She forced a bracing gulp of ice water past a knot of repulsion forming in her throat, then picked up the picture. Had this ever happened to Sheridan or Alyssa? If so, what did they say? "Your family?" she asked numbly.

Franklin met her gaze directly. "Yes."

She shook her head. "Your daughters are . . . lovely."

"They are, aren't they? They take after their mother."

"Your wife."

"Yes."

Maggie's emotions shifted. Anger took over the controls. "Your current wife, to be more specific, meaning you're still married and living together."

"That's right, Maggie." Franklin reached across the table and slipped the picture from her still fingers. "Under the circumstances, I thought you should know."

"How considerate of you."

Maggie felt as if someone had dumped a bucket of slime over her head. She felt dirty, degraded. While she struggled to recapture what was left of her dignity, Jack's words echoed in her ears. *Be careful, Princess. There's something about him that doesn't sit right with me. Frankly, I don't trust the guy.*

Score one for you and your instinct, Jack.

So Franklin had three daughters and a wife. A family not unlike Maggie's before a terrible accident on the loading dock had punctured her father's lungs and snatched him away from his wife, Maggie and her two sisters. With the last air in his lungs, Harold Kincaid had struggled to convey a message. He asked that his co-workers tell his girls how sorry he was he wouldn't be there for them.

And Franklin flipped his lovely girls' picture around—intentionally, Maggie was sure—to notify any potential paramours that they could count on a roll in the sack with him, but nothing remotely permanent.

This dating business wasn't all it was cracked up to be, Maggie thought dismally. She started to excuse herself, to put as much distance as possible between her and this disgusting man. But Franklin's audacity kept her rooted to her chair. Someone needed to teach that man some manners.

Maggie recalled a scene from a sitcom that provided inspiration for the task. Pretending for the moment she had the talent, the dramatic flair of her sister, Alyssa, she tossed her hair over her shoulders and smiled coyly at Franklin.

Comprehension sparked in his eyes. He stuffed the picture back into his billfold. Holding his gaze, Maggie tapped her pink linen napkin to one corner of her mouth, then the other. She pulled a compact and lipstick from her purse. Giving Franklin a hot glance over the mirror, she slowly slid the tube of creamy red over her widely parted lips.

Franklin's gaze riveted to her mouth. "Nice color."

"You like it?"

"It's my favorite. I like almost anything red. Hair. jumpsuits." He lowered his voice and rubbed his leg against hers beneath the table. "Lingerie."

"How nice," Maggie said and drew out the last word, in an insulting Southern style. She tucked her compact into her purse and pushed back her chair. Franklin, being a northern type, apparently didn't detect the sarcasm in her voice. He wouldn't get another warning. "You'll excuse me for a moment?"

Franklin dropped his napkin into his plate and shot out of his chair, looking frantically for the waiter.

Maggie patted his hand. "Relax, darlin'. I'm just going to freshen up."

"You could do that in my room."

"Yes, I suppose I could," she said and batted her eyes outrageously. "But before I join you, I thought

I'd check out the lingerie in the boutique. The red lingerie," she added with an arched brow.

"I like the way you think," Franklin mumbled and lifted a finger to signal for the check. "Buy plenty. We can spend the entire day in my suite, if you like." He leaned down and gave her a buzz on the cheek that had her stomach churning with distaste. "I'll order dinner up," he said on a hot breath. "We can eat on the balcony and watch the sun set."

"How delightful," Maggie responded and noticed the tempo of Franklin's breathing had picked up. "You will wear those attractive white pants, won't you?" She let her gaze slide briefly to his golf slacks, where a mound had swollen noticeably in his crotch.

Franklin looked at her strangely. "If that's what you want."

By now assured she had attracted the attention of many diners in the room, Maggie spoke with what she hoped looked like a seductive smile. "We're talking about what I want?"

"We sure are, Maggie."

"Fine. I want you to sit down."

"Anything you say," he said with a perplexed smile and took his chair while she slipped back into hers.

The waiter arrived at the table. Franklin waved him off. He propped his elbows on the table and spread his hands wide. A broad grin tucked his cheeks into folds of tan-weathered skin. "Now what? More coffee?" He leaned forward and ran a finger over the back of her hand. "Or maybe you'd like some creamy cheesecake."

"Shh," she said in a naughty whisper, then glanced over her shoulder as if to make sure no one was looking. Someone was. Several someones. She tamped down the urge to smile.

Angling her head seductively while she held Franklin's amused gaze, she dipped one shoulder, reached under the tablecloth, and touched Franklin's knee.

A jolt of surprise widened his gaze. One brow shot up. One corner of his mouth lifted in a smile of ribald amusement. "Maggie, Maggie. You're full of surprises, aren't you?"

"I hope you remember that," she murmured, running the tip of her creamy red lipstick over the knee and up the thigh of his pants leg, "when you try to explain to your wife the stain on the front of your pants."

Maggie wasted no time returning to her suite. There she pulled on her trusty Docs, packed the overflow from her tote into a plastic laundry bag and bade farewell to her Cinderella weekend. Somehow she'd lost her taste for the affluent lifestyle. She hiked to the bus, which dropped her within a block of her apartment.

She stomped up the stairs, unlocked her apartment and discovered Homer wasn't home.

"Well, this is a fine kettle of fish," she grumbled and reluctantly descended the stairs to Jack's apartment. She wanted her cat home, and she wanted to be alone. What she didn't want was a confrontation with Jack. She didn't want him to know how much he had hurt her by breaking their date. His excuse that he thought she ought to be free to do her own thing at the hotel was hogwash. She probably wasn't sophisticated enough for Jack. Men—to hell with all of them.

She sounded the brass knocker on Jack's door twice, telling herself she could do this. She could pretend Jack had never kissed her. Make believe he'd never held her in his arms and aroused her.

"I'm coming. I'm coming!" he boomed from the other side of the door before he yanked it open. He was wearing a rubber apron and smelling of developing solution. "If my prints are ruined, I swear . . . Maggie! What are you doing here?"

"I live here. Remember?" She stalked through the door, chin held high, heart thumping erratically. "Where's Homer?"

"His Highness is in the bedroom. On my pillow probably. I'll be plucking cat hair off my sheets for days."

"You could wash them," Maggie returned. "Or is it that time of year?"

"Oh, boy," Jack mumbled and shook his head, "it's going to be one of those days, I can see."

Until last night, Maggie would have ducked in and scooped Homer from Jack's bed. Now the thought of entering the room where Jack slept had her conjuring up thoughts of tangled sheets, his musky male scent and several particularly hot fantasies from her dreams. "Would you get him for me?"

"Homer? Sure. Why not? I can wash the cat hair from my hands and my apron before I go back in the darkroom."

"Jack?"

"Yeah, Maggie."

"Stuff it."

"Maggie," he said, his eyes wide, a smile splitting his face as he followed her into his bedroom. "Do you realize what you just did?"

"Yes. I told you to get lost."

Once in Jack's bedroom, Maggie tried not to catalog the contents of his intensely personal space, but she couldn't help it. He'd negligently tossed the white oxford-cloth shirt he'd worn Friday night, plus the tie, over the back of an overstuffed armchair. His underwear—Bullwinkle boxers—dangled from the post of a queen-sized bed. The pillow closest to her still bore the impression of his head.

Regret tugged low in Maggie's abdomen. She had hoped that today they would pursue the intimacy that had sprung up between them on Friday and Saturday nights.

Fat chance.

The trouble was, Maggie's desire for Jack was being stubborn. It had wrapped its tentacles around her and refused to let go. She wished she weren't in Jack's bedroom. She wished Jack's vanilla-laced cologne wasn't everywhere. In the twisted wad of sheets on the bed. In the laundry piled high in the corner. In the open bottle of Obsession that sat on his dresser.

Maggie's gaze moved back to the bed where Homer had laid claim to Jack's other pillow. Something shiny drew her attention back to the dresser. A dozen little foil packets, like the one that had been thrust into her hand on the UT campus by safe-sex demonstrators, lay there in plain view.

Condoms.

A least a dozen of them!

A man bought one condom in case. He bought twelve because he anticipated—Maggie gulped—because he planned multiple exposures.

Maybe that was the real reason Jack had broken their breakfast date. He had other plans—that required the use of condoms. Her gaze flicked to the overflowing wastebasket. No opened, empty packets in view, at least. Still . . .

A burning flush crept up Maggie's cheeks. "Come on, Homer, baby," she said and snatched him off Jack's pillow. "Momma's home. Let's get out of this dump."

Homer lifted a haughty chin. When Maggie scooped him up from Jack's pillow, the cat cried out in disgruntled protest. Maggie buried her face in his fur. Careful not to look at those foil packets, she swept out of the room.

Jack caught up with her at the door. "How'd your breakfast go?"

"Fine."

"Fine?" Jack waved his hands. "What does fine mean? Fine the food was good? Fine you liked Franklin? Fine you're going to see him again?"

"I don't see that it's any business of yours," Maggie said coolly, the vision of all those condoms looming in her head. When—with whom—did he plan to use them?

She was relatively certain he'd noticed that she'd seen the foil packets, yet he made no effort to scoop them in a drawer or otherwise hide them from view. He hadn't even squirmed. If anything, his attitude had been blasé. Like, what did you expect? Every man has cologne, keys, and condoms on his dresser.

If that's what sex had become in the nineties, no wonder women immersed themselves in romance novels for stories of traditional love. "I don't think I'll be seeing Franklin again," she told Jack.

"Why not?"

"Let's just say I'm learning to stand up for myself. That and I don't think he likes red anymore."

Jack shook his head, as if by doing so he'd get Maggie's logic to filter through his brain. "Red. You mean your hair?"

"Not exactly."

"I was going to say, if he doesn't like your hair, he's got lousy taste. I like your hair. The color and the waves and—"

"Save your compliments for your model friends." Maggie turned to go, but Jack was fast on his feet. He got to the door first, leaned back against it and crossed his arms over his chest. "You're not leaving."

"Oh, great. First you don't want to see me, then you won't let me leave."

"I didn't say I didn't want to see you."

"You didn't have to. Breaking our date said it succinctly."

"I did that because I thought that's what you wanted. To be left alone so you could meet men. This afternoon, I got to wondering why."

"Because I prefer them to women," Maggie quipped, not willing to admit that her desire to connect with the opposite sex had narrowed from plural to singular. Jack.

"Cute. What I mean is, why now? Why not six months ago?"

"Well . . ." Maggie stroked Homer's head, trying to decide if she should bother explaining herself to Jack. Judging from the size of his condom supply, *he* had a very active social life. How could he possibly understand her need to find that one special person to marry and have children with?

Jack's expression, though, was serious. He was, after all, her best friend. She didn't want to lose the one person who understood her, who was always there for her. If they could get past this detour into the sexual potential of a relationship that existed between any man and woman, they could revert to their casual, relaxed status.

So, she took a chance. "I turned twenty-nine last month."

"Uh, oh," he said with a comprehending nod. "The fourth decade and biological clock panic.

You think if you don't find the right guy soon, you won't have the goods for the competition."

"It isn't so much that," she admitted, realizing after the events of the weekend that she wasn't as plain and unattractive as she'd thought. "It's more the family thing."

Jack cocked his head and waited for her to continue.

"You know, babies."

"Babies," he repeated flatly.

"Yes. I want several. If I don't start my family soon, I'll run out of time before I run out of desire."

The old Jack would have landed with both feet in her last statement and made her blush big time. But he just stood there, looking at her as if she were crazy. "Isn't that putting the cart before the horse?"

"You want to explain that?"

"Maybe I'm crazy, but the way I hear it, it's supposed to go love first, then marriage, then babies."

"Of course it is."

"But you're not looking for love. You're looking for a—a damned stud!"

She lifted her chin defensively. "I'm sure there are a lot of men who have the same priorities. I wouldn't want to marry a man who didn't want children."

"And what if you met a guy who wanted them real bad?"

"That would be wonderful."

"Women!" Jack threw up his hands and paced

in front of his door. "You can't make them understand a damned thing."

"It would help if—"

Jack stuck a finger in her face, his expression
dead serious. "Look, Princess. I'll spell it out for
you. With that agenda of yours, you could fool
yourself into believing you love a guy. You get
married. You have babies. The old man loses his
job. The babies get sick. The bills stack up. Your
mother-in-law comes to visit. She doesn't approve
of the way you're raising the kids. Suddenly Daddy
doesn't look so good. You know why? Because you
didn't love him in the first place. You two split.
Who gets hurt?"

"Everybody, but—"

"Especially those sweet little kids," Jack pointed
out.

"Don't you think I'm mature enough to make
sure I loved a guy before I married him?"

"I don't know. You were obviously wrong about
Franklin."

"Wait a minute. There's a leap in logic here,"
Maggie pointed out. "I didn't marry him. I only
had one date with the man."

"Even though I warned you he was scum."

"How was I to know he was married!"

"That dirty bastard!" Jack took Maggie by both
arms. "What did he try to do to you? You didn't
let him take you to his room, did you?"

"No, and believe me, I took care of him. He'll
never bother me again, unless perhaps to send
me a cleaning bill."

"Come again?"

Maggie waved away Jack's query and pushed his hands away. She couldn't let him touch her. When he did, her thinking got fuzzy. "Trust me. He's history."

"You see what I mean, Princess? You've got lousy instincts when it comes to people."

"What makes you think yours are so good?"

Jack looked at her for a long moment, then shifted his gaze briefly to a bookcase in the corner. The only thing of any consequence Maggie could see on the shelves besides a disorderly array of books and magazines was a picture of his father.

"Believe me," Jack stated with stern authority, "when it comes to reading people, I'm the king."

"And kings blow it sometimes," Maggie retorted, then cuddled Homer close to her chest. "Come on, baby. Let's get out of here. We wouldn't want to keep Jack from his work." Thinking of his condom stash, she added under her breath, "Or whatever else the king has planned for the evening."

Early Sunday evening, after Jack had developed, cropped and printed the remainder of his film, he ripped open one of the shiny foil packets and extracted the condom.

Positioning it just so in one hand, he applied the hot tip of his glue gun to the outside of the rolled rim. He clicked the gun trigger twice. Thick, hot glue spurted out and seared the tip of Jack's forefinger.

"Hot damn!" he muttered and stuck the stinging finger into his mouth.

By the time he'd glued all twelve condoms onto the forking twigs of the cheap, artificial plant he'd bought, his finger throbbed with the pain of several additional glue burns.

"You'd better get a laugh out of this, old buddy," Jack muttered to himself as he stuck the condom-bearing plant securely into a pot filled with florist's clay.

He stood back to admire his creation. His version of a rubber tree plant would be his contribution to the wake the poker buddies were throwing tomorrow tonight for Buck. The object of the tongue-in-cheek party was to perk Buck up. Alleviate the guy's pain and suffering, if only for a couple of hours. Tomorrow marked the first, official, miserable day of Buck's unwanted return to bachelorhood.

Three years down the tube. Surprise, surprise. How Buck had thought his marriage could survive when his lovely wife worked in Seattle, and he in Austin was beyond Jack's comprehension.

Buck's morose situation reminded Jack all too much of his dad's. There was one mighty big difference—the broken-hearted, confused kid Jack had been. At least Buck's marriage hadn't been blessed with children who would be torn up by the divorce.

Before Jack tied the knot, he'd have to be damned sure his and his intended's vows were backed by an iron-clad determination to do what it took to keep the family together. Jack didn't

want any kid of his having to endure what he
had. No momma telling him to get lost. No
string of potential parents drifting in and out of
his dad's life, treating him as if he didn't matter.

Better to not marry than risk screwing up an
innocent kid's life.

He poked artificial moss around the base of his
rubber tree plant. He thought of the unfulfilled
maternal urge that had Maggie determined to
leap into the dating scene again. Because she
wanted kids, she was looking for a husband. The
nineties version of an M.R.S. degree.

Trouble was, she'd probably convince herself
that the first single guy who treated her well was
her meant-to-be, true love. Jack had seen it happen several times to models who tired of the demanding regimen of their career.

He thought of the jolt that shot through him
like lightning when he saw Maggie in all her glory,
beautiful. For a while there, she'd mesmerized
him with looks that would put any woman to
shame. So soft, so sweet, so pulse-pumpingly stunning he almost didn't listen to his inner voice that
was screaming, "Stop it, you idiot!" Although Jack
planned to do some knee-bouncing, shoulder-
burping of his own someday, he sure as hell wasn't
going to let himself get sucked into marrying
Maggie so he could be her stud.

That is precisely why he'd kept his big mouth
shut when she'd spotted what for him would be
more than a year's supply of condoms. Better let
Maggie think he had the morals of an alley cat

than wind up siring babies with a woman who didn't really love him.

And probably wouldn't stick around for the duration.

Eight

To keep from thinking about Jack's lecture—
and all those condoms—Maggie spent Sunday afternoon and evening doing a week's worth of
homework in advance, waxing her furniture, and
packaging up the Mont Blanc pen with a thank-
you note for her Aunt Barbara.

On Monday she arose an hour early to do her
best at imitating the artistry of the Grand Perimeter's makeup and hair stylists. Then, her morning
newspaper tucked into her tote bag, she walked
the three blocks to work.

She knew she still needed hours of practice before she could make herself look anything close
to glamorous again. Still, she couldn't wait to see
if Kayla, Desiree, and Juliana noticed the difference in her appearance.

The bell above the shop's door tinkled as she
walked in on the dot at nine, later than her usual
early arrival. At her entry, Kayla, Desiree, and
Juliana exploded from the back room.

"Maggie, you lucky dog!" Kayla gushed. "Oh,
my gosh! Look at her hair. It's red. Maggie's hair
is red, and it looks . . . gorgeous! And you aren't
wearing those ugly boots."

"Lucky?" Maggie asked.

"You know—the hotel! Your free weekend."

"You know about that?"

"Are you kidding?" Desiree thrust the Monday *American-Statesmen* under Maggie's nose. "All of Austin knows. See, your picture's right here, on page eight. Tell us all about it. What's the Presidential Suite like? Why didn't you call us? We could have come up and had a giant party!"

Being not only a part of but the nucleus of her co-workers' conversation was a seductive experience for Maggie. The episode reminded her of the closeness she had shared with her two sisters in the dormitory-style room their father had built over the garage before he died.

The major difference was not to be overlooked, she reminded herself, with a red-hot flash of resentment. Her sisters had loved her. Sheridan and Alyssa had shared with her. They hadn't envied her successes in her areas of interest while they pursued others.

Until this morning the only emotion the other seamstresses had exhibited toward Maggie, with the occasional exception of Juliana, was undisguised envy. Just once she was tempted to do what Jack had urged her to do. Stand up for herself and give them a piece of her mind.

She opened her mouth to do just that, but the words wouldn't come. She had to work with these women. Being shut out by them was uncomfortable enough. If she made them angry, Maggie wasn't sure she could bear the added tension.

Instead, she told them about the Presidential

Suite's seven phones, the view of Town Lake, the dozens of roses in the hotel's signature crystal vases. She whirled self-consciously to show off one of the garments she had selected with her gift certificate.

"But who did your hair? And your makeup?" Desiree wanted to know.

"People from the hotel salon."

"You really do look beautiful, Maggie," Juliana murmured respectfully.

Kayla lifted her chin and crossed her arms over her chest. "I hope you know how to keep it up. On your salary, you'll never be able to afford regular appointments at that salon. And in a couple or three weeks, your roots will begin to show."

"We could help her," Juliana offered. "Desiree, you color your hair. Surely you could give Maggie some tips."

Desiree shot Juliana an acid look. "I'm a natural blonde. I only lighten my roots."

Miss Caroline rounded the corner, wearing a taupe suit Maggie had designed to complement the former model's lean figure and patrician features. "Girls, girls, we have gowns to sew. Maggie, you look lovely. That was a nice article about you in the paper."

"Thank you, Miss Caroline. I'm afraid I haven't had time to read it yet."

"Perhaps on your break." Maggie's boss gave her a measuring look. "What's on your schedule today?"

"Finishing that bridal gown."

"How would you like to help me staff the Save

Our Springs benefit fashion show? I could use an extra hand."

"I appreciate the opportunity, Miss Caroline, but as it is, I'm worried about meeting the tight deadline on that gown."

"What do you have left to do?"

"The handwork mostly."

"If that's all, Kayla can work on it for you while you're gone. You won't mind, will you, dear?"

"Mind? Why no, Miss Caroline," Kayla said through a forced smile.

Maggie couldn't have effected a better put-down of Kayla if she had tried. Handwork was something all the seamstresses could do; it required the most basic of skills. Besides, Maggie knew that if Kayla helped on the bridal gown, her own schedule would suffer. That meant Kayla would have to work late hours, which would put a crimp in her social schedule.

After all the catty remarks and slights she had endured at Kayla's instigation, Maggie supposed she should feel a measure of victory. She didn't. Watching the high color flame on Kayla's cheeks, she knew Kayla would find a way to make her pay dearly for this latest privilege granted Maggie. Miss Caroline had never asked any of the seamstresses to accompany her to fashion shows where she displayed and sold designer labels ordered on trips to the Dallas Apparel Market. The savvy proprietor wanted her seamstresses there in the shop, producing the expensive garments for which she made the highest markup.

Why was Miss Caroline making an exception this time?

Her answer came when they arrived at the Driskill, the grand dame of the Texas capital city's restored hotels a few blocks away in the heart of downtown Austin. One of Miss Caroline's models had called in sick. Maggie was the right size for the garments.

"I couldn't," Maggie insisted, sure she would trip and fall on the ramp that had been erected in the Crystal Ballroom.

"Of course you can," Miss Caroline assured her. "I'll announce you're filling in, so no one will expect you to be smooth and polished. The main thing is to have fun with it. Pretend you're someone else. A movie star."

"But my hair—"

"Is lovely. I have to apologize to you, Maggie. I never knew you were so beautiful. Consider this your contribution to saving Barton Springs."

That did it. Austinites put Californians to shame in their strident efforts to clean up and preserve the local environment. Their favorite local cause was saving the aquifer that fueled Barton Springs, a community swim resort south of the river. Maggie and her sisters had splashed in the natural pool of pure, cool spring water as children. While walking down that ramp Maggie would think of the early years when the entire family picnicked beneath the spreading arms of live oaks and pecan trees.

Nine

Once in a rare while the *American-Statesman* pitched Jack a crumb when the news demand exceeded the supply of photographers.

Today was one of those days. The assignment came at a good time. Now Jack would be able to pay next month's rent on time.

The call came while, coffee cup in hand, he stared bleary-eyed at page eight of the Monday morning edition. There was Maggie—the new Maggie—hair fluffed and shining. Makeup enhanced glorious features only God had known she possessed until her recreation at the hands of the hotel beauticians. She was smiling up into the face of that hotel president, Raleigh Cordell. He was looking at her as if he'd like to eat her for breakfast.

Lounging now against the back wall of the Driskill Hotel's Crystal Ballroom, Jack felt a snarl coming on. Resentment tightened in his gut. He didn't like the hot glances Maggie was drawing from admiring men with her glamour girl looks. Men like Raleigh Cordell.

This morning Jack had tried to catch Maggie before she left for work. He needed to let her know he'd forgotten Buck's party when he talked about getting together with her tonight. He barely missed her but caught sight of her walking through the parking lot. She almost caused a rear-end collision when Buck slammed on his brakes to let her pass in front of him. Jack half wished he hadn't encouraged her to alter her Laura Ashley-in-combat-boots image.

Now she'd have to fend off advances she had little experience at deflecting. She'd have to cope with guys who wanted to run their hands all over her. And didn't he know how it felt, because last Saturday night it had been all he could do to keep his hands to himself.

Maybe, Jack thought, as a silver-haired lady took the last empty chair in the Crystal Ballroom, he'd have to have a talk with Maggie. Tell her what to expect from these guys. The time between what's-your-sign and hop-in-my-bed had shortened drastically since Maggie had been out in the dating world.

Her brush with that married guy, Franklin, had been scary enough. When Jack got home, he'd leave a message on her answering machine. If she was free, they'd get together Tuesday night, instead of this evening.

Overhead, the glittering lights of the antique crystal chandeliers dimmed. Caroline McCann moved to the microphone. Not a bad-looking chick, Maggie's boss. Not Jack's type—too old by a half dozen years—but a classy-looking dame nonetheless.

Jack sidled around the packed ballroom and assumed his spot against the far wall. From the speakers came the lively jazz for which Austin was known. From behind a hunter green curtain, the first model sashayed onto the ramp and strutted down the runway.

Nice hair. A blonde, but skin and bones. No sparkle in her eyes. Maggie was a hell of a lot more attractive, Jack thought, but tripped the shutter anyway. The society editor had asked him for one shot of each model in each outfit. The more pictures he sold, the more money he'd make. Who was Jack to argue?

"Our next model is wearing a versatile ensemble," Maggie's boss announced. "The suit will take her into the high-powered offices of professional women, then out for an evening of dining and dancing."

The music picked up tempo. A dynamite redhead in an electric blue suit stepped hesitantly onto the runway, a nervous expression on her face.

Holy cow, Jack thought and shot up from his crouched position. "Maggie!"

"Sit down," a female voice behind him complained.

"I see our photographer knows our model," Caroline McCann said and slanted Jack a warning look.

Jack barely caught it. His eyes were rooted to Maggie. She looked like she belonged in a board room or on the set of the evening news. The straight, snug skirt barely skimmed the top of her knees. Her great legs swished smartly down the ramp.

Jack's chest burst with pride. That was his Maggie. His upstairs neighbor. He pressed his eye against the viewfinder and snapped away.

"Maggie Kincaid is one of the designers at Miss Caroline's Couturier, where all our fashions today can be purchased," Maggie's boss explained. "Maggie, show the ladies what happens when you remove your jacket."

Maggie reached up and unfastened a button on one shoulder. Turning her back to the audience, she slipped out of her jacket to reveal a figure-hugging dress. The footlights reflected points of shimmering light off rhinestones that studded strips of fabric crisscrossing a broad oval opening on Maggie's back.

The crowd gave a collective round of admiring oohs and ahs. Face flushed, Maggie turned, slung her jacket over her shoulder on one finger and resumed her walk.

Her gaze fell to the crowd to her right and collided with Jack's. A broad grin split her cheeks. She gave her shoulders a slight little hitch and wobbled slightly on her heels.

Jack's pulse hammered in his ears. He lifted his camera and shot. Once. Twice. A knot swelled in his throat. He watched the gentle sway of Maggie's hips as she walked back up the ramp.

"You may have seen our Maggie's picture in this morning's paper," her boss announced. "She was a real-life Cinderella this weekend when she won a free stay in the Presidential Suite at the

Grand Perimeter. Let's give Maggie a special round of applause for filling in for one of our models today."

That's when it hit Jack like a sledgehammer. Maggie was a class act. She had the looks and finesse to carry off anything that struck her fancy.

Where did that leave an underpaid, underappreciated photographer like Jack? A guy who was trying like hell to forget her but couldn't get her out of his mind?

Make up your mind, bozo. Either you want her, or you don't. Better decide quick. And pray like hell Maggie cares as much for you as she thinks she does.

Miss Caroline told Maggie she was such a hit in the blue cocktail suit, she could have sold the design ten times over.

As her thanks for Maggie's good-natured help with the fashion show, she gave her favorite seamstress several remnants of beautiful fabrics and the rest of the day off.

Maggie was still pinching herself when she knocked on Jack's door at six o'clock. He answered in snug jeans, an ironed plaid sport shirt, his wavy hair still shower damp.

"Maggie, what are you doing here?" Jack asked, smoothing a hand through his hair.

"Maybe I'd better come back later and try again," she said with a half laugh and turned toward the stairs.

"I didn't mean that the way it sounded." Jack

glanced at the tray in her hands. With her short workday she'd had time to whip up dinner for the two of them. "I hope that tastes as good as it smells. What is it?"

"Your favorite. Spaghetti. Heavy on the garlic, hold the mushrooms." She breezed past Jack into his apartment. "You didn't need to get dressed up, just for me."

Her gaze fell to a new potted plant on Jack's coffee table. The blooms looked . . . strange. Dear, Lord, they were condoms! Gesturing with her hand at what she could see now was an artificial plant, with unusual embellishments, she said, "What, may I ask, is that?"

"A rubber tree plant."

With about a dozen condoms glued on the branches. So that's what they were for! The pocket of uneasiness that had niggled at her because of Jack's healthy stash of prevention vanished in a blink. "So now they grow those things on trees. How handy."

"It's a gift, smarty pants."

"Not for me, I hope."

"Of course, not. It's for Buck. His divorce was final today. The poker gang's throwing him a wake. I thought, under the circumstances, the occasion called for a little humor."

"You're having a party for Buck? Tonight?"

"Sure. You got my message, didn't you?"

"What message?"

"The one I left this morning on your machine."

"I haven't checked it since I got home," Maggie

admitted. She rarely got calls. "What was the message?"

"I'd forgotten about Buck's party. It's been planned for weeks. I suggested we get together tomorrow night instead." He gave the dinner a wistful look. "Tell you what. I'll run over, pay my respects and call you when I get back. If you don't mind eating late, that is."

"If it's dinner you want, go ahead. Eat. Be my guest." She looked around for a place to set down her tray. "I can't believe you're standing me up again."

Jack caught her arm. "We didn't have a date, Maggie. We were just going to talk, *friend* to friend."

Jack's pointed emphasis on the word *friend* told Maggie *Back off. Forget I kissed you. That was just recreation. You're a friend. Only a friend.*

The old wimpy Maggie would have smiled and said, whatever you say, Jack. I'll wait for your call. But events of the last few days had a new starch stiffening her spine. Strangely, the backbone reinforcement was a result of Jack's goading.

The anger rose inside of her and spilled out in words. "For your information, I refused a date tonight because you and I had plans. If you had called me earlier, I could have gone."

"A date?" Jack thundered, wiggly vertical lines furrowing his brow. "Who with?"

"A director from Save Our Springs," she said haughtily and turned to leave.

" 'A director from Save Our Springs,' " he mimicked. "Then why don't you call him and tell him you can go after all."

"I think I will."

"Fine."

"Fine." She turned to leave, her dinner still in her hands. It would be a cold day in hell before she would cook for Jack Lewis again.

"Where was he going to take you?"

Ha! Maggie had gotten a rise out of Jack, or he wouldn't have asked. She lifted her chin, refusing to face him. "To Olay's."

Jack snorted and came around to glare in her face. "You mean that place where the motto is, 'If it burns the lips, it frees the mind?' The guy's got real class."

"At least *he* was going to buy my dinner. Besides, I like hot food."

Jack jammed his hands on his hips and glowered at her. "How about hot men?"

"Jack! You're out of line."

"You think you're ready to get back into the dating scene, but I'll tell you, Princess, you don't know diddily about it."

"I wasn't born yesterday," she said coolly.

"You just think you weren't. The rules of the dating game have changed a hell of a lot since you were out there."

"Like how?"

"Like how long it takes before a guy tries to get you in bed."

"How long is that?" she asked aloofly.

"Ten minutes maybe."

"Oh, sure. A guy's going to say, hello. How are you? Would you like to go to bed with me?"

"No, now it's hi, babe, what's your sign, let's hop in the sack."

"You needn't worry about me, Jack," Maggie said, furious that he saw her dating other men but not him. "I can take care of myself."

"Okay, let's play a little game, and I'll show you."

"Can I put this thing down?" she asked and lifted the tray.

"Here, let me have it." Jack took the tray from her hands and looked for a place to set it. There being no uncluttered surface, he swept a pile of junk mail off the coffee table with his elbow.

"Now, let's say I take you to dinner. Afterward, we have a drink or two in the bar, listen to some jazz. Are you with me?"

"That would take more than ten minutes," Maggie commented dryly. "Even with your eating habits."

"Cute. So you've had a couple of glasses of wine, and I say, 'You know, I'm real excited about a new program we've developed to help save our springs.' And you say—?"

"I'd love to hear about it."

"And I say, 'I'll do one better. I've got a brochure in the car that outlines the whole program. I'd like you to see it.' And you say . . . ?"

" 'Sure. Why not?' "

Jack's eyes gleamed. "So I signal for the check, leave a hefty tip and take you to the car. I tear the car apart looking for the brochure. Then I say, 'Stupid me. I left it in my apartment. It's only a few minutes' drive from here. I'll just run over and get it.' When we get to my apartment, I start to get out. I hesitate. I shake my head. I say, 'Maggie, I don't feel right leaving you sitting out here in the dark by yourself while I go inside. Come on. It'll only take a minute.' So you . . . ?"

"Go inside."

"Wrong!"

"Why not? We've got gangs around here, like any other city. And an occasional weirdo."

Jack took her arm, anger sparking in the crystal blue of his eyes. "Because once director boy gets you in his apartment, he's going to be all over you like pigs on . . . potatoes."

"Give me some credit, Jack. I can say no."

"He may, uh, how shall I put it? Find other things for you to do with your mouth."

Maggie felt a flush creeping up her neck. "Are you saying I should never go to a man's apartment?"

"Not unless you're ready to go to bed with him."

"I'm in your apartment, and you're not trying to get me into your bed."

Jack said nothing. He merely stood there, glaring into her eyes, his grip on her arm tightening until it hurt. He was so close, she could feel his moist, minty breath on her face. A muscle in his jaw flexed. His nostrils flared. He grabbed the back of her head with one hand and pressed his lips insistently to her slack mouth.

Her mouth didn't stay slack for long. Her lips matched the pressure, the desperation of Jack's kiss. She twined her arms around his neck and responded openly to the sensations Jack sparked in her quivering body.

Jack didn't just kiss her; he devoured her. He sampled the textures of her mouth, then shoved her hair aside to trail hot, wet kisses down her neck and into the open V of her jumpsuit.

Maggie knew he could feel her wildly thumping pulse beneath his lips. She let her head loll back and surrendered to the sensation of being one hundred percent alive—mind, body and spirit. Of knowing Jack was responding to her as she was to him. His breath feathered into her cleavage. Deep in her abdomen a flickering need roared to life.

With one last, deeply exhaled breath, Jack lifted his head. His hot gaze burned into her like a searing flame.

Maggie lifted a hand to brush a lock of hair from his sweat-dampened forehead.

Jack batted her hand away, then took her by her forearms and shook her once, hard enough to make her blink. "That," he told her with hands trembling, "is what I've been trying to tell you. You can't trust a guy once he has you in his apartment. Now go on, get out of here."

"But—"

"Maggie . . ."

Hauling in a deep breath to clear her head, she turned her back on Jack. Tears welled up inside her. She couldn't stop them from spilling over her lids and streaming down her cheeks. Not wanting Jack to see what he'd done to her, she lifted her chin and moved toward the door.

Jack's voice halted her. "Maggie, wait. I'm sorry."

"For what?" she forced past the tightness in her throat.

"For the mix-up about tonight. I'll call you when I get back from Buck's. It shouldn't be long. We'll . . . go for a burger and fries."

"Don't bother," Maggie replied and swept out of his apartment. "I won't be home."

$\mathcal{T}\varepsilon n$

There might have been a time when Jack felt lower than he did after he sent Maggie teary-eyed from his apartment.

Maybe when he stuffed laxatives in the chocolates he thought his dad had bought for a lady friend. The woman who told him she'd find a way to get rid of him once she had her name on the marriage license. In fact, the candy had been a present for the elderly lady next door who sometimes cooked for Jack and his dad.

That same remorse for having hurt someone he cared for ate at his belly like an oncoming case of stomach flu. Mentally flogging himself, he took the sidewalk across the courtyard and followed the noise to Buck's apartment. He banged on the door with his fist and wondered if he was destined to live the empty life of a single guy forever.

Before he'd left for the party, he'd called Wilson to check on Polly. Jack hadn't heard from him since the poker party and was worried Polly might have gotten sick. While Wilson told Jack that Polly was feeling fit as a fiddle, Polly had apparently run her hand over a sensitive area of her husband's body. Chuckling, Wilson had told Jack to drive on over some evening and bring a date. They'd all go to dinner. Then he'd excused himself from the phone and hung up abruptly.

That's what Jack wanted. Instead of partying with the guys, tonight he'd much rather curl up on the couch with a very special woman.

Maggie, he thought, with sudden clarity as Buck threw open the door. Even as the roar of Monday night football and male camaraderie filled the foyer, Jack couldn't get the sweet taste of Maggie, the drugging scent of her cologne out of his mind. But damned if he didn't have to.

"Jack, come on in out of the heat."

"Hey, buddy, sorry about the divorce. Here, this is for you." Jack shoved his gift into Buck's hands, heaved a sigh and clapped his friend on the back. "I could sure use a beer."

"What is it?" Buck asked and followed Jack into the kitchen.

"A rubber tree plant."

"I'll be damned. Only you. You think I could use these things?" Buck asked skeptically.

"The condoms?" Jack asked and thought of the amused look on Maggie's face when she saw the tree.

Maggie, hell. He had to get her out of his mind. Every time he thought of her, he saw her holding her tray of spaghetti, her expectant smile fading into disappointment, then pique.

But Jack had to push her away from him, for her sake, as well as his own. She needed to learn what kind of man she wanted, not just him because he was the first who happened along. Besides, she had programmed herself for disappointment by keying in on the baby-making thing. Even though Jack would take great physical pleasure in making her a momma, he couldn't let himself get sucked into her program and its screwy priorities. Not even if he could tell by the few times he'd held her close that she was incredibly responsive and would be a passionate lover.

"Of course the condoms," Buck said, penetrating Jack's thoughts. He gave Jack a boldly appraising look. "Hey, bud, if you don't mind my saying so, you look like hell. Who's the one who got the divorce, anyway?"

"Yeah, well, I feel like hell." Jack yanked open the refrigerator and snagged an ice cold Celis long neck. He uncapped it and knocked back a slug.

"Only one thing gives a guy that haggard look. Women."

"You said it! They drive a man nuts."

"Damned right."

"Who needs 'em?" Jack boasted and hooked an arm around his friend's shoulders.

Buck's face crumpled. "Me."

"Oh, hell, I forgot." Jack led Buck out onto the balcony, where they could talk over the roar of booming male voices. "Sorry, Buck. How're you doing? How'd it go in court?"

"She didn't show up," Buck lamented and propping his forearms on the wrought iron railing, stared out over the tree-shaded neighborhood with misted eyes. "She sent her attorney.

She said since it was over, there was no use in her spending the round-trip airfare from California."

"Fits," Jack commented. "Look at it this way. At least you didn't have kids."

"I wanted kids," Buck commented with a regretful sigh and wiped a knuckle under his nose. "I wanted a lot of things. I failed at all of them, except my job. I still got my job."

"Don't be so hard on yourself. Next time you might think about finding a wife who'll at least live in the same city, though."

"That's for sure."

"Me, I'm going to be mighty careful before I say, I do. I made a promise to myself," Jack said, to himself as much as to Buck. "I wouldn't get married until I found a woman who was as intent on staying together as I was, who'd make the necessary compromises."

"Good luck. My attorney says too many people are getting married with the idea if it doesn't work, they can always get divorced. Kind of like picking out a dog at the pound, taking it home and finding out it pees on the carpet, so you take it back.

"That reminds me. Did you see Maggie Kincaid's picture in the paper? Modeling? Who would have thought all that woman was hiding under those dumpy clothes she's been wearing."

"Yeah, who would have thought?" Jack grumped and wondered at the screwy workings of Buck's mind.

"Have you thought about asking her out?"

"Thought about it," Jack admitted.

"And?"

Right now Maggie was across the courtyard, in her spotless apartment, either madder than a hornet or crying buckets. Neither image made Jack feel like much of a man. He hated hurting her, but better he derail her now than both of them suffer the consequences later. "Nah. Not my type."

Buck slanted Jack a questioning look. Jack steeled himself not to show the emotions on his face that were wrestling in his stomach.

Apparently convinced Jack meant what he said, Buck went on. "The boys and I were talking about Maggie before you got here. She's a hell of a good-looking woman these days since she started doing something with her hair and wearing different clothes. We figured you had first rights, you being friends and all. If you're sure you're not going to ask her out, I thought, well, she's awful sweet. After a month or two, I might give her a call. Take her to a movie. She doesn't seem the type who'd get all wrapped up in her career, you know? And one time I helped her carry her groceries in. She had something cooking in the oven that made my mouth water. If her cooking tastes half as good as it smells, man, I'd be in heaven."

The thought of Maggie going out with Buck had the hairs standing up on Jack's arms. Not that Buck didn't know how to treat a woman, but he wasn't . . . smart enough for Maggie. Or mannerly. Yes, that was it. Buck didn't have the finesse a woman of her genteel nature needed.

But Buck had one thing going for him. He didn't intend to stay single long. He wanted to remarry. Have kids. Maggie could have a man who'd gladly give her the babies she wanted.

A picture of Maggie lying naked in Buck's arms popped into Jack's head. The beer churned in his empty belly. He didn't want any other man touching Maggie. He didn't want anyone else kissing her. He didn't want—

"Hey, buddy," Buck said and jabbed Jack with his elbow. "You sure you're not sick? You got sweat popping out all over your forehead."

When Maggie's pulse slowed to a roar, she called the Save Our Springs director who had asked her out after the fashion show. She agreed to have dinner with him the next evening.

Still stinging from Jack's dignity-robbing lesson, she went on that date. All she could think while she poked at her perfectly good meal in one of Austin's finest restaurants was that it was Jack she wanted to see across the table.

Only since Jack had kissed her at the hotel had she begun to admit that she'd always hoped something would develop between them. Many times she'd left his apartment after Monday night football and gone up to bed. Although tired, she'd lain awake and fantasized about what it would be like to stay in his apartment. Crawl into his bed, run her hand over his chest and have him treat her as if she were as desirable as his women model friends. Now that she had an inkling of what that felt like, she couldn't get Jack off her mind.

She apologized to her date for her mopey atti-

tude at the end of the evening and told him the
fault was hers.

He quit calling two weeks later. However, when
Kayla informed her a guy was on the line for her,
at three in the afternoon the next Wednesday,
Maggie assumed her SOS director had more per-
sistence than brains.

"Please," she said into the receiver, "don't take
this personally, but I'd appreciate it if you didn't
call me again."

"Mademoiselle Kincaid?"

Maggie only knew one man who had ever addressed her as *Mademoiselle*. The international
president of the Grand Perimeter chain. She wondered why in the world he was calling her and
where he'd gotten her work number. Then she
remembered he had been there, during her press
conference, when she told the reporters where
she worked. "Mr. Cordell? Is that really you?"

"Yes," he responded with a chuckle.

Maggie pressed a hand to her cheek, already
feeling the heat of embarrassment. "Please, forgive me. I thought you were someone else."

"The gentleman with the lipstick on his slacks
perhaps?"

"Oh, dear," Maggie cried, knowing now why
Raleigh Cordell had called. "Did he turn in a
complaint about me?"

"I don't think he would dare, my dear. But gossip
flies in hotels. After you left, your breakfast companion told the waiter he'd spilled something on
his slacks. He asked if he could borrow a tablecloth
to wrap around him when he left. Instead the

waiter said he thought he could help him remove the stain and offered to bring him some club soda and a washcloth. Finally your breakfast companion explained that club soda wouldn't work on his particular stain, because it was lipstick.''

Hearing the amusement in the hotel president's voice, Maggie relaxed her grip on the receiver and listened to him continue.

"Apparently the man had earned quite a reputation for himself among the hotel's female employees following his check-in two days earlier. He had extended, shall we say, inappropriate invitations to any number of our staff before he met you. They would have risked losing their jobs if they'd attempted to teach him the lesson that you did. So the waiter brought him a tablecloth. A pink linen one. When he walked out with it tied around his waist, the entire staff was grinning. They were extremely pleased you took the initiative.''

"Then you aren't upset with me?''

"Of course not, mademoiselle.''

"I hope he returned the tablecloth.''

"He left it in his room. He checked out and moved to a different hotel.''

"I'm sorry you lost business because of me,'' Maggie said, yet the embarrassment Franklin had suffered served him right.

"I'm the one who should apologize,'' Cordell said. "I was distressed your weekend in our hotel was ruined by having to suffer the indignity of a man's unwanted advances.''

"It wasn't your fault or the hotel's," Maggie reminded him.

"You're very kind. But the lipstick incident isn't why I called."

"Did I charge too much food on the bill?"

Cordell chuckled. "About half what the public relations department budgeted."

"Oh, good," Maggie said on a sigh, then realized three pairs of eyes were glued to her, six ears listening unabashedly to her side of the conversation.

"Who is it?" Juliana mouthed, her eyes wide with curiosity.

Maggie shook her head briskly and mouthed, "Later."

"The reason I'm calling," Cordell continued, "is to ask if you'd have dinner with me and our local manager a week from tomorrow."

Why? Maggie wondered, then chided herself for thinking like Jack. After all, Mr. Cordell had asked her to have dinner with him *and* the manager. No doubt this was a business meeting of some kind. "I'd be delighted," she responded. "What time?"

"What time do you get off work?"

Maggie took a quick look at next Thursday's schedule on the back wall. "I should be able to leave by five-thirty."

"Excellent. I'll send a limousine over to pick you up. We'll dine at the hotel. Good-bye, my dear."

Not being one to tell untruths, Maggie had a difficult time keeping the identity of her dinner companions a secret from the wildly curious Kayla, Desiree, and Juliana.

But being somewhat confused about the purpose of her dinner with the hotel administrators, Maggie preferred not to mention names. The article about her that had appeared in the *American-Statesman* quoted both men. The clipping was still displayed on the Couturier's bulletin board. The girls' memories were sharp. They would match the names up in a flash. Maggie was generating enough attention as it was after receiving a phone call from what Kayla called that sexy French guy.

Although Raleigh Cordell's invitation had sounded innocuous enough, Maggie couldn't help wondering why the hotel chain's president and the Austin property's manager wanted her to dine with them. She suspected they wanted to pick her brain about her experiences at the hotel. Learn from an outsider what they could do to improve their service, their food selection and preparation, their decor. That was the only reason she could think of to explain why Mr. Cordell was sending a limousine to pick her up.

Wanting to look professional at that dinner, Maggie used her evening hours during the following week to design and sew a black business suit in classic lines. She wore the suit to work on the warm, mid-October day of her appointment.

The garment prompted another round of questioning spearheaded by Kayla. Why was she so dressed up? Did this have anything to do with the French guy who had called her a week or so ago? Even Miss Caroline was curious.

At five-fifteen, Maggie slipped a plastic bag over the debutante gown she was sewing and hung it in the appropriate closet. By five-twenty-five she had tidied her work station, brushed the lint off her suit and was on her way to the restroom to freshen her makeup.

Tediously beading the bodice of her current project, Kayla looked up as Maggie walked by. "Leaving early?"

"It isn't early. It's five-twenty-five."

"For you, that's early."

Maggie shrugged. "I have plans."

Kayla ran a pondering look up Maggie's suit, then comprehension prompted a wide-mouthed, "Oh. Tonight must be your dinner date." She glanced over her shoulder and gave Desiree a look of amusement before smothering a smile and pretending to concentrate on her beading.

If only Kayla weren't so condescending, so openly hostile when anything good happened to her, Maggie lamented while fluffing her hair. Maggie would like nothing better than to have someone with whom to talk, to share all the exciting developments in her life. She and Jack hadn't spoken more than a few words since the night of Buck's party. She missed their friendship, their easy give and take.

More than anything, she needed to discuss her frustrations over Jack's hot-and-cold attitude toward her with a woman who could sympathize and understand. She missed her sisters terribly and vowed to call them both over the weekend.

A fresh coat of lipstick applied, Maggie stepped

out of the rest room. She hoped she could slip
out without attracting more attention.

Her hopes for a noneventful departure fizzled.
There, crowded around the front window, were
the other seamstresses, staring out. Beyond them
Maggie could see the late afternoon sun glinting
off a sleek black limousine parked at the curb of
the tree-lined street. "Oh, no," she groaned.

"Is that limousine here for you?" Miss Caroline
asked behind Maggie.

"I'm afraid it is."

Miss Caroline patted her on the shoulder. "I
heard the girls talking about a phone call you got
last week from a new gentleman asking you to
dinner. Is this the evening?"

"Yes."

"From the looks of that limousine, he must be
quite well-to-do."

"He is that," Maggie allowed.

"Someone you met during the Save Our Springs
benefit?"

"No, someone I met at the hotel," Maggie answered vaguely.

"Well, enjoy your evening." Maggie's boss patted her on the shoulder, turned toward her office,
then paused. "I've been meaning to tell you all
day. That's a lovely suit. The lines would compliment many figure styles."

"Thank you."

"You designed it?"

"Yes, I did," Maggie replied modestly.

"Terrific," Caroline responded brightly. "When

you have time, I'd like to see you make it up in
several sizes."

The plush limousine had its own bar, a television set and telephone. The amenities would have
made Maggie feel like Cinderella if she hadn't
been grumbling to herself all the way to the hotel
about Miss Caroline's thievery.

When she walked into the lobby, the manager's
personal assistant was waiting for her at the concierge desk. Smiling broadly, he escorted Maggie
to the glass elevator that whisked them to the Marseilles Room. There Maggie discovered she was to
dine not only with the president and Austin property manager, but also with Armand Foster, the
corporate public relations vice president. She remembered him as the escort the hotel had provided should she wish to have one during her free
weekend.

Maggie remembered his condescending manner and greeted him stiffly. This time he was almost overly attentive in his greeting. Amazing
what a little hair color, a snug-fitting suit and a
splash of lipstick could do.

If the purpose of the dinner was to encourage
Maggie's ideas on ways to improve the hotel, Armand's attendance at the dinner made sense. Yet
one aspect of such a session didn't figure. She
wasn't a woman of means. She didn't possess the
perspective of those who might wish to stay at a
luxury hotel. If the sheets were clean, the roof

wasn't leaking, and bugs weren't scurrying around the room, she was satisfied.

They dined at the manager's table. Set behind a privacy screen, it provided a breathtaking view of Town Lake. From the western sky the declining sun splashed the waterway with a glistening sheen of gold. Back in the public portion of the dining room, an accomplished pianist played in the elegant style of Eddie Duchin.

While they dined, Maggie said a silent prayer of thanks to her mother. Although their family had struggled financially, Wilma Kincaid had demanded that her brood observe the finest manners at her table, whether they ate tuna fish sandwiches or a budget-stretching casserole.

Good thing. Maggie discovered her opinion was desired on a number of dishes the president had asked the chef to prepare for menu consideration. That meant a seemingly endless sampling of appetizers, entrees and desserts, many calling for the use of special cutlery.

Maggie forced down tiny bites and hoped her stomach wouldn't revolt from the mixture of rich, creamy sauces; tender shellfish and spicy Southwestern cuisine. All the while she felt as if the manager and two hotel officers were watching everything she did. She waited patiently for someone to explain her function for the evening besides that of a taste tester.

At sundown they participated in a bizarre Austin ritual. They watched the bats that slept beneath Congress Street Bridge during the day swoop out to pepper the darkening skies before disappearing until dawn.

Maggie turned from the spectacle to see Armand Foster engrossed in a quiet conversation with Raleigh Cordell. When they noticed that she was looking at them, they ceased talking and smiled at her.

A funny feeling crept up Maggie's spine. She had the distinct impression they had been discussing her. Still sitting at the table, she was sure a slip showing below the hem of her skirt wasn't the problem. The front crossover neckline of her white silk blouse was respectfully high. What then?

"Well, now," Cordell said and pushed back his chair to assist Maggie from hers. "Shall we adjourn to the executive offices for coffee?"

Maggie gave herself a strict lecture as the glass elevator ascended to the executive floor. She was a plain Texas woman with basic values who hadn't pretended to be anything else. She needn't be nervous about being in the company of powerful men. She should relax and enjoy an evening her co-workers would give nearly anything to experience.

She took the proffered chair in a conversational grouping in the executive living room. A waiter served them coffee. Thinking how her life had changed since the last time she'd been in that office, Maggie sipped the savory blend that tasted of vanilla and hazelnut.

Cordell cleared his throat. "I'm afraid, in asking you to dine with us this evening, we've been less than candid with you, Mademoiselle Kincaid. We have a proposition to make. A strictly business proposition," he tacked on with a cosmopolitan wink.

So much for feeling relaxed and composed in the presence of corporate power. So she wouldn't rattle her coffee cup in its saucer with her suddenly shaky hands, Maggie set both on the table.

Her mind raced like a computer along corridors of possibility. What proposition could the Grand Perimeter Hotel possibly make that would involve her?

When the hotel's boutique owner had brought fashions to the Presidential Suite for her to select from, she had admired one garment's superb construction. That led to a discussion of the fact that she was a seamstress who occasionally designed dresses. The owner of the exclusive shop could have relayed that information to management. Maggie supposed it was possible that Mr. Cordell could want to talk to her about designing garments for the chain's boutiques.

Possible, but unlikely.

"What do you have in mind?" she forced past a clot swelling in her throat.

"Have you ever done any public speaking, Maggie?" Armand asked.

Public speaking? There went Maggie's dress designing theory. Shaking the cobwebs of disbelief from her mind, she replied, "None to speak of. Why do you ask?"

Raleigh Cordell and the public relations vice president exchanged glances. "We could coach her," Armand said as if her inexperience had no appreciable effect on what they were considering.

Cordell leaned back in his chair, propped his elbows on the upholstered arms and smiled at Maggie over the tips of steepled fingers. "We happen to think you would make quite an effective hotel spokesperson for us, Maggie."

"Spokesperson?" Maggie squeaked. She blinked twice, hard, to make sure this wasn't one of her dreams where she had been granted her younger sister's moxie. "Me?"

"Of course. Why are you so shocked?"

"I've never done anything like that. I'm a seamstress. And a designer," she hastily added. "I—I wouldn't know the first thing about representing your hotels."

"My dear, we've been considering you in this role since your press conference. You probably weren't aware of it, but we taped the session with the media. When you made such complimentary comments about the hotel here, we thought, what can we do with this? We ran the interview by all our public relations people."

"The overwhelming consensus is you're a natural," Armand informed her. "Even uncoached, you can field reporters' questions like a pro."

"As I explained to Mr. Cordell then, I only told the truth."

"So much the better."

"We saw your picture that appeared in the *American-Statesman*," Armand continued. "The one of you modeling in the Save Our Springs benefit. It proved that the publicity photo of you we released wasn't a fluke. You are extremely photogenic."

"Did you suspect that we were watching you to-night?" Cordell asked.

"As a matter of fact, I did," Maggie answered candidly. "I couldn't figure out why, or the reason you asked me to join you for dinner."

"Any man would be honored to dine with you, mademoiselle," the gallant president murmured. "Be that as it may, Armand wanted to see for himself why we had raved about your gracious demeanor. You passed his tough scrutiny with flying colors, my dear. You have a freshness about you, a certain glow."

"A Kathy Lee Gifford appeal," Armand explained.

This sounded suspiciously like one of Maggie's dreams. "Forgive me. I'm not accustomed to such flattery," she said. "I know that at any time I'm going to wake up and discover I'm dreaming."

Cordell inclined his head at the manager. The executive handed him a glossy presentation folder. Cordell passed it to Maggie. "This is what we have in mind. What do you think?"

Maggie took one look at the folder, and her mouth went dry. Scrolled diagonally across the navy enameled folder in gold were the words, "Cinderella Girl." Through a die-cut hole in the shape of a high-heel shoe, a picture of her smiling face clearly showed.

She opened the folder and gasped. There she was on the dance floor of the Marseilles Room in the arms of an unidentifiable man. Although all that showed of her dance partner was a back view, Maggie knew without question Jack was the one holding her loosely in his arms. She was smiling at him, her eyes glowing with an exotic blend of affection and desire that even now kindled a warm place in her abdomen. The memory of how something inside her had sparked to life that night in Jack's arms prompted a bittersweet heaviness in her chest.

If only Jack shared the feeling.

In addition to their picture, the layout showed several squares that had been blocked with tiny horizontal lines. Maggie had helped Miss Caroline design advertising on occasion and realized these squares were proposed copy blocks.

"Naturally, I'm flattered," she said and handed the folder to Cordell. "But I don't understand exactly what you're asking me to do. If you want to use my picture in your promotions, you already have my consent. I'd—ah—have to secure approval for you from my companion for that evening."

"It's quite simple, Maggie," Cordell said. "We'd like you to become the Grand Perimeter Hotel Chain's Cinderella Girl. You'd be the focus of an international promotional campaign. If you agree, we'll begin the creative work next week."

Eleven

Since Buck's party, Jack had done his damned best to make Maggie think he was avoiding her.

What she didn't know was that he made sure he was home each night by six. He stood behind his drawn blinds, waiting for her to turn the corner and walk down the sidewalk to the building. He had to know she got home safely; he wanted to know if she was returning alone.

He wanted her to date, and he didn't. If she was seeing other men, as he had encouraged her to, he wanted to size up his competition.

After dark he found excuses to stroll outside so he could check out her apartment for lights. Knowing her habit of staying home evenings, he figured if she was gone, that meant she was on a date. Every time he heard a man's voice in the hallway, he darted out to check his mailbox. But so far he hadn't seen her coming or going with any strange men. He figured the Save Our Springs director must have bombed out, or he'd be around.

Jack peered through the miniblinds and muttered a few choice obscenities. At 9:07 on a Thursday night, Maggie still wasn't home. Even though her boss had a habit of stretching Maggie's work-

day as long as possible, Maggie never returned
this late.

Maybe she was with Buck. At the thought of her
practicing the flirting gestures Jack had taught on
Buck, the blood thundered in his ears. Buck had
been neglected by his wife for months. He had honored his wedding vows, but no promise of fidelity
bound him anymore. If Maggie tossed her hair,
preened, held Buck's gaze too long, Jack figured
his buddy wouldn't sit around holding hands. In
that event, Maggie would have to make a decision
she might not be ready for.

Buck's car was not in the parking lot. Was it
possible right now his affection-starved lips were
closing over Maggie's?

Jack pounded the window frame with his fist.
The miniblinds clattered; the glass shook. Then
reality penetrated his haze of anger and frustra-
tion.

Maggie could be a lot worse off than in Buck's
arms. But Buck worried Jack the most, for two
reasons. One, the guy wanted to get married and
have kids. Two, he and Jack were friends. Any day
now Buck could haul himself out of his pit of
misery and ask her out. Once he did, Maggie
would be off-limits to Jack. Buddies didn't date
the same woman.

Jack dropped the miniblind slat, but a flash of
black outside tripped his curiosity. He lifted the
slat again and peered outside.

In the light of the parking lot's halogen lamps,
he saw that a black stretch limousine had rounded
the corner. The sleek vehicle stopped in front of

his building. A uniformed driver got out and circled the car.

Jack pulled the sheet of blinds back to get a better look. If anybody in his complex could afford the services of a limousine, Jack hadn't met him—or her. Whoever had enlisted the services of that limousine was probably a visiting friend or relative.

Jack remembered that Maggie's Aunt Barbara in Charleston was a clothing rep who did fairly well for herself. Maybe she was visiting Maggie. If so, Aunt Barbara was in for a disappointment. Maggie wasn't home.

Shapely legs in dark hose and black high heels swung out of the limousine. Jack ran his palm across his mouth. If that was Maggie's aunt, she had great-looking legs. Lacking anything better to do, he pulled the blinds up for a better look.

The chauffeur extended his hand and gave the lady an assist from the limousine. Whoever she was, she wore a fashionable suit Maggie would like. She had great red hair, long and wavy, a lot like Maggie's new hairstyle. She was—

Damn! She didn't *look* like Maggie. She *was* Maggie!

While Jack stood, framed in the glaring light of his window, Maggie glanced his way. Recognition registered in her features. She lifted her chin and looked away.

Ah, hell, Jack thought, and headed for the door. Now that she'd caught him spying on her, he might as well take advantage of the opportunity to try to make up for pissing her off. Since she was dating, she probably needed a sounding board too. Someone to keep her from getting ahead of herself—from jumping the matrimonial gulch so she could have kids. Someday, after she'd dated a good bit, maybe she'd decide to go at things slow and easy. Jack'd be right there waiting.

In the meantime, by damn, he'd find out who the hell had paid for Maggie's limousine!

On the way out the door, he grabbed his keys. He was nonchalantly unlocking his mail compartment when the chauffeur opened the building door for Maggie.

"Hey, Mags," he said over his shoulder. "A little early to be getting home from a date, isn't it?"

She sailed past him with her chin lifted at a snotty angle. "A little late to be getting your mail, isn't it?"

"I—uh—had a late assignment. Just got home."

"Oh, really." She pivoted on the first stair and looked him up and down. "Shorts. No shirt. No shoes. What kind of work were you doing? Underwater photography?"

Before he could think of a plausible explanation, she whirled around and finished climbing the stairs. Her hips swayed gently, prompting all kinds of teeth-gritting fantasies in Jack's mind.

"I saw you spying on me through the window, Jack. Not nice."

Jaw clenched, he slammed the door to his empty mail slot and extracted his key. Apparently, dear, sweet Maggie had learned to bear a grudge. She wasn't going to make it easy for him to mend fences.

He listened to her humming a dreamy version of "One Moment in Time" and reluctantly followed her up the stairs. "You mind me asking who the lucky guy was?" he called after her.

"I mind. But I'll tell you this much. He was a gentleman," she retorted with a disparaging glance. She walked into her apartment and left him to follow her or endure a closed door in the face. He opted for the former and caught a strong whiff of that exotic perfume she'd bought at the hotel.

She slipped out of her heels, padded into the kitchen in smoke-colored nylon hose and tossed coolly over her shoulder, "I'm fresh out of beer. You want a Coke?"

What Jack wanted was some answers. For one, did the perfume work on her date as well as it did on him? But Jack could tell if he didn't finesse the reconciliation of their friendship, he would wind up on the other side of her apartment door. "Think I'll pass. You look like you've had a long day." He snuck up behind her, settled his hands over the curve of her shoulders and dug his massaging thumbs into the tight muscles of her back.

As she had weeks before, she tensed into a ball of knots.

"Relax, Princess," he murmured into her ear. "Let me do the serving for a change."

Maggie's head lolled back, the long, lustrous waves of auburn hair shifting over his hands like spun silk. Jack inhaled the taunting scent of her and restrained his urges. He wanted her to have time to relax, to let his hands accomplish what his words couldn't. Put a teeny reminder in her brain what it felt like when he touched her. Make her think about it when some gentleman jerk with the bucks to hire a limousine tried to kiss her.

Just when he felt the tenseness fading from her muscles, Maggie jerked her head forward and left him with his hands suspended in air.

"I'm really tired, Jack." She opened the refrigerator and took out a Diet Coke. Jack followed her into the living room and watched her settle onto the couch next to Homer. She crossed one slender leg over the other on a footstool she had needle-pointed back when she was just Maggie and hadn't churned up Jack's libido. She sighed deeply. "As you said, it's been a long day."

Jack plopped into the overstuffed chair and slung one leg over an arm draped with hand-crocheted doilies. "You want to talk? I've got a couple of hours."

"You're sure you can afford the time?" she asked with a caustic glance.

"Maggie, my girl, I've got all the time in the world—for you, that is."

Maggie made a big show of checking her watch. "Nine-fifteen, on a Thursday night. What's the matter, Jack? Did somebody break a date with you?"

Jack opened his mouth to tell Maggie he had turned down three promising offers for the evening. All he could think about all day while he was shooting the renovated state capitol building was getting home to see Maggie, if only for a few minutes. But before he could utter a word, the phone in her kitchen jangled.

"You'll excuse me?" she asked and crossed in front of him to answer the phone.

Jack picked up the remote control for Maggie's television and pressed the "on" button with his thumb. Pretending to search for a show that interested him, he turned down the volume so he could listen to Maggie's end of the conversation.

He was flipping from station to station when he heard the lilting laughter of her voice. He pushed the mute button, wondering how many men were calling her these days and if he knew any of them.

"No, Buck, I didn't win the lottery," Maggie said. "But it was fun. It had a bar and a TV and everything."

Jack nearly broke his neck scrambling off the couch. He skidded into the kitchen over Maggie's slickly polished tile floor as she twined the phone cord around her wrist and said, "Tomorrow night?"

Jack's gut took a hard punch. What the hell was he going to do? Buck was asking her for a date. He slipped his palm over the receiver and muttered gruffly, "Tell him you got plans."

"But I don't," Maggie whispered.

"You do now. You're having dinner with me."

"Funny," Maggie said icily. "I don't recall you asking me out."

"I'm asking you now."

"I'm not sure I want to go anywhere with you."

"Maggie!" Jack forced through gritted teeth.

"All right, all right," she relented with the

slightest hint of satisfaction in her haughty expression. She peeled Jack's hand off the mouthpiece, holding his gaze. "I'm sorry, Buck. I just checked my calendar. I already have plans. Another time? Of course. I'd like that. Bye now."

A sigh of relief slipped past Jack's lips.

Maggie hung up and leveled him with a stony glare. "Now, what's this about you and me going to dinner tomorrow night?"

"I've been meaning to ask you," Jack improvised, recalling Wilson's invitation to come over and bring a date.

"Are you sure you won't change your mind and back out at the last minute?"

Jack took Maggie's hand and led her back into the living room. "Cross my heart and hope to die."

Maggie pulled from his grasp. "What time will you pick me up?"

"For Pete's sake, Maggie, we live in the same apartment building. We'll go about seven or seven-thirty."

"If I don't hear from you by then, I'm calling Buck."

"You'll hear from me," Jack groused and remembered the time when Maggie wouldn't have had the nerve to issue such an ultimatum.

"If you expect me to cook dinner, the answer is—"

"I'm not asking you to cook."

Maggie resumed her position on the couch and lifted Homer to her lap. "Are you sure that won't be putting you out?"

"It's no problem. Really."

"I thought all you wanted from me was a whole lot of letting alone."

Jack spread his arms and let them fall to his sides. The truth was, when Buck had asked her out, he'd called Jack's hand. Go for her, or stand back. The way Jack felt about her, he had no choice. He had to figure out a way to make things move slow, though. Maybe date her casually while she saw other guys. But not Buck. Yes, that was it.

But how could he explain all this to Maggie? "So, I was wrong," he said vaguely. "I apologize."

Maggie nailed him with a narrowed gaze. "For what?"

"For being rude."

"And?"

"And what?"

"If you don't know, you can't possibly be sorry for it," Maggie said and stroked her hand over Homer's fur in a slow, graceful movement.

Shaking off the unnerving vision of that stroking hand, Jack realized he knew damned well what Maggie wanted him to apologize for. For breaking their breakfast date at the hotel and for pushing her away the night of Buck's party.

The truth was, he was sorry. Sorry for hurting her. Sorry she hadn't had a chance to find out how he measured up to other guys. Sorry she was going about this finding a mate business with screwed up priorities.

If he out-and-out apologized, they'd be right back where they left off. With Maggie in his arms, marriage on her mind, and Jack wondering if sev-

eral years and a few troubles down the road, she'd
be content to stay with him and their kids.

At least tomorrow night would be a formal date.
A dinner table would separate them most of the
evening. Wilson and Polly would cool the ardor.
Between now and then Jack could plan how to slow
Maggie down. Stall her determined agenda. Get
her to let things happen, see if she and Jack had
what it took to stick it out in the long run.

She lifted her chin and glared at him. "Are you
going to apologize?"

He cleared his throat. "Yeah. I am." He searched
for something to be penitent about. "I'm sorry
I . . . hurt you. Yes, that's it."

Her hand froze on Homer's back. Homer stared
at Jack with wide, yellow eyes and arched his tail
upward. "Do you mean it?" Maggie asked.

"I wouldn't have said it if I didn't. Who paid
for the limousine?"

Maggie examined her nails. "Raleigh Cordell."

"So *he's* back in town." Remembering how Cordell had looked at Maggie—touched her—Jack
paced the braided rug in front of the couch. "I
knew he had the hots for you."

"If he does, he hid them admirably. We had
dinner at the hotel."

"Then what?"

A sly smile lifted the corners of Maggie's mouth.
"We went upstairs."

"That bastard—"

"To the executive offices."

"Oh," Jack said flatly. "Why?"

"Raleigh said—"

Jack threw up his hands. "Oh, it's Raleigh now, is it?"

"Raleigh," she said with a smug grin, "wants me to be the spokesperson for Grand Perimeter Hotels."

"Spokesperson," he repeated flatly. "You mean like Michael Jordan used to be for Nike?"

For the first time that evening, the old Maggie spoke. Cradling her soft drink in her hands, she leaned forward. "I can't believe it, Jack. They want me to be their Cinderella Girl. Me! I'm beginning to understand how my younger sister felt every time they cast her in a new role."

Maggie's eyes were shining, her cheeks flushed. Jack couldn't remember ever seeing her this excited. He had a hard time thinking of her as a celebrity. Not because she wasn't beautiful. She was that. And she had apparently handled her press conference like a pro. But he'd seen the way Cordell had looked at her, touched her. Maggie might have missed the old goat's lecherous potential, but Jack read him like a book. Was this offer on the level? Or did Cordell have plans to exploit Maggie for personal pleasure?

"That's a hell of an offer," he told Maggie. "Congrats, kid."

"I have you to thank," she reminded him. "If I hadn't gone to the hotel for the weekend, none of this would have happened."

Great. If Maggie took Cordell up on his offer and anything happened to her, Jack would feel personally responsible. "Cinderella Girl, huh?" He resumed his pacing, trying to think of a tactful

way to help Maggie examine this offer from all
angles. "What would that involve? Trips to the
home office? Dinners out with Raleigh boy?"

"Jack, Jack. Why must you be so cynical?" She
took a delicate sip of her soft drink and stroked
Homer again. Jack couldn't help wondering how
Maggie's hands would feel sliding over the bare
skin of his back. Did Cordell fantasize about the
same thing?

"I'm not cynical. I'm not trying to rain on your
parade. But surely you've heard about guys like
Cordell who demand favors from the young, beautiful models they discover."

"Let me assure you *Raleigh* is treating me with
the utmost respect."

"So far," he pointed out.

Homer clumped off the couch, rubbed against
Jack's leg and meowed a loud complaint. He
turned his eyes from Jack to Maggie and blinked,
as if agreeing that the president at least deserved
watching. Jack scooped Homer up. Homer licked
his knuckle.

Jack gave the old boy an appreciative pat. "Tell
her," he murmured into the cat's ear under his
breath. "Not that she'll listen."

Maggie went on, disregarding Jack's warning.
"Raleigh wants me to appear in a series of magazine and newspaper ads. If the ads produce the
desired results, I'll do some TV spots. Make some
public appearances."

The magnitude of what Maggie was telling Jack
gradually sank in. If Cordell's offer was on the
level, Maggie would become an international ce-

lebrity. What would that do to her? To them, if they did manage to become a couple?

Insecurity niggled at Jack's self-confidence. He was no Richard Gere. He was a struggling commercial photographer. Talented, sure. But how long until he established himself so he could afford to take Maggie to fancy restaurants for dinner? "Does that mean you'd have to quit your sewing job?"

"Not initially. I'd only work for Grand Perimeter when they needed me. I'd be paid by the assignment, with residuals on TV commercials. If I made any public appearances, they'd pay me per diem, plus expenses."

"Per diem. Expenses. That sounds a whole lot like travel."

"Yes, isn't it exciting?"

"Yeah, it's peachy keen."

Maggie patted the now-empty cushion beside her. "Sit down, Jack. I can't wait to tell you all about it. The offer's one-hundred percent on the level. Ever since Raleigh told me, I've been floating on a cloud. I want you to be happy for me, too."

Hesitantly Jack sat beside her on the couch. His insecurity faded enough for the reality to filter through his brain. This was the chance of a lifetime for Maggie. If he cared for her at all, he would be happy for her. "Does that mean you're going to accept the offer?"

"I think so. I told Raleigh I wanted to think about it overnight. I'm not much on snap decisions, not when they're this important."

"Is this really what you want to do, Princess? Fly around the country, making appearances? Eat room service? Live out of a suitcase?"

Maggie didn't answer him right away. Jack reached for her hand and squeezed it. He tilted her chin with his knuckle and smiled into her troubled eyes. "What's the matter, kid?"

"It's all so new. I look in the mirror and see this woman and think, who is that? Now they want that woman to represent them. I'm not sure I can be her."

Pride swelled inside him for the real Maggie, the genuine, unaffected woman he wanted to protect. Regardless of his concern for her, or his personal insecurities, he wanted her to know how special she was. "You can be anything you want, Princess." He kissed her reverently on the tip of her nose. "Anything else bothering you?" he asked in a husky voice.

"I'm excited about the prospects of the position—I don't want you to think I'm not—but I hope it doesn't interfere with my plans for a career in design."

"How much would you be gone?"

"Just now and then."

"How often is that?"

"Once a month, twice occasionally."

"Your boss lady already makes you put in extra hours to keep up with the orders. How's she going to do without her best seamstress while you fly off somewhere a couple of times a month?"

"I'd have to clear it with her first, of course."

"What about night school?"

"Raleigh said he'd work around my classes."

"Where would you have to travel?"

Maggie shifted sideways on the couch. "Wherever Grand Perimeter has a hotel. The brochure in my room listed Seattle, San Francisco, Atlanta and New York, among others." Her eyes lit up. "And Paris! Oh, my gosh. The fashion capital of the world. Maybe this wouldn't be so bad for my career after all."

Jack could see the gears in Maggie's bright mind shifting smoothly like the shutter on a good camera lens. "I can't believe this is happening to me. A few weeks ago my idea of excitement was Monday night football in your apartment. Now I have the chance to go to all those exciting places. And be paid for it!"

Jack flicked a strand of Homer's hair off his jeans. "I didn't think our Monday nights were so bad."

Maggie's expression softened. She slid her finger across the back of the couch and touched the knotted muscles of his shoulder. "They were great fun—until you kissed me."

Jack's head came up. Insecurity and what he took to be an insult had him saying things he didn't mean. "Well, forgive me. I'll make sure I never do it again. Maybe you'd like Raleigh to kiss you." Jack crossed his arms over his chest, kicked at the braided throw rug and glowered. "Maybe he already has."

"Men!" Maggie exclaimed and threw up her hands. "Not that it's any of your business, but my relationship with Raleigh is strictly professional.

He's quite the gentleman. In fact, you could take a few lessons from him."

"You think so, do you?" Jack shifted sideways so they sat face to face, knee brushing knee on the upholstered couch. At the contact, a shiver of awareness swept up Jack's thigh and set off a quickening of muscles. "Well, watch out, sweetheart. I can guarantee you one thing. Raleigh Cordell may act like a gentleman, but he has his eyes on you, and I don't mean in a professional manner."

"You're way off base!" Maggie glared at her red-faced neighbor, not wanting to acknowledge the crazy things he was doing to her composure. She took a deep breath and tried to speak calmly, but she couldn't. "In fact, you sound like a jealous adolescent."

"An adolescent, huh?" Jack clamped his hands around Maggie's waist and hauled her onto his lap. He cupped the back of her head in his insistent hand and angled his face over hers. "Does this feel like a pimple-faced kid?"

Maggie opened her mouth to reply, but Jack smothered her words with a hot, insistent kiss. She muttered a muffled version of her complaint into his mouth, but her objection faded in the onslaught of his practiced lips.

Her bottled-up desire for Jack filled her with a honeyed warmth. She opened her heart to him and her arms. Jack took what she offered and gave her more pleasure in that one kiss than she thought she could bear.

In moments they were horizontal on the couch.

Jack's hands were caressing her, his mouth plundering regions that heretofore she'd reserved for the discreet coverage of lace.

In the blink of an eye, Jack's teeth nudged her nipple into a tight, twisted bud of need. This is what had kept her awake at nights. The need to feel Jack's hands, his lips, his teeth bringing her flesh to the flash point of surrender. She prepared to give herself to him, willingly, fully.

Then, suddenly his hands stilled. "Princess?" he muttered over the taut skin of her abdomen.

"Uh-huh," she replied in a desire-induced haze.

He patted the lace-covered mound of her femininity. "Don't let any other guy touch you here. Especially that hotel creep. He won't make you an honest woman. He won't give you the kids you want."

What about you, Jack? she wanted to say. Are you willing to think about marrying me? Will you ever be?

Jack tensed above her. She could feel the hard, swollen insistence of him pressing into her thigh. Apprehension had Maggie's hands trembling, her breath freezing in her lungs. She licked her lips, released a shuddering breath. "What are you telling me, Jack?"

"To be careful. Don't let yourself get sucked in. I don't want to see you hurt."

"I'm confused." She placed her hand over his, amazed by the heat of their combined flesh. "You're touching me here. What makes you dif-

ferent? Will you make me an honest woman? Will
you give me those kids I want?"

Jack's head drooped. As he shook it, the softness of his blond hair brushed over the bare skin
above her bikini panty line. A shudder tore across
her abdomen.

Jack heaved a deep sigh. At the rush of moist,
warm air over the sensitive skin below her navel,
she slid her fingers through his hair and squeezed
her eyes shut to the sweet torment of the moment.

She cared for this man. Too much. The past
seventeen days had been torture, not seeing him.
If only he would open the tightly closed door to
his heart wide enough for her to squeeze in. She
would love away the mysterious hurt she suspected was keeping him from her.

Jack lifted his head. Maggie opened her eyes
and found him staring at her. He pursed his lips
and hauled himself into a sitting position. "I'm
sorry, Mags." He patted her thigh in a much too
platonic gesture. "It's late. You've got some serious thinking to do. I'd better get going. Lock your
doors. Sleep tight. See you tomorrow."

Gathering up the loose ends of her dignity was
getting to be a habit for Maggie after being with
Jack.

She watched him adjust the swollen front of
his shorts and walk awkwardly away. His hand
was on the doorknob when he turned for a
heart-pounding moment and let his gaze slide

over her. The look was as intimate as a physical caress.

Still, he walked out, without giving Maggie a satisfactory answer to her question.

She posed another to herself. What was wrong with her that Jack couldn't even discuss a future with her, making love, fathering her babies? How could he walk away from the explosive chemistry between them so easily when all he'd have to do is come back through that door, and she would give herself to him?

The next morning Maggie got to work early. She found Miss Caroline struggling over the design sketch of a bridal gown in her office. Maggie hauled in a steadying breath and asked for a few moments of her boss's time. Forcing troubling thoughts of Jack from her mind, Maggie explained her opportunity to represent the Grand Perimeter Hotels.

Miss Caroline sat back in her chair and gave that genteel smile that courted not only the old Austin monied families but the political power brokers in the state capitol. "I can't say I'm surprised. You went through a Cinderella transformation at that hotel. They were smart to hook into the promotional opportunities you could provide them."

"I don't want to lose my job here," Maggie insisted.

"It will take an occasional shuffling of schedules, but I see no reason why we can't make allowances for any trips you need to make. Just be sure to give me advance notice so I can make sure your work is covered."

"I'll be happy to work weekends for days I miss."

"Nonsense," Caroline replied. "But you can do this. Whenever possible in your media interviews, mention that you work here. The publicity would more than compensate me for the hours you miss."

She tapped her pencil on the desk and let her gaze drift out the window. The first golden leaves of fall were drifting past the window. "I'd love to see the demand for my designs spread beyond Austin and San Antonio."

Her designs? Resentment was a bitter taste in Maggie's mouth. During the past week Maggie's boss had asked for help in scheduling production for the next three months. It came as something of a shock that fully fifty percent of the special orders had come from Maggie's personal designs. She was being paid as a seamstress, with no bonus or commission for her design work. She knew she should stand up for herself, demand better pay, as well as recognition for her creative ability, but what if Miss Caroline fired her?

Maggie's mother's struggles to support the family after her father's death burned in her memory. The hotel work would be lucrative when it came, but she needed a steady, dependable income to pay her bills.

"I'll do what I can to help you," Maggie grudgingly told her boss, yet she strengthened her resolve. One day Maggie's designs would bear her label, not Miss Caroline's. She would not let her work for Grand Perimeter interfere with her career plans.

A knock sounded at Caroline's door. When told to enter, Juliana poked her head around the door. "Phone for you, Maggie. It's that man with the sexy French accent again. Is he the one who sent the limousine for you last night?"

Maggie exchanged glances with Caroline. "That was him."

"Lucky you!"

"I don't know," Caroline said with a conspiratorial smile at Maggie. "I think we're all going to share in the luck. When are you going to tell them?"

"Tell us what?" Juliana wanted to know.

"I sort of have another job," Maggie said and ducked out to answer the phone. If she stayed another moment, she might let the resentment burning through her veins induce her to do something bold and brash, like quit her job.

Twelve

Maggie's caller was indeed Raleigh Cordell, encouraging her to give him a decision on his offer so they could proceed with their plans.

Pressing a palm to her diaphragm, Maggie said a shaky yes on an exhaled breath. Raleigh told her he would send her contract by express mail to Austin with a modest signing bonus. He then turned the call over to Armand Foster.

Not accustomed yet to the speed with which corporate America worked, Maggie sat numbly on the break-room couch and jotted notes about her first assignment. A photo shoot in two weeks at the Austin Grand Perimeter. The plan called for recreating some of the weekend scenes the photographers had missed.

That evening while she and Jack drove northeast to Lake Travis for a double date with some of his friends, Maggie recounted the day's events. She could hardly contain her enthusiasm and was secretly pleased to have something, anything, to talk about but what had happened last night.

"Will you help me get ready for the photo shoot?" she asked. "I don't know the first thing about relaxing in front of a camera."

"I've got a better idea." He poked the station selector on the car stereo to a country-western station. "I'll ask one of the models I've worked with to give you a few pointers."

"I'd feel better if you helped me."

Unsmiling, he slanted her a glance and drove his fingers through his hair. "I'll call her tomorrow."

Maggie studied him for a moment. Not once since he had knocked on her door had he flashed his cocky grin. As a matter of fact, he hadn't smiled at all. "Did you have a bad day?"

"I had a great day. I got a couple of the jobs I bid on."

"Why the sour look, then?"

"Leave it alone, Mags."

She folded her arms over her chest and stared out her window. "It's last night, isn't it?"

"No."

She turned to him. "What then?"

"I was just thinking."

"Obviously. About what?"

"About how much you've changed."

"You're the one who wanted me to. Are you telling me you wished I hadn't?"

"I didn't say that. Although, I have to admit, at times I miss the old Mags."

"As I recall, you thought the old me was frumpy and sexless. Only capable of being mildly attractive. Now that I've—what did you call it? Oh, yes— 'fixed myself up,' you miss the old me. Is there any pleasing you?"

Jack reached across the gear console of his Mus-

tang and gave her hand what could only be re-
garded as a brotherly squeeze. "Give me some
time. Okay, kiddo? You're just taking some getting
used to, that's all."

"How so?"

"You're becoming a celebrity."

"Jack Lewis, if I didn't know better, I'd say you
resent my success."

"Hell, Maggie, you know I don't. I'm proud as
hell of you. It just makes me think a bit about a
few things."

"Like what?"

"Maggie, I said, leave it alone."

She drummed her fingers on the armrest, wondering if it was ever possible to satisfy a man. Soon
her fingers picked up the heavy country-western
beat of a female vocalist. She was admonishing a
guy not to deal her aces if he didn't expect her
to play them.

Indeed!

A few minutes later, Jack wheeled off the main
road onto a driveway that led to a private residence
overlooking Lake Travis. A couple Maggie judged
to be about Jack's age emerged from the house,
arm in arm.

After the three exchanged hugs, Jack introduced
the couple as Polly and Wilson Jamison. Maggie
recalled seeing Wilson, a tall, slender man with
dark brown hair, once or twice at the apartment
building. A member of Jack's infamous poker
group, Wilson had twinkling eyes and a slightly off-
center nose. Combined, they gave him a boyish appeal. His wife was short and blond, with freckles

sprinkled across her nose. It wrinkled when she smiled. She smiled a lot. Especially at her husband.

He took her hand and gave it a squeeze. "You want to tell them now?"

"Maybe we'd better."

"Tell us what?" Jack asked.

Polly picked up a piece of gravel and pitched it into the lake. "What are you doing May first?"

"May first. May first. Flying to Bora Bora. What gives?"

"Really? Bora Bora?" Polly asked.

Jack threw up his hands. "All right, you don't leave me any choice." He advanced on Polly, scooped her into his arms and headed down the dock toward the lake. "This'll only take a minute," he told Maggie. "I had to do this all the time when we were kids. You'd think a grown woman would learn not to be so stubborn, though."

"Honey," Polly yelled over her shoulder, "maybe we'd better tell them now."

"Put her down," Wilson called to Jack.

"Why?" he called back.

"Because you don't throw pregnant women in the lake."

Jack stopped dead in his tracks and looked at Polly strangely. "Pregnant? You?"

"Sure, me. Why not?"

"I always think of you as that snotty little girl with a pitcher's mitt on her hand. Now you're going to have a kid of your own. Gee, Polly, that's great." He set her carefully on her feet. "I mean, that's wonderful! Can I get you anything? A drink? No, you can't have alcohol, can you? How about milk? Or a banana?"

"I think you'd better get Jack a chair," Polly said with a laugh that echoed over the water. "We wouldn't want him keeling over from the shock."

"Maggie," Jack said, his eyes wide, his chest expanding, "I'm going to be an uncle."

"Polly's your sister?"

"Closest thing to it," Wilson remarked.

"Maybe you'd better get *him* that drink," Maggie said with a chuckle. She loved the look of wonder in Jack's eyes. She let herself think for the briefest of moments how proud he would be to have his own children. For months she had admired him secretly. Now he was regarding her not as the female version of a buddy, but as a desirable woman. She dearly hoped his vision of her would continue to change until he saw her as his wife, as the mother of his children.

They adjourned to the deck where Wilson ordered Polly to relax. He served everyone lemonade and a tray of hors d'oeuvres.

"You don't mind if we ride over to the restaurant in the car instead of the boat?" he asked Jack. "The water's a bit rough, and—"

"No explanations needed." He turned to Maggie. "We'll take a spin on the lake some other time."

Some other time. Maggie liked the sound of that. She smiled at Jack and thought how very accustomed she could get to being with him and his friends like this.

They arrived at the restaurant an hour later and

dined on a glassed-in terrace overlooking the lake. The sun lingered on the horizon, then dipped into the water, tinting the sky and the sails of boats at anchor with a pinkish glow. A jazz quintet played softly in the background. The aroma of a mesquite fire and Texas barbecue spiced the air.

After dinner, Polly and Maggie excused themselves to go to the ladies' room.

"When Jack told us he was bringing you to meet us, we figured you were special," Polly said in her warm, friendly manner. "We were right."

Wilson's wife was a delightful mixture of Maggie's older and younger sisters. Maggie had liked her immediately. "Thanks, Polly. That means a lot to me."

"You're the first woman Jack's introduced us to in years."

"I am?" Maggie asked with wide-eyed shock. "But I thought . . ."

"He was a ladies' man? I can see how you'd think that with that rascal's silver tongue and the nature of his work. How long have you been dating?"

"Not long," Maggie replied, still trying to assimilate this latest bit of news about Jack's social life. "We live in the same apartment building."

"That," Polly said with a waggle of her brows, "could be delightfully convenient."

Maggie flushed but figured now was her chance to gain some insight into this man who was driving her nuts with his inconsistency. "How long have you and Wilson known Jack?"

"The guys played Little League together in Dallas from the time they were five. They hung out at the park near my house. I was the neighborhood tomboy. When I bugged them enough, they let me pitch. It irritated the heck out of them that I was better than both of them."

"I haven't heard Jack talk much about his family."

"That's not surprising." Polly studied Maggie in the mirror for a moment, then said, "Judging from the way you look at each other, I gather this thing between you isn't casual. It might help you to know that he didn't have the happiest of childhoods. Jack's mother abandoned him and his father when Jack was a little tyke. If it weren't for Wilson and his folks, I don't know what Jack would have done after his mother left."

Rage ripped through Maggie's mind at the hurt his mother had inflicted on him. "What kind of woman could walk away from her child?"

"In this case, one from a very wealthy family." Polly crooked her finger. "Highland Park, dahling. Rich, glamorous, and spoiled rotten."

"Did Jack's father ever remarry?"

"My mother says he worshipped Jack's mother. When she left, he was destroyed. After a while, he dated, but no one steady. Jack was hell on wheels for a while—until Wilson's parents set him straight. Come on," she said with a glance at her watch, "we'd better get back before the guys come looking for us. By the way, I love the color of your hair."

"If you like it enough to want it for yourself, I'll give you the name of my hairdresser," Maggie said, thinking that was the least she could do after the very illuminating information Polly had shared with her.

Steering with his left hand, Jack reached across the narrow gear shift console and draped his arm around Maggie's shoulders.

The first evening of what he hoped would be many hadn't gone exactly as he'd planned. He had expected that the fresh air and a boat ride would tire them and take the edge off the desire building between them.

Guess what? No boat ride, no diffusion. Still, the company of friends had been a deterrent to hands-on activities. And Maggie had enjoyed herself, Jack was sure.

As if to confirm his opinion, she turned and gave him a smile of contentment. He nudged her head closer, gave her forehead a quick kiss and steered his Mustang around a sharp curve in the road. Overhead, through the open sun roof, countless stars winked down at them from a blanket of jet black. The clean, country air had the slight bite of a south Texas fall night.

Maggie angled her body to snuggle against Jack's chest. Her warm breath soughed into the open placket of his shirt, lapping at the barriers he'd carefully erected to restrain his desire.

Maggie smelled like fresh air and mesquite smoke. Her skin tasted slightly salty with just a hint of something exotic, like a lotion scented with honeysuckle. He let his fingers tangle in the soft mass of her windblown hair and wished for the enduring happiness Polly and Wilson shared.

Polly and Wilson were going to have a baby. The need for the happiness and fulfillment such a child would bring them twisted powerfully in Jack's gut.

Wincing from her cramped position, Maggie straightened. She rubbed a massaging palm over the nape of her neck.

"Got a stiff neck?"

Maggie nodded. "My boss said I could get off at five if I didn't break for lunch."

"That's some slave driver you work for."

"She is that," Maggie agreed.

"If you like, I could show you some exercises to help you work the kinks out."

"Or you could give me a rubdown," she countered, slanting him a look that told him her alternative was more an offer than a request.

No way, Jack thought, and stared at the black-topped road rising and falling before them like a ribbon. If he touched Maggie again, he wouldn't be able to stop himself this time. He wanted to go slow with her, but he was human, dammit.

"I like Polly and Wilson," Maggie said, and Jack relaxed a little at the change in topic. "She told me the three of you grew up together."

"They're the closest thing to a family I've got," Jack found himself admitting.

"What about your father?"

"Dad died a couple of years ago."

"Polly told me about your mother."

Jack tightened his grip on the steering wheel. "Polly has a big mouth."

"She didn't mean any harm. It's obvious she loves you like a brother."

"And bugs me like one."

"To do what?"

"Get married. What else?"

"And that would be catastrophic."

Jack thought about that for a moment, wanting to be fair with Maggie about his answer. "It could be if I rushed into it."

"I see. And that's what you think I'm trying to do. Rush you."

"No, I think you're trying to rush yourself, and I'm handy."

"Oh, my, Jack." Maggie laughed softly. "I thought your ego was stronger than that."

Jack gave a slight shrug.

"When was the last time you saw your mother?"

"I don't know. A long time ago."

"If you don't want to talk about her, I understand."

Talk about his mother? Where would he start? he thought bitterly. Where would he end? Better yet, what could he tell Maggie about the middle? There wasn't much. Two years in Jack's life. Most of it he couldn't remember. Mainly just her leaving. And the aching need to have her come back, pull him on her lap and tell him she loved him.

But sooner or later Maggie would need to know the details of his family's dirty laundry. Thanks to Polly, that time might as well be now. "When did I last see her? Let's see, ten years ago, I think. Yes,

that was it. I'd just graduated from UT. Got my
degree in photojournalism mid-term. Jobs were
scarce in Austin, so I spent a few months knocking
around Dallas. Spent the holidays shooting Santa
Claus pictures in Northpark Mall. One day I looked
up and there she was."

"Your mother?"

"Yep. My dad had called her and told her I was
in town. Told her what I was doing. Said the least
she could do was stop by and say hello."

"How long had it been since she'd seen you?"
Maggie asked softly.

"Far as I know, since the day she left. But I
recognized her immediately. She looked just like
the picture of her Dad kept around. Blond hair,
tall, regal, eyes like blue ice."

"Did you talk?"

"Oh, yeah, we talked. She introduced me to
her three stepsons. Stair-steps. Five, six, and seven.
Then she had me take their picture. She tipped
me ten bucks, turned the kids over to their nanny
and left with her rich husband."

"That's it?"

"Uh-huh, and I haven't seen her since. What's
more, I don't care to."

"No wonder you're scared of getting married."

"I'm not scared. I'm just . . . cautious."

"I'm not like her, Jack. I wouldn't leave you."

"If it's all the same with you, I'd prefer not
talking about getting married, to you or to anyone
else."

"But you have to be thinking about it. It's natural to think about it when you're dating someone,

and you're feeling things like we felt last night, and . . ."

Maggie expanded on what happened last night. Jack tried to ignore what she was saying but couldn't. The more she talked, the more he thought about her on that couch and why he couldn't take what she'd offered.

Suddenly an armadillo appeared in the road in front of them. Jack swerved and swore. That wasn't like him, not keeping his mind on his driving. He had to find a way to get her to drop the discussion of sex, marriage, and babies—or they might have a wreck.

Jack crested a hill, then swooped into the next valley before mounting another easy rise. He recognized the road to his attorney's ranch where he'd shot several rolls of film earlier in the week. Impulse and frazzled nerves had him steering onto the side road and blazing a bumpy trail south. Dust billowed in his rear-view mirror behind them and filtered through the sunroof.

They hit a chuck hole. Maggie grabbed the armrest. "Where are we going?"

"Up the road a piece."

"That's obvious. What I want to know is, why?"

"So we can talk."

"We can talk while you drive."

"Not about what's on your mind. I almost hit that armadillo back there. If I had, we might be wrapped around a tree right about now."

"But surely this is private property."

"Yes, it is."

"It's dark, Jack. Someone's liable to come after us with a shotgun."

"The owner's a friend of mine." He rounded a curve and braked his car at a scenic overlook beneath the spreading arms of an ancient live oak.

He propped his wrist over the upper curve of the steering wheel and tamped down the emotions that were playing havoc with his ability to think straight. "I want you to back off, Maggie. Quit talking about marriage and babies. That scares the hell out of a guy."

"If you drove out here to tell me that, you needn't have bothered. Now that you've said what's on your mind, may we go, please?"

"Dammit, Maggie! What I'm trying to say is, can't you let this thing between us develop naturally? Do you have to have a commitment up front?"

Maggie gazed off at the inky contours of gently rolling hills. "I was merely trying to tell you I'm not like your mother. You blew it all out of proportion. I'm beginning to think you might not be capable of making a commitment to a woman. If that's so, I'm truly sorry, Jack. For you and for me. But I have to know. I want a family. Your honesty could save us both a whole lot of grief."

"You're saying I'm screwed up."

"I'm saying your mother may have hurt you so deeply that you can't trust your heart to another woman. Without help anyway."

"Do me a favor," he replied hotly. "Keep your amateur psychology to yourself. For your information, I wouldn't have any trouble making a commitment. *I* also don't have any trouble getting my priorities straight."

"You're implying I do," she said, turning a resentful stare on him.

"You're the one who told me your damned biological clock's winding down. You want kids, so bingo. You start looking around for a husband."

"What's wrong with wanting to settle down and have a family?"

"As I said before, I like the traditional way of doing things. *First* you fall in love, which makes you want to get married and have kids."

"And as I explained to you, as far as I'm concerned, all three go together. It's only a matter of time."

"There's one step you're overlooking, Princess. Staying together. You put anything on the agenda before love, you run the risk of everything blowing up in your face. So, please. Quit thinking of me as a baby maker. If a baby's all you want, you can accomplish that with a reputable sperm bank."

"That does it!" Maggie said and slammed out of the car, needing to put some distance between her and that stubborn man so she didn't scream at him what a fool he was.

A door behind her banged shut. Hard. "Get back in the car, Maggie. You can't walk around out here by yourself."

"Stay away from me," she called over her shoulder.

"You could step on a snake."

"The only kind of snake out here has two legs. And he's got grits for brains."

"What about the fire ants?"

"What about them?"

"You can't see where you're going. You might walk right into an ant hill. If you get stung, those pretty legs of yours'll have blisters for weeks."

"Now he's trying to flatter me," Maggie groused. "Go back to the car."

Jack's hands clamped over the curve of her shoulders. "I'm not going to let you get hurt." He scooped her into his arms and turned for the car.

"Put me down."

"No way." He labored to talk as he walked. "For a wisp of a woman, you weigh a ton. Have you put on weight?"

"No! Who asked you to carry me anyway?"

"My dad raised me to be a gentleman."

"When it suits you," she observed wryly.

He stooped to open the passenger side of the car with one hand, then dumped Maggie unceremoniously on her feet. "Get in."

"Not yet."

"Ah, Maggie. It's late. We aren't getting anywhere with our talking. I won't change my thinking. Neither will you. So, I'd like to go on home and get some decent shut-eye. I have a job at eight in the morning."

"You should have thought about that before you made plans for tonight."

"You had a good time. Admit it."

"I had a marvelous time, until you accused me again of working on an M.R.S. degree."

"Well, aren't you?"

"I want to get married. I want to have kids. Why should that surprise you? I'm twenty-nine. Of course, I could go to that sperm bank you mentioned and have a baby by myself."

"That's stupid thinking."

"You're the one who brought it up. Besides, a lot of women are doing it these days."

"Not women who care about their babies. A kid needs a dad and a mom."

Maggie couldn't argue that one with him. The truth was, she didn't feel like arguing at all. She was so tired she was ready to drop. The only thing that was keeping her awake was their bickering and the realization that Jack's deeply-felt hurt had kept him from finding someone to share his life with. Could he break out of that mold? Could he give what they shared a chance to grow? Or would he run like a rabbit every time she brought up the subject of marriage?

The wind gusted, ruffling Jack's hair and whipping Maggie's across her face. She lifted her hand to brush her hair out of her eyes. When she opened them, she found Jack staring at her. For once she was compelled to be quiet.

They stood there, toe to toe, not moving. Overhead, dry leaves clinging to the gnarled branches rustled in the breeze. Jack's hand settled on the curve of Maggie's shoulder. His thumb traced lazy circles on her neck. His fingers skimmed the tender skin beneath the weight of her hair.

Even though Jack was doing an effective job of dispelling the barrier of irritation their differences of opinion had created, another question occurred to her. She didn't want to disturb the temporary truce, but she needed an answer. "If you're so afraid of getting snared in a trap you think I've set, why did you ask me out tonight?"

"So you wouldn't date Buck."

Maggie blinked, not at all happy with Jack's answer. Surely he was leaving something out. "That's the only reason?"

"No, but I had to move fast. He asked you out. If you'd accepted, I'd have to wait until you figured out if you liked him or not."

"Why?"

"Come on, Mags. Friends don't date the same woman."

"I don't believe it," she muttered with a disbelieving shake of her head. "We've been arguing about priorities when it comes to love and marriage. Now you tell me you wouldn't have bothered to ask me out if your poker buddy had beat you to the draw. No wonder you don't want to talk about commitment. You don't really feel much for me, do you?"

"The hell I don't."

She poked him in the open placket of his shirt, hard, with her forefinger. "Then why didn't you listen to this thing that goes thump-thump in your chest? Why don't you act on it?"

Now that Maggie's finger had connected with Jack's bare skin, his heart wasn't just thumping.

It was beating like the hooves of a damned quarter horse.

He took Maggie's hand and pressed her palm over the pulsating beat in his chest. "You feel that?"

"If I couldn't, I'd be dead."

"That isn't just hormones pumping blood, Princess. That's my heart there, and I don't mean just an organ. It's getting involved. I'm scared shitless."

Finally, they were getting somewhere. "What are you afraid of, Jack?"

"Something like me telling you I love you, and you returning the sentiment. Then, down the line, you deciding love isn't all it's cracked up to be, so you walk out, like Buck's wife did."

"You're not talking about Buck's wife, are you?" Maggie asked softly. She brushed a lock of hair from his forehead and wished she could make Jack forget all the hurt he had endured as a child abandoned by his mother. "You're talking about your mother, aren't you?"

Jack gave a casual shrug. But even in the dim light of the stars, Maggie could see the hurt flicker in his eyes.

"Maybe I'm talking about both," he admitted.

"You're not going to get any one-hundred-percent guarantees when it comes to love, Jack. Your mother walked out on your dad. I'm sorry for that. But my dad left my mother, too."

"Your dad died. That was different."

"True, but the fact is, one day he went to work and never came home. My mother was only thirty when it happened. She had expected to grow old with Dad, but she didn't have ten gray hairs when he died."

Maggie's throat tightened around the memory of the gnawing, empty hole that had opened in her stomach when her father disappeared from her life. "I asked her, once, 'Mom, if you knew Dad was going to die when he did, would you have married him, or would you have married somebody else?' You know what she said? She said, 'Sweetheart, if I never love again, what your dad and I shared will be enough to last a lifetime. Does that answer your question?' "

Maggie looked Jack straight in the face, her gaze direct, unflinching. "I want that kind of love, Jack. I want babies that grow from that deep commitment. I've always told myself, when love hits me, I'm going to go for it, whether it's convenient or not. Until you, I was beginning to think I wasn't going to find it. I didn't feel attractive. I didn't think I had much to offer a man. Now, thanks to you, I know I do. The trouble is, I also know who the man is I want to spend my life with. But he's too damned chicken to risk seeing if it might work."

Jack slid his hand under her hair and curved his hand around the nape of her neck. His expression was reverent and more tender than Maggie thought possible of him. "Is that your way of telling me you love me, Princess?"

She lifted her chin, tossing pride and caution over her shoulder with her hair. "It is. Do you have trouble with that?"

Beneath her fingertips, Jack's heartbeat stuttered, a good sign, she hoped.

"When did you figure out you felt this way about me?"

"I don't know. It just happened. It came out of my mouth, by way of my heart."

"You're sure."

With another man, Maggie would have been irritated by the doubt. Jack, she realized, needed assurances. "I think I've loved you for a long time, but I wouldn't admit it to myself because I thought there was no way you'd ever think about me in the same way." She bit her lip and swallowed her pride. "You remember when you got that terrible case of the flu?"

"Yeah," Jack said. "You made me chicken soup. I was lying on the couch, burning up with fever. You got a bowl of ice water and bathed my forehead."

It pleased Maggie that Jack remembered so much about that weekend. "When I touched your forehead, I felt this burning this tingling. I thought, my, his fever must be high to affect my skin that way. But the tingling didn't stop when I left and went back up to my apartment. I was burning all right." She rolled her eyes and fanned her face. "In a most frustrating way!"

"That was in March. More than seven months ago," Jack said, as if he couldn't believe it.

"I also remember sitting on your living room floor with you a couple of months later." She fingered the collar of his shirt. "The air conditioning was out. You weren't wearing a shirt. I was supposed to be helping you pick out your best prints for a magazine article. My eyes kept straying to your chest. You'd catch me looking at you and ask if something was wrong."

"I remember that. You said you were hungry."

Maggie grinned. "Guess what for? Or should I say who?"

"I can't believe I was so dense," Jack said. "I never knew you thought of me like that."

"If you had, it wouldn't have made any difference, except maybe to ruin our friendship. I wasn't the kind of woman you were attracted to," she said matter-of-factly. "I finally accepted that and settled for what we could share. Friendship. But the truth is, I didn't fall in love with you last week or last month. It's been happening for about a year."

Jack reached up and scratched his head, as if trying to decide how to tell her something. A tug of amusement twisted his mouth.

Dear Lord, he was laughing at her! Just as Melvin had done when she'd walked into the interior design shop next to Miss Caroline's and found it unattended. Hearing what sounded like cries for help, Maggie had swallowed her fear and searched for the proprietor in the back room out of concern for her safety.

Maggie would never forget the hot flush of humiliation that had swept over her when she found that designer with Melvin. He had been backed against the wall, the woman's legs hooked around his waist, her head thrown back while she rode him to climax. Melvin had looked over the designer's shoulder and given Maggie that same smile that lurked on Jack's lips now.

She extricated herself from Jack's arms. "I'm glad you find my feelings for you amusing," she snapped and pushed at his unyielding chest so she could get to the door handle.

Jack didn't budge. "I didn't hear anybody laughing."

Deciding he just might be getting a sadistic kick out of humiliating her, Maggie chilled him with a haughty, composed look of indifference. "You don't have to laugh out loud." Her gaze shifted. She tapped a stiff finger to the side of his mouth. "You're doing it here. With your lips."

"Is that so?" Jack clamped his hand around her wrist and moved her hand to the back of his neck. Before she could protest, he shifted his legs apart, pulled her against his chest and anchored her in place with unyielding arms. "What makes you such an expert at reading my thoughts?"

"It doesn't take a genius." Staring stubbornly into Jack's glinting eyes, Maggie struggled to wedge an arm between them. Jack only tightened his hold on her. A shaft of desire shot through her. Apprehension made her tremble as the male scent of Jack, the texture of his warm flesh against hers, the heat of his breath assaulted her senses. "What do you think you're trying to do?"

"Something with my lips you couldn't possibly misinterpret." A muscle in his jaw flexed. Angling his head, he shifted his arms higher on her back, clearly determined to make her submit to his kiss.

At the last moment, Maggie turned her head.

Jack's lips connected with her hair. "I don't want you to kiss me right now," she informed him tightly.

"You don't make a very good liar, Mags." Jack cupped the back of her head in one insistent hand and forced her to face him. The pace of his breathing had quickened. Eyes fixed on her mouth, he lowered his head and laid claim to her lips.

Determined not to submit to him, Maggie pursed her lips. A chuckle rumbled deep in Jack's chest. "My, but you're frisky, aren't you?" he murmured over her lips and, backing her against the side of his car, made her his prisoner. "But I got to warn you. I really want you."

Want her? As in all of her? Although that's what she'd craved the night before, what she'd fantasized about today, now that Jack's desire appeared to be matching Maggie's, insecurity had her stomach churning. What if she couldn't satisfy him? What if she disappointed him, as she'd disappointed Melvin?

She gulped as Jack's turgid maleness pressed into her abdomen. She glanced quickly down the dirt road toward the highway. "Take me home, Jack."

"No way. Not yet. I'm enjoying this."

"Just what do you intend to do with me out here?"

"Kiss you. Then . . . we'll see."

"Jack, I-I'm . . ."

"Scared? No need to be. I won't bite." He lowered his head, then chuckled. "I take that back. I just might."

He slanted his mouth over hers. "Kiss me, Maggie." Jack took her chin in his hand. Holding her gaze, he rubbed his thumb slowly over her lower lip.

Maybe if she kissed Jack, proved to him he couldn't arouse her just now, he would take her home. Maggie closed her eyes and waited. She expected a kiss that would leave her lips swollen and her dignity bruised.

When Jack's lips closed over hers, though, the one word that leaped from Maggie's mind was tender. His arms held her close; his body pressed her into the hard, cool metal of his car, but his lips coaxed; they teased.

Incredibly, she felt cherished. In the assault on her senses, her restraint ebbed; reason vanished like droplets of dew in the wind.

She opened her eyes, hoping to find a look of love on Jack's face.

"That's right," he murmured over her mouth. "Look at my eyes. See the heat burning in them. See what you do to me, Mags. Know I'm fighting myself here, as much as I'm fighting you."

He tilted his hips forward slightly, showing Maggie with the hardness of him what other effect she was having on his body.

Lust wasn't love. She balked. Yet, a traitorous part of her had her meeting the increased pressure of his body with an involuntary ripple of desire.

Jack pounced on the first sign of her submission. "Oh, God, Maggie. Don't you know how much I want you?" He gathered her closer and traced her lips with the tip of his tongue.

His breath smelled minty. He tasted of the hot, syrupy chocolate of their dessert. Deep in Maggie's abdomen, flames of longing licked at her long-suppressed need.

There was only so much a woman could take. Maggie's eyes drifted shut. All the knotted muscles of her restraint relaxed their tenuous grip on her control. Her tongue darted out to meet Jack's.

Jack wasted no time in taking what Maggie offered. His lips closed insistently over hers. His tongue slipped over the barrier of her earlier restraint and teased her tongue to tangle in a mind-dazing sample of what could follow.

Huge, long-fingered hands that Maggie had watched handling cameras with the gentleness of a caressing lover turned their tenderness on her. They roamed her back, then moved over her ribs to graze the outside curves of her breasts.

There on a dirt road on the eastern fringe of the Hill Country, hands skimmed bodies, mouths tasted skin. Pulses hammered until desires swelled with the need for release. Confident now that Maggie wouldn't try to slip from his grasp, Jack found the handle to the door and opened it.

Maggie broke the kiss and glanced up with passion-glazed eyes. "Jack?"

"Yeah, Princess?"

"Are you taking me home?"

"Nope."

"Then why—?"

"Shh," he said and silenced her query with a kiss while he drew her aside and swung the car door open. At the creak of metal hinges something skittered across the rocky soil and gave Maggie a start. "Probably a field mouse," he noted. "Come on. Let's go where the critters can't get you."

Jack released the catch on the front passenger seat. The upholstered back snapped forward. Jack gestured to the back seat with one hand and waited for Maggie's reaction. She climbed inside without complaint, the fabric of her jumpsuit stretching taut across her rump.

Maggie laughed while Jack followed her. The tenor of her voice conveyed a telltale nervous quality. "The back seat of a car. Wouldn't the Sisters of Mercy be mortified?"

Jack pulled her into his arms, already hungry for the return of her soft body against him. "I can take you home, if you like. Just say the word."

Maggie propped her chin on his chest. "That comes as somewhat of a surprise."

"Why?"

"I thought you were going to do with me as you wished."

"What makes you think I'm not?"

"You just gave me the choice of going home. You said, 'Just say the word.' "

He chucked her on the chin. "I didn't say when I'd take you home."

"And I," she reminded him, "didn't say the word."

Back in his wild and woolly days of high school and college, every time Jack got a different car, he initiated it by steaming up the windows of the back seat with his favorite girl. He ultimately gave each car a nickname that only he knew related to the nature of the night of steamy sex. These days every time a guy had sex with a woman, he risked his life. Jack preferred to nurse his memories and take a lot of cold showers. He also jogged, pumped iron, and was prone to erotic dreams.

Tonight memories of those cars and steamy nights paled for Jack in contrast to the mere anticipation of making love to Maggie. Knowing she had experienced only one lover, and a crass one at that, he dedicated himself to making their joining pleasurable for her.

Sliding the zipper of her jumpsuit down her torso with teeth-gritting slowness, he murmured, "I won't hurt you."

"It isn't in you to hurt," Maggie assured him in a tender voice that warmed him deep inside.

The zipper parted to reveal breasts spilling over the tight constraints of a white lace bra. The flimsy contraption showed as much as it bound. Jack's libido kicked his pulse into roaring speed. His breath came out in a whoosh of desire. He skimmed his fingertips over the boundary between lace and bare flesh. Rational thought shot through the top of his head.

At first Maggie reacted to his touch with the hesitant shyness of a virgin. She lowered her head and dropped her gaze. Jack cupped his hands around the softness of her breasts and eased open the front closure of her bra. Released from their constraints, Maggie's breasts swung free with a be-witching jiggle.

Jack filled his eager hands and looked to Maggie's eyes for reassurance. She took the corner of her lower lip between her teeth and slanted him a smoky look. No more the demure woman who had been merely his friend, she became his willing, eager lover. Her hands dipped impatiently under his T-shirt. Her fingers splayed across his chest; her palms molded to his sweat-slickened pectorals. Fingernails lightly raked his nipples.

Zippers unzipped. T-shirts flew. Maggie's jumpsuit went the way of her bra. In the time-honored tradition of back seats, hands sought and pleasured, mouths lathed and suckled. Maggie tasted of manmade lotions and natural juices. The musky scent of her desire spiced the humid night air.

Driven to feel the moist heat of her close around him, Jack knelt on the bench seat between her parted legs and cradled her head in his hands. "I wasn't laughing at you earlier. I was laughing at myself."

"Why?"

"I've been watching you for months. The way you walk, the way your rear end sways when you climb the stairs. I've been thinking there's a whole lot more woman to Maggie Kincaid than she's showing. If you hadn't become such a good friend, I might have crossed the line earlier. I wish I had. I might have figured out a lot sooner you're the woman . . ." He blew out a hot, quick breath.

"I can't believe I'm saying this, but here goes. I love you, Mags."

Maggie's eyes misted over. "Oh, Jack. I'm so glad. I'm thrilled you could say it. I love you, too."

"Touch me," he moaned and captured her mouth, "and let's make it complete."

Her fingers closed around him and guided him to the tight, moist center of entry. Trembling from restraint, Jack sank into her one heavenly inch at a time. He stroked slowly and deeply until she came, crying his name while her sweet female muscles quivered around him.

He smoothed her damp hair from her face and waited. In a few moments her desire rose and crested, this time taking him with her. Jack's last coherent thought as he buried himself deep inside her and gave her a part of himself was that that night in a fogged-up car in the Texas Hill Country he'd found what had been missing from his life.

Thirteen

Maggie snuggled back into the spoon of Jack's body and gave a contented sigh.

Jack slung his leg over hers and nibbled at her ear. "I've got a great idea."

"So have I. Let's go back to my apartment and give each other massages."

"Ah, Maggie, I thought you were a romantic."

"Isn't a massage romantic?"

"Not like lying here together and watching the sun rise."

"Jack, we couldn't! Farmers get up early. Your friend will probably be out here plowing his fields or something by that time."

"So, we can get dressed."

"But you have an early . . . shoot."

"What's the matter?"

"I've been feeling this tickling along my calf." She sat up and brushed at her leg, the same sensation creeping over her arms and her back. "You don't suppose it's fire ants."

"Nope. None around here. Your blood's probably just beginning to cool."

"How can you be so sure it isn't fire ants?"

Jack circled her nipple with one finger. "I was here earlier this week. There weren't any then."

Maggie grabbed Jack's finger and pulled it away from her. "Wait a minute. Did you set this up?"

"What?"

"This," she said, gesturing emphatically with both hands.

"Oh, you mean *this,*" Jack said and sat up to cover her lips with a kiss that left little doubt as to his stamina or his intentions.

Maggie broke the kiss, attempting to think through the fog of desire clouding her brain. "I think you get the idea. Did you bring me out here for the sole purpose of—that is, did you pretend you didn't want me, when all along you planned to—?"

"Make love to you?" He slid his thumbs over the tight buds of her nipples. "Yeah, I did, Princess."

Maggie batted his hands away. "Then this *was* a set up." She reached for her panties, suddenly feeling the need to cover up. "And I fell for it. Oh, boy, I thought parking went out with drive-in movies."

"I didn't say this was a setup. I said I planned to make love to you . . . someday."

"Oh. Well, I guess that's okay then. When did you plan to . . . you know?"

"I'll have to check my calendar. It might have been the fifteenth of November, or it might have been the seventeenth."

"You're making fun of me."

"No, I'm not. I'm trying to tell you, I didn't

plan anything. I just decided I was going to ask you out. Can I help it if we made love on our first date?"

"Jack! You make it sound like I'm a tramp."

"Lighten up, sweetheart. We've known each other for a year. We love each other. We made love."

"What now?" she asked, glad the dark of night hid the flush of heat creeping over her cheeks. She knew she was acting like a fool. Last night she wanted Jack to make love to her. Tonight she'd balked when he'd pressed her. Now she'd accused him of pulling off on a country road to take advantage of her. But all this was so new to her.

"What now? We let it happen," Jack responded. "What are you doing tomorrow night?"

"I don't know," she replied and ran a finger down the length of his arm. His skin had the texture of satin. "What do you have in mind?"

The early rays of sun were slanting over Maggie's bed the next morning when a shrill ring intruded on her dream.

Eyes still closed, she reached over and batted the top of her nightstand to turn off her alarm. But the source of the piercing sound wasn't her alarm. It was her damned telephone.

Moaning, she squinted one eye open on the third ring and focused her bleary gaze on the clock face. Seven-thirty. On a Saturday. And she didn't have to work. She'd let the darned phone ring. It was probably somebody selling something she didn't want. No one she knew ever called on a weekend before nine o'clock.

Dreamy remnants of her night with Jack brought a smile of remembrance to her lips. The tender tissue between her legs verified that their lovemaking had not been another frustrating dream.

Jack. Seven-thirty.

"Oh, my gosh!" she muttered and grabbed for the phone. Jack had a photo shoot at eight. Seventhirty would be about the time he'd leave. What if he needed help? What if he simply wanted to pick up the phone and hear her voice? Make plans for the evening? Yes, she was sure her caller was Jack.

She cradled the receiver to her ear and snuggled back into her pillow. Since Jack had made love to her, there was a new richness, a lushness to her body. She was warmer, more aware of the vibrancy of color, the resonance of sound, the luxuriant feel of textures. "Good morning," she murmured and let her eyes drift shut. Her voice came out sounding a lot like a satisfied purr. "Is this who I think it is?"

"That depends," a male voice replied with a hint of amusement.

"Jack?"

"No."

"Buck?"

"Wrong again."

"Then I don't know you. Which means you're selling something. Look, it's early. I had a late night. I'm not in the mood for a sales pitch. I—"

"Have a plane to catch."

Maggie's eyes snapped open. "Who is this?"

"Armand Foster. Sorry for the early call. I waited as long as I could."

"You must be an early riser," she mumbled and pushed up onto her elbow.

"It's two-thirty in the afternoon here."

"Where are you?" she asked in a daze.

"Paris, and believe me, I'm not too happy about having to give up my Saturday to work, but Raleigh and I agreed we can't pass up this opportunity."

The fact that someone in Paris even wanted to talk to her had Maggie shaking the cobwebs from her brain. "What's this about catching a plane, and what opportunity?"

"We got a call this morning from our PR liaison in San Francisco. He's been working on the producer of 'Lifestyles of the Rich and Famous' to feature Raleigh on our property there. The show's producer called our man in the middle of the night in a panic. It seems one segment fell through on the show in production. Some star had a falling out with her famous live-in lover and canceled. And—get this—the producer heard about our Cinderella Girl promotion and decided to fill in on a segment about you. How lucky can we get!"

This was a dream; Maggie knew it. She sat up to force blood to circulate better to her foggy brain. "Armand, I'm neither rich, nor famous."

"Trust me. By the time the segment airs, the public will perceive you as both. Maybe you don't realize it, but you're going to be as famous as Cindy Crawford before we're through."

Maggie was tempted to tell Armand he had

called the wrong sister, but by now she was fully awake. She was thinking how exciting it would be one day when she was a mother and cooking breakfast for her family. She could tell her children she had once starred in "Lifestyles of the Rich and Famous." Of course, they'd never believe her!

She glanced in the mirror and wrinkled her nose at the distinctly unglamorous apparition staring back at her. "You want me in San Francisco— this evening? As in tonight?"

"The weatherman's predicting no fog, which figured into the producer's decision. The conditions should be perfect for filming. Take a cab to the airport. There's a flight out of Austin at noon. You'll find tickets in your name at the American Airlines will-call desk. You'll change planes in Dallas and be in San Francisco at four. A hotel limousine will pick you up there. You'll arrive at the Grand Perimeter in time for hair, makeup, and wardrobe. If all goes as planned, you'll be ready for filming at dusk."

Flights. Tickets. Limousine. Armand wasn't kidding. He expected her to be in San Francisco about the time she and Jack were to have begun their second date. "I'm afraid it's out of the question, Armand. I have plans for the evening."

A dead silence followed her protest. When Armand spoke, his words were drawn out, his tone intimidating. "More important than this? And before you answer, may I remind you that you have a contract with us?"

A contract. What had the fine print defined?

Maggie wasn't sure, nor did she want to irritate Grand Perimeter management at the outset by appearing to be difficult.

She hesitated. Things could be worse. Armand's call could have come during the week when she would have had to miss a day's work without the advance notice Miss Caroline had requested when Maggie needed time off. She could catch an early flight out of San Francisco in the morning and be back in Austin by late afternoon.

Surely Jack wouldn't mind postponing their date for one night. She would slip a note under his door and call him when she changed planes in Dallas. Homer could keep him company until she got back.

"Maggie?"

"All right." She swung her legs over the side of the bed and came down on Homer. The poor thing screeched and shot out of the room. "I'll be there."

By the time Jack got home at 5:00 P.M., he'd developed what promised to be the best mood of his life.

He slung his camera bag over his shoulder and reached into the back seat of his car to load up the half dozen assorted bags from his shopping trip. Kicking the door shut with his foot, he glanced up at Maggie's balcony. He hoped to catch a glimpse of her buffing a spot on the glass.

Through the sliding door he saw only Homer.

The cat's alert gaze was riveted to a fat blue jay taunting him from the balcony's iron railing. Jack was so pumped up at the prospect of spending the evening with Maggie, he felt like sharing his happiness with Homer. Maybe he'd open Maggie's balcony door and give the old boy a chance to sink his pointy teeth into the damned squawking bird. Then maybe Homer would forgive Jack for stealing Maggie away for the evening.

This morning he had shot the joggers and scullers on Town Lake for an Austin travel piece for *Texas Monthly*. While he worked, Jack thought and thought on his plans for the evening. Instead of going out, he would treat Maggie to a fantastic date in his apartment. He wanted her to remember it for its contrast to the usual beer and Monday night football sessions that had characterized their friendship before he'd fallen in love with her. He'd finally come up with a plan.

First they'd take the phone off the hook and indulge in a bit of reacquainting. After all, it had been ten whole hours since Jack had held Maggie in his arms. Since he'd felt her bare breasts brush against his nipples until he thought they'd pop off, like buttons on a snug shirt.

Then they'd uncork the bottle of wine he'd picked up at the liquor store. Pour some gardenia-smelling bubbly from the bed and bath store into his tub. Fill that sucker up and soak their tired bodies while they polished off the wine.

Afterward, he'd give Maggie a leisurely massage, with the aromatic oil he'd found in an organic products shop on Sixth Street.

Then he'd make slow easy love to Maggie in the softness of his bed, to make up for the backseat gyrotechnics of the night before.

When those appetites were duly sated, he'd make Maggie curl up on his couch while he cooked her his famous pasta primavera. Carbohydrates were supposed to be energy renewers. He figured by then they'd need recharging. Jack wouldn't hear of Maggie lifting a finger to help, before, during, or after dinner.

He hoped he'd find a way to persuade her to stay the night. Grinning at a couple of ways he'd come up with to do just that, he took the three steps to the door in a jaunty leap. When he walked into the building, he saw Buck angling across the courtyard. "Hey, buddy, how goes it?"

Buck gave a wry grin and followed him inside. "Okay, I guess. You?"

"Great. Just great."

"I hear you're dating Maggie."

"Yeah, well . . ." Jack gave a nervous laugh. "No hard feelings?"

"Nah. She probably wouldn't have gone for me anyway. When's she coming back?"

Jack looked at him blankly.

"You know, from San Francisco. I saw her climbing into a cab when I got back from jogging this morning. I asked her to a movie. She told me you guys were dating."

"Maggie, in a cab?" Jack asked his poker buddy.

"You're sure she said she was going to San Francisco?"

"Sure. I offered to give her a lift to save her the cab fare. She said, 'Thanks, but it's paid for.' I asked her where she was going, and she said to the airport. She had to catch a plane for San Francisco."

"We had plans. It must have been something important." Jack remembered Maggie saying one sister lived in Phoenix, and the other on the East Coast, but he couldn't recall where her mother lived. As disappointed as he was that he wouldn't be seeing her that evening, he couldn't help worrying about her. What if her mother was sick? What if—God forbid—Maggie's mom had died. "Did she say why?" Jack asked.

"No, she told me she really had to go or she'd miss her plane."

"How did she act? Upset? Worried?"

Buck thought on Jack's question for a moment. "I wouldn't say worried. Flustered's more like it. And she was frowning."

"I expect she'll call and let me know what's going on."

"If I have to spend another Saturday night staring at the walls of my apartment, they'll have to check me into a loony bin. I wouldn't mind taking in a movie. You game?"

"I'll let you know," Jack said and wished he could find someone sweet like Maggie for Buck. Someone who would gladly stick around to share the day-to-day things. "I want to wait until I hear from Maggie. If she calls in time, I'll give you a buzz."

"By the way," Buck said with a sheepish dip of his head, "if it doesn't work out for you and Maggie . . ."

"I know, I know. Give you a call. Don't plan on it."

Jack unlocked his apartment, scooped up his packages and pushed his door open with his hip. As he stepped across the threshold, his gaze fell on a pastel blue envelope staring up at him from the floor. His name was penned across the front in Maggie's graceful writing. He felt a tug in his gut, and smiled. How like Maggie to leave him a note when she had to leave unexpectedly.

He dumped his packages on the table, slipped his camera bag off his shoulder and snapped up the envelope. He retrieved a beer from the fridge while he thumbed open the gummed flap. Inside he found a single sheet of paper and what looked like a hastily written note:

"Had to fly to San Francisco for filming of a TV show. I fed Homer. Will you check his food bowl in the morning? Or let him sleep with you? I hate missing our date this evening. Can I have a rain check for tomorrow night? Love you (really), Maggie."

"Well, hell!" The all-too-familiar feeling of being abandoned vaulted from Jack's memory and jabbed him in the gut. He wadded up the note, threw it against the wall and tasted the acrid bite of disappointment. He knocked back a long, thirsty slug of beer. The icy liquid cleared the fuzz from his brain and doused his initial, irrational flash of irritation.

In his logical mind, he knew this trip was something Maggie had to do. But how much could they expect of her, calling at the last minute like this and expecting her to jump? She could have informed the hotel people she had plans. If she hated missing their date so all-fired much, she could have told Raleigh and his troops they'd have to wait a day because she had important plans with someone who meant a lot to her.

Between flights in Dallas, Maggie tried to reach Jack, but he hadn't returned yet from his shoot.

The moment she walked off the jetway in San Francisco, the hotel's driver spotted her and escorted her to the limousine. There she found a carry-out tray waiting for her with a sumptuous meal from the hotel. Before she took a bite, she used the limo's cellular phone to call Jack. Still he didn't answer.

Since then she had been whisked from wardrobe to hair to makeup. She made it through what felt like a never-ending series of takes with Raleigh Cordell by pretending she was her confident, experienced younger sister. The shoot had been exciting, but exhausting.

Her body was a bag of aching bones. Her feet would have been numb if they hadn't hurt so much. The stage makeup still on her face was so thick she felt claustrophobic.

She slipped out of her heels and glanced at the clock. Ten past midnight. In Austin, it would be ten past two. Surely Jack would be asleep by now, but she had promised to call, and she would. Truth to tell, she didn't want to go to sleep without hearing his voice.

Too tired to undress, she picked up the phone and flopped back on the bed. On the fourth ring, Jack's answering machine kicked in.

Frowning, Maggie rolled over and plucked at the quilting on the designer comforter. Jack wasn't home. On Saturday night. Not that he didn't have a right to go out, but who was he with? Maggie wondered.

Ten kinds of insecurity niggled at her while she waited for the message beep to sound. "I just got in," she said. "I'm sorry it's so late, but we had to do this one shoot at sunset, overlooking the bay. Then I had to change into a cocktail dress for pictures in the nightclub. Anyway, I wish I were there, or you were here. This bed is huge. Jack?" Maggie's voice took a decided, husky dip. "I love you."

She started to hang up, then heard a scrambling sound over the line, as if the phone had been dropped, followed by, "Damn it, Homer! Get out of here. Maggie, are you still there?"

"Jack! I'm so glad you got home before I hung up."

"Yeah," he said. "Me, too."

"I'm sorry about tonight."

"Not as sorry as I am, Princess. What's up?"

"If you were here, I'd ask you to pinch me to make sure I wasn't dreaming."

"If I were there, I'd do a lot more than pinch you. You sound excited. And tired. What was the big emergency?"

Maggie told Jack how she came to be scheduled for a "Lifestyles of the Rich and Famous" segment. She and Jack shared a good laugh over the irony, but he didn't sound like himself. His laugh was dry. It sounded forced.

"So, when will you be home?" he asked.

"Tomorrow afternoon. Can I have that rain check?"

"Well . . ." he said tentatively, and Maggie decided from the trace of resentment in his voice, he was covering up his real feelings about their broken date. "I guess. But I already drank half your bottle of wine."

"You bought me a bottle of wine?"

"That ain't all, sweetheart."

"Oh, Jack."

A knock sounded at her door.

"Someone's at the door. Can you wait a minute?"

"Maggie, come back! You can't answer your door now. It's after two there."

"I won't open it. I'll talk through it," she compromised.

"Well, okay. But if you're not back in sixty seconds, I'm going to hang up and call hotel security."

The fact Jack was so concerned about her had

Maggie smiling as she padded wearily to the door in her bare feet. "Who is it?"

"Raleigh."

"Raleigh who?" she asked suspiciously, although the man spoke with the president's decided French accent.

"Raleigh Cordell. Maggie, will you please open your door? I have a message for you. From Armand. He's called your room twice, but your line was busy. Since I'm staying here tonight, he prevailed upon me to deliver the message personally."

Maggie unlocked the security bolt and opened the door so the president could enter. "Please, make yourself comfortable," she said self-consciously and motioned for him to sit at the conversational grouping in the sitting room of her suite. "I'll only be another minute or two. Then we can discuss Armand's message."

"I'd appreciate it if you'd conclude your conversation quickly," Raleigh said with a weary sigh. "We need to talk about tomorrow."

"Tomorrow?" Maggie asked him blankly.

"Yes, it appears we'll need you to stay over another day or two. The producer isn't satisfied with the rushes. The shadows were all wrong. He wants to reshoot, only earlier in the day."

"I'm afraid that's impossible," Maggie said and lifted her chin with more assertiveness than she felt. "I have to be back in Austin by tomorrow evening. And at work Monday morning."

"My dear, the film crew leaves Tuesday morning for Milan. If you won't agree to extend your stay, we'll lose this fabulous opportunity to appear on 'Lifestyles.' "

Maggie thought of Jack, who wanted her to spend Sunday evening with him. Of Miss Caroline who expected her to report Monday morning as usual. Lastly, of Raleigh Cordell, the president of an international hotel chain, politely insisting she not make them forego a promotional opportunity.

The experience reminded her of the time she and her two sisters had fought over a Raggedy Ann doll. They had tugged and pulled until the poor doll lost an arm and a leg. She was being pulled in three different directions, at risk of losing an arm or a leg in the fray. She couldn't satisfy everyone. That distressed her. Of the three demanding her devotion, though, Jack meant the most to her. She wouldn't let him down, not again.

"If you want to replace me, go right ahead," she told Raleigh. "But I *will* be on the plane to Austin tomorrow morning."

"Is there anything I can do to change your mind? Anything at all?"

Maggie thought for a moment. A switch tripped in her brain. It was because of Jack that she was the Grand Perimeter's Cinderella Girl. If she used her head, she could return the favor. The prospect had her grinning. "There might be something," she told Raleigh. "Wait here just a moment."

She scurried into her bedroom. Halfway to the bed, she heard Jack's voice hollering out of the receiver. She picked it up and heard, "Six, five, four—"

"Jack! It's okay. I'm fine. Settle down."

"Another seven seconds, and you would have had the cops beating down your door. Who is that man in your room, and what's he doing there at this hour?"

"It's only Raleigh, and he isn't in my bedroom. He's in the sitting room. I have a suite. Armand has been trying to reach me, but he hasn't been able to get through because I was talking to you. He phoned Raleigh and asked him to deliver the message in person."

"What message?" Jack growled.

"I'll let you know in one minute. Hold on again. I'll be right back."

Maggie darted back to her sitting room and found the president checking his watch. "Raleigh?"

"Yes, my dear?"

She took a deep breath and flattened her hand over her diaphragm. What she had in mind would disappoint Jack at the outset. That distressed her. Standing up to the president of an international hotel chain had her pulse thumping and her throat constricting. Anticipating Miss Caroline's fury if she showed up late for work Monday, if at all, had Maggie's head throbbing.

She was sick of trying to make everyone happy. It was her life. She deserved to take her wishes into consideration for a change.

"I'll stay one more night in San Francisco," she told Raleigh.

"Merci," Raleigh said and, taking her hand, kissed the curves of her fingers.

"But only one. In return, you and Armand are going to do something for me, and I want it kept a secret."

Fourteen

Had Maggie lost her mind?

At two in the morning, she'd let Raleigh Cordell into her hotel room. Right now the king of cultured sleaze could be plying her with champagne. He could be weakening her exhausted body until she didn't have the strength to resist his groping hands.

If he dishonored her, the prez would probably warn Maggie if she violated her contract because of what he'd done, he would nail her butt in the press. It wouldn't hurt Cordell to be accused of sleeping with his Cinderella Girl. He was too rich, too powerful to be affected by reputation sabotage. But poor, sweet Maggie would be destroyed.

Jack stormed about his apartment, fury pumping his blood until a tide of rage roared in his ears. At the same time, insecurity destroyed the last, lingering traces of his euphoria. One day after he'd lost himself inside Maggie, she was acting as if they'd merely gone to a movie Friday night. As if they hadn't made earth-shattering love that had made him feel as if maybe Jack Lewis was worthy of a woman's enduring, gentle touch.

Maggie could have told the hotel mucky-mucks

to stick their request that she fly to San Francisco at a moment's notice. Clearly, Maggie's choice had been between Jack and the job. It appeared she had made the decision easily and without remorse. Judging from her excitement over the attention in San Francisco, she didn't regret her decision a bit.

What was it about Jack that made him come last when the female gender had to make choices? Just once he wished a woman would say, "Sorry, Jack's too important. Kiss off, stick your job," or words of similar conviction.

He yanked the receiver off the hook and called Buck.

"H'lo," his friend mumbled in a sleepy voice.

"Hey, Buck, the offer still good for a beer?"

"Beer?" Jack heard a fumbling from Buck's end, then, "Are you crazy? It's . . . Jesus, two-thirty in the goddamned morning. Did you hear from Maggie?"

"Yeah. A few minutes ago."

"Is she okay?"

"I can only hope."

"What was the emergency?"

"Her new job. Does that ring a bell?"

Buck met Jack's announcement with a long stretch of silence. In the way of men, no words had to be spoken for understanding to link between them.

"I got a six-pack in the fridge," Buck said. "Come on over."

* * *

As luck would have it, the "Lifestyles" crew wound up their filming by midnight Sunday. Exhausted from the emotional drain as much as the physical aspects of the shoot, Maggie fell into a shallow sleep on the red-eye back to Austin.

Feeling anything but glamorous, she arrived Monday morning at eight. The old Maggie would have changed clothes and reported to work. But she was too tired to sew a decent seam. She said to hell with it. She called her boss, told her about the "Lifestyles" shoot and said she was taking the day off.

Not only did Miss Caroline not complain, she encouraged Maggie to get plenty of rest before she returned. Maggie found out why when she opened her Monday *American-Statesman* that evening. Next to her picture on page five, a headline read, "Local Seamstress Named Hotel Chain's Cinderella Girl." Miss Caroline's Couturier was named as Maggie's Austin employer. Armand Foster hadn't wasted time launching his PR campaign, Maggie mused.

While her boss had been easy to placate, Jack was another matter. It wasn't so much that he blew off steam. He didn't. He didn't express much emotion at all. His welcome kiss when she knocked on his door Monday morning was guarded. His hands didn't roam her body. When Maggie dipped her fingertips into the waistband of his jeans, he broke the kiss. He grabbed her suitcase, hefted it up the flight of stairs and kissed her pristinely on the cheek.

Before leaving, he told her he would be away

for a few days on a job. They would have to post-
pone their date indefinitely.

Indefinitely. How long would that be? Maggie
wondered, realizing now how disappointed Jack
must have been when she couldn't make their
date.

She hugged Homer to her chest and pressed
her forehead to the window glass. Jack pulled out
of his parking space and waved to her through
his open window.

Homer yowled a complaint and twitched the
tip of his tail. "I know. He isn't gone yet, and we
already miss him, don't we, baby?"

She knew Jack's cool demeanor had been an
effort to disguise his hurt feelings, his insecurity
over his place in her life. She hoped all that would
change soon.

"Raleigh and Armand had better deliver," she
told Homer on the way to the kitchen. "And Jack
had better be back in time."

"Where is that damned photographer?"

Jack gritted his teeth over the acid retort that
sprang to his mind. He'd just returned last night
from his shoot on a shrimp boat in Galveston Bay,
and he was beat. This being Saturday, he'd planned
to sleep in and spend the day developing his film
and cleaning his lenses. But the phone call this
morning had changed that. A guy'd have to be a
fool to turn down the chance to make a cool thousand in one day.

For his bank account's sake—and Maggie's—he

decided to ignore the foul mood of the Grand Perimeter's PR glory boy. He stepped forward and gave his hand a solid, businesslike shake. "Jack Lewis. You must be Armand Foster. It's a pleasure to be working with you."

"That's yet to be determined," the wise guy returned. "Maggie tells us you're as good as the guy we had lined up for this shoot. Let's see you prove it."

He shoved a sheaf of papers at Jack. "Here, these are the photo specs. We're on a tight schedule. Mr. Cordell has a noon flight to Paris."

The Dallas photographer hired to do the Austin Grand Perimeter shoot had waited until this morning to fly in. Because of a violent morning thunderstorm, all flights from Dallas had been grounded. Jack's call at seven to fill in had roused him from bed. He'd busted his ass to show up by eight. Now Armand Foster was treating him like a first-year photography student.

Jack was tempted to stuff the wad of papers down Foster's throat. But Maggie's reputation, plus the big bucks and the opportunity to prove himself to a client with the stature of Grand Perimeter had Jack swallowing his resentment.

He scanned the spec sheets. Maggie wandering through the lobby in awe. Maggie checking in at the registration desk. Maggie chatting with a male model on a lounge at the pool. Maggie shopping in the boutique, having her nails done in the salon.

B-O-R-I-N-G. For a corporate PR man, Foster

was short in the imagination department. "Mind if I turn in a few extra shots?"

"Suit yourself," Foster responded. "You'll only get paid for what we use. *If* we use any at all."

Hey, buddy, who needs you? Jack wanted to tell the jerk, but he knew the answer to the question. *Jack* did. He had no doubt Maggie had used her influence to get him the fill-in job, but he couldn't blow this chance for a choice credit on his resume. He would shoot the pictures and do his best to earn the hotel's respect, and hefty fee, with the quality of his work.

"Where's Her Highness?" Jack asked, glancing around the lobby for Maggie.

"Miss Kincaid is with Mr. Cordell—in makeup. If you're smart, you'll put a lid on that attitude of yours, buddy," Foster advised him. He glanced over Jack's shoulder and broke into a smile. "There they are now. She's one good-looking lady, isn't she? You used to date her—right?"

Used to? Who said? Shaken by Foster's comment, Jack turned in the direction of his gaze. Maggie waved to him from across lobby, resplendent in a clinging gown of shimmering sequins the color of a summer Texas sky. With her hand tucked in Cordell's arm, she walked toward them with a regal air, her head held high. Her hair was exotically styled, her makeup flawless, her nails perfectly polished. Only the flicker of insecurity in her expression hinted at the woman Maggie had been a couple of months ago.

She met his gaze, inclined her head with a polite smile, then lifted her chin. Had he made a mistake blowing her off during the two weeks while he got his head straight? While he gave Maggie time and space to decide if she'd made a mistake giving herself to him?

They used to date. At the thought what they had shared might truly be history, a burning knot swelled in Jack's throat. Then reason gave him a bracing shake. Maggie might have told the hotel folks there was nothing between them so she could help get him this job. Thin, mighty thin, Jack realized, but the possibility gave him reason to hope for the best.

Going along with the past tense version of their relationship for a number of reasons, Jack answered Foster evasively. "What made you think we were dating? Maggie and I are friends, neighbors."

"We knew you joined her here for dinner during her free weekend. Our president asked me to question you about your status. I'm afraid he's quite taken with our Maggie."

Their Maggie? Where was their tag of ownership?

Jack glared at Cordell. If that hotel Romeo touched her, he would whack off body parts—Cordell's hand or a couple of things more appropriate.

"Good thing Raleigh didn't see her before I sicced our beauty staff on her," Foster said with a chuckle. "If he had, he probably would have thrown her a dog bone instead of a spokesmodel contract. She was a major woofer, wasn't she? You should give me an award for neighborhood beautification."

"You supercilious bastard," Jack grumbled and knotted his hand into a fist.

"Go ahead. Deck me," Foster told him. "Then you're out of here, and I can hire a first-class photographer."

Careful not to look like more than a friend to Maggie, Jack worked through Foster's spec sheets.

He learned that putting a camera between himself and Maggie was an effective way of keeping his hands off her. The lens put her at a distance, made her seem more like an object than the warm, passionate woman she had been in his arms.

At ten-thirty, in the lobby, he wound up the shots that included the president. Cordell turned to Maggie. Taking her hands, he gave her a kiss on the cheek. "You did magnificently, my dear."

Maggie shot Jack a nervous glance. "I'm sure you'll like Jack's work."

"If so, he'll be hearing from us."

Maggie pulled her hands from Cordell's grasp. "Have a nice flight, Raleigh."

Have a nice flight, Raleigh, Jack muttered under his breath as he collapsed his tripod and looked around for Foster. *I hope you get air sick, you old goat.*

Maggie returned as the president was stepping into his limousine. "Now what?" she asked.

Jack ignored the breathless quality of her voice. He would treat her like any other model.

And next week he'd fly to Pluto.

"We need to do the pool shots," he told her. "But before you go to the trouble of changing, I'd like to run up to the Presidential Suite." He motioned for the bellhop to load up his lighting equipment. "I have a couple of ideas I'd like to pursue there."

Maggie's face lit up. Her eyes twinkled. She whispered behind her hand, "Me, too."

"Cool your jets, Princess," Jack said, inclining his head at the bellhop. He signaled to the makeup specialist to follow them. "We aren't exactly alone."

"You've been ignoring me."

"Me?" Jack asked innocently. "Why would I do that?"

"Because you're still mad at me for breaking our date when I went to San Francisco."

"Now where did you get an idea like that?" Jack asked and followed her into the private elevator for the trip to the Presidential Suite.

Once upstairs, Jack pretended this was like any other shoot, purely business. He went about setting up his equipment while the makeup artist freshened Maggie's face and refluffed her hair. A bellhop walked in the open door, pushing a cart with four signature Grand Perimeter crystal vases filled with long-stemmed red roses.

"Who are the flowers for?" Maggie asked.

"You, of course," Jack answered distractedly, then told the bellhop, "Put them over there, on the sofa table, behind the green couch."

"They're part of the shoot?" she asked.

"Yeah."

"Oh. I thought maybe they were from . . ."

"Cordell?"

"No, you," she mouthed when the makeup artist turned her back.

"Right," Jack mouthed back and pretended to turn his pants pockets inside out.

Maggie gave him a smug look. That's when Jack knew it. He'd been right. She was responsible for him getting this job.

She wouldn't be sorry, nor would that Armand guy. Jack would give him Cinderella pictures that would blow his socks off.

"Okay, I'm ready," Maggie announced and exhaled a breathy sigh. "Where do you want me?"

On the couch. On the table. On the bar. "Stand over there, behind the couch," Jack said with a wave of his hand. He was determined not to touch her or look directly into her doelike eyes.

She moved obediently into place. "Now what?"

"Since the hotel's made a big deal out of crystal, I want two vases of roses on either side of you. I want a champagne glass in one hand. I want your fingertips dangling on the marble tabletop near the phone. The message I want to give is, 'I can call and get anything I want when I want it.' Got it?"

Maggie nodded. Angling her body at the camera, she picked up the champagne glass and brought it almost to her lips. She slanted Jack a sultry look. "How's this?"

A muscle in Jack's groin tightened. "Perfect."

He tripped the shutter instantly, then straightened. "Where did you learn to do that?"

"What?"

"Give a photographer exactly what he wants."

Maggie slanted a glance at the bellhop, then mouthed over her shoulder, "In the back seat of a car."

Jack snapped the shutter—and adjusted the waistband on his pants.

He led Maggie through a series of three more poses—reclining on the rug in front of the fireplace while she raked her hand through her hair like a temptress. Checking the back of her dress over her shoulder in the gilt-edged mirror in the foyer. Looking over the room-service menu while curled up in a chair.

By then Maggie was showing signs of fatigue. "Why don't we all break for an hour or so," Jack suggested and told the bellhop and makeup artist, "I'll call you when we're ready."

"Thanks," Maggie mumbled as the two disappeared out the door. "I'm beat."

"Good." Jack closed the door behind them and grabbed his favorite camera. "Go take off your clothes and get into bed."

Maggie looked from the camera to Jack. "Now, wait a minute. If you think I'm going to pose for any kinky pictures, you're . . ."

"Save it, Mags. You'll find a negligee on the bed. I asked Armand to have it sent up from the boutique. Put it on, and I'll meet you in the bedroom in five minutes."

"But—"

"Trust me. I won't take any shots unless you say yes."

Maggie lifted her chin and shot him a stubborn glance. "Promise?"

The fire in her eyes told Jack if he violated her trust she would make him pay, big time. He'd decided the odds were good that one day he would pay the price of falling in love with her. While on that shrimp boat, he'd looked at things dispassionately and decided before long Maggie's career would probably eclipse her personal life. That's what happened with successful models. They gave up everything for their careers. If that happened with Maggie, Jack would wind up on his butt on the bottom of her priority list.

But that wasn't Maggie's fault. If that time came, he wouldn't complicate the process of her disentangling herself from him by making her feel guilty.

Logical thinking aside, that old weakness of his for the sweet woman inside the bodacious wrappings had him reaching for her chin. He ran his thumb over the softness of her skin, then let his hand drop. "Don't you know by now, you can trust me, Princess?"

"Well . . ."

He gave her fanny a little slap. "Run along. Change. I'd like to shoot this and one other pose before the inquiring minds and peering eyes return. Don't worry. I won't send any prints to Foster without the official Kincaid stamp of approval."

"If you do, you're history," she said and flounced into the bedroom.

"I'm already history," Jack mumbled to himself. He collapsed onto the couch and dragged his hands down over his face. If he had been asked to design the perfect instrument of torture for himself, what he was about to do would be better than plucking pubic hairs.

Maybe he ought to move. To Dallas. Houston, maybe. Nope, further away. In order to forget Maggie, he might have to put a continent between them.

"Ready?"

Maggie plumped the pillow behind her and tucked the cream-colored comforter and burgundy sheets strategically at her waist. "Anytime you are."

Jack opened the door to the bedroom and backed in, his arms full of camera equipment. "Relax. It'll take me a couple minutes to set up."

"I'm in no hurry," she said with a yawn. When Jack turned her way, and she was sure she had his attention, she arched her back and stretched like Homer. She'd practiced in front of the mirror before climbing into bed. She knew without looking that she was giving Jack an eyeful of cleavage. The royal blue negligee with the teeny-weeny straps draped seductively over her breasts. Someday she would have to thank Armand for his good taste—if her little plan worked.

Jack took one look at her and dropped his light deflector. He stood there, gaping at Maggie, for several seconds. The tips of his ears turned bright red.

"I think you dropped something, Jack."

"Yeah. You're right." He stooped down and patted around the carpet, his gaze riveted to her cleavage.

Maggie smothered a grin. Her older sister, Sheridan, had been right when Maggie called her last night for advice. This was going to be a piece of cake. Maggie knew what she wanted, and by golly, for once, she was going for it.

"Now," Jack said, when all his equipment was in place, "there should be a wicker bed-tray around here."

"Over there," Maggie said and pointed to the chaise longue.

Jack fetched the tray, which contained a bud vase with a rose, a platter of fresh fruit, and a crystal glass filled with orange juice. He brought it to Maggie and positioned it over her lap.

"Hmm. This looks good," Maggie said, and ran her tongue slowly, deliberately over her lips. She picked up the fork and speared a banana segment.

"Wait! Don't eat that."

"Why not?"

"You'll ruin the picture."

"But I'm starved," Maggie pleaded with an exaggerated pout.

"This will only take a minute or two," Jack said, backing into the armchair on his way back to his camera. "Then you can eat before the hot tub shots. We'll do the pool last."

Hot tub shots, huh? This was going to be more fun than Maggie had imagined.

Jack flexed his knees and squinted his eye behind the camera. "I want you to pretend you're famished."

"I won't have to pretend," Maggie complained.

"Okay, here's the setup. Prince Charming just brought you that tray."

Maggie clamped her mouth over her reply that he had, indeed, done that. She wouldn't have to pretend.

"You're waking up from your fairy-tale night. Memories of the evening are still fresh in your mind. I want you to look dreamy-eyed."

Maggie dipped one shoulder slightly. One negligee strap slipped down her arm, revealing the upper fullness of her right breast.

Jack's head shot up from his camera. He cleared his throat. "Fix your strap."

Maggie slipped one finger up the strap and dragged it slowly, deliberately back in place. She wiggled her shoulders, as if to reposition the flimsy bodice of the negligee. "There? Is that what you want?"

Jack dug in his pants pocket for a handkerchief and mopped it across his forehead. "Damn lights are sure hot," he said and crammed the linen square back into his pocket. He ducked behind the camera again. "Let's see if we can't get this over with quickly."

"I kind of like it here," Maggie remarked with a tilt of her head and a plastic smile.

Jack tripped the shutter, then frowned at her. "Something isn't right."

"Perhaps I should scoot the covers down a bit more?"

"No! It's your face."

"Is my makeup smeared?"

Jack appeared to think for a minute. "That's what it is. You look too perfect. This is supposed to be morning. Can you mess up your hair a little?"

Maggie rubbed the sides of her hair. "How's that?"

Jack looked at her through the camera's lens but came away shaking his head. "Better. But still not right. I'm going to call the makeup artist."

"You gave her an hour off. I'll just go to sleep while we wait on her." Maggie lifted the tray to one side, scooched down into the bed and closed her eyes.

"That's good. Hold it." Jack snapped a couple of frames.

Maggie gave a smoky sigh and snuggled deeper into her pillow. Beneath the covers she tugged on the negligee so that it slipped down, revealing one whole breast. The cool sheet grazed her skin. She knew without looking that her nipple was twisting into a tight bud. She waited, wondering what she would do if her subterfuge didn't work.

Eyes securely closed, she waited. And listened. She heard Jack swear under his breath. Heard his feet clump across the carpet to her bed. The vanilla scent of him teased her nostrils.

"Maggie, come on. I know you're not asleep. We've got work to do."

The moment she opened her eyes, Jack averted his gaze.

"Jack?"

"Yeah?"

"You remember telling me I needed to learn not to be a doormat? I needed to learn not to let people walk all over me?"

"Can't this wait until we're through with the shoot?" Jack asked. "I like the angle of the light coming through the window."

"This'll only take a minute. You told me I needed to learn to stand up for myself."

"Yeah, yeah."

"Well, I'm doing it."

"What?"

"I'm telling you what I want." Beneath the sheets, fear of rejection had Maggie trembling. Her insides were a painful mass of quivers. What if she told Jack, and he laughed at her?

She reached for his hand. Hesitantly he took it. "What is it, Princess? You want a drink?"

"No."

"What then?"

Maggie's heart was thumping like a wild, crazy thing.

Go or no go time.

Go.

Arching her back for effect, she lifted her chin, closed her eyes and slowly tugged the sheet and the comforter to her waist. The chilly air hit her bare breast.

She waited what seemed like endless moments.

Then Jack's husky voice broke the fragile silence. "God, Maggie, I . . . ah, hell!"

Beside her the mattress shifted. She opened her eyes to see Jack's head descend, to see his tongue dart out and flick the tight peak of her nipple.

"Oh, Jack," she murmured and, taking his head in her hands, sifted her bright red nails through his glorious, silky hair. He tensed when she touched him. "Don't stop. Please. I want you. See." She took his hand and pulled it beneath the covers, positioning his fingers in the hot, moist center of her feminine need.

Jack's fingers plunged into her possessively. His mouth claimed her lips. The pleasure was so exquisite, tears formed in the corners of her eyes and trickled down her cheeks. She wanted to tell Jack she loved him, but she was afraid he would pull away from her. Instead, she showed him, with her heart and her body.

So intense was her need for him, she climaxed against his plunging fingers. When the quivers of her sated muscles began to ebb, she opened her eyes and found him fully on the bed, one leg slung over hers. His eyes were glazed, his shirt rumpled. The bedroom bore the intoxicating, musky scent of their lovemaking.

Jack's breath was hot against Maggie's bare breast. A questioning filled his gaze. "Why did you tell Foster we *used* to date?"

"I had my reasons," she answered him evasively.

Jack thought about what Foster had said about Cordell having the hots for Maggie. Was that one of the reasons? "What do you want from me, Maggie?"

"To give you what you gave me. To please you." She tugged the rest of his shirttail from his pants and raked her fingernails up the hard contours of his chest. "To love you, Jack. Let me."

Later the maid would find buttons in the carpet. They popped from Jack's shirt when she tore it from his chest. Maggie gave no thought to how he would explain his telling appearance to the staff. She loved Jack. She poured the intensity of her passion into pleasing him as if this might be her last chance to prove to him that hers was the body of a woman in love. She could give more, open wider, sate longer than any woman he would ever know.

Fifteen

Jack's shot of Maggie in that bed after they made love became a classic in the annals of hotel promotion, as did the subsequent shots of her in the hot tub.

If the truth were known, no hair stylist could have effected the freshly love-tousled look of her hair. No makeup artist could have given her body the same sheen of satisfaction, her lips quite that pouty, swollen quality. No soft lens could have perpetuated the heavy-lidded look of satisfaction in her glowing eyes as she lifted a cup of coffee from the breakfast tray to her lips and smiled into the camera.

The photo session not only bridged the gap between Maggie and Jack, but the resulting prints earned him Armand Foster's respect. The PR guru took one look at the pictures and saw dollar signs. Jack had transformed Maggie into every woman's fantasy—freshly loved, reveling in the lushness of her surroundings and her sated body.

Humbled by Jack's abilities, Armand Foster signed him on as the Cinderella Girl's director of photography.

For three months Maggie and Jack flew to Grand

Perimeter hotels all over the world for Cinderella appearances. The work was demanding and exhausting. Many weekends, they worked late into the evening. Not once did Maggie complain.

Jack developed a new and abiding respect for her. Other models would have whined and balked at the hours. He'd found a partner in Maggie, in front of the camera, behind the scenes—and in bed.

Their only problem was their decision to keep the nature of their relationship a secret from hotel personnel. Jack didn't really mind the subterfuge. It added a delicious touch of the forbidden. He merely rumpled his sheets and spread wet towels around his bathroom, then snuck into Maggie's room at day's end.

What Jack minded was what happened on a raw, drizzly January evening in Seattle. He, Maggie, and Cordell were scheduled to attend a watch party in the posh, revolving restaurant of the Space Needle. The segment featuring Cordell and Maggie was slotted for that evening's "Lifestyles of the Rich and Famous."

While the beauty wizards touched up the tint in Maggie's hair, Jack slipped into his tuxedo and ducked down to the lobby. He found the hotel limo waiting out front. Both football fans, he and the driver had hit it off on the way in from the airport. Jack slipped him twenty bucks and asked him to take him on an errand that had his heart thumping overtime.

Unable to sit still on the way back, he opened the lucite panel between the passenger section and the driver and proceeded to shoot the bull. Jack half listened while the retired bell captain spouted statistics about the Seattle Seahawks.

They pulled up to the hotel a couple of minutes before Jack was due to meet Maggie in the lobby lounge for a cocktail.

"What time's this shindig over tonight?" Jack asked, hoping for an early evening.

"That depends," the driver responded.

"On what?"

"On who you're talking about."

"What's the difference?"

The driver turned around, a sly smile adding a deep crease to his wrinkled face. "Mr. Cordell told me to bring everybody back to the hotel after the party. It's over at ten."

"Ten," Jack repeated, fingering the velvet box in his tuxedo jacket pocket. "No after parties?"

"Only for Mr. Cordell—and the lady."

Jack's hand froze on the box. "Which lady?"

"The Cinderella Girl, of course."

"Where are they going?" Jack asked suspiciously.

"Your friend from Texas seems like a sweet lady. Seeing as how you and her seem to be good friends, maybe you ought to know. Mr. Cordell's my boss, but he's a creep."

"What are you saying?" Jack pressed him.

"If you tell him, he'll fire my ass."

"I can keep a secret," Jack told him.

"Well, okay. After I drop you off, the boss is taking her to his boat. Alone, if you know what I mean."

Jack heard the rain peppering the car, but he couldn't see the drops on the windshield. A red haze clouded his vision. He schooled himself not to let his voice betray his rage. "When are you supposed to bring them back to the hotel?"

"Don't know for sure." The driver lowered his voice, as if someone might overhear what he was about to say. "Your flight's leaving for Austin in the morning, isn't it?"

"Yeah, at ten."

"If you wait on the girl and the boss has his way, you might miss your plane."

"How can you be sure?"

"The son of a bitch asked me to stock the boat for breakfast."

Jack strode into the cocktail lounge, trembling with the need to wrap his hands around the bastard president's neck and squeeze until his eyes bugged out.

He found Cordell sitting close enough to Maggie in a cozy corner booth to nibble her earlobes. Maggie saw Jack approach the table and she lit up like a Christmas tree.

A ball of disgust swelled in Jack's throat. There his trusting Maggie sat, oblivious to the fate Cordell had planned for her. Once on that boat, she'd be at his mercy.

She was dazzling in a floor-length gown of white that emphasized her high breasts, her narrow waist. The beaded crystal stuff that dangled from the fabric sent refracted light swirling about her corner of the lounge. The knockout gown was a Maggie Kincaid Original she'd beaded during their evenings back home. A pair of lucite heels that looked like Cinderella's glass slippers completed her outfit.

If Jack hadn't wanted to avoid getting blood all over Maggie's pretty dress, he'd have punched Cordell's lights out, then got Maggie the hell out of his hotel.

Any man with a healthy libido could recognize the blatant intention in the old guy's gaze. A bottle of uncorked Dom Perignon sat chilling in a silver champagne bucket beside the table. Cordell's champagne glass clinked ominously against Maggie's. He was already working on her.

Jack's temples throbbed from the blood surging through his veins. His hand formed into a fist. He restrained it. Maggie's career was at stake.

For her sake, Jack hauled in a deep, bracing breath and calmly approached the table. Refraining from slugging the skinny bastard took a great deal more control.

Jack cleared his throat.

Maggie turned to him. He could tell by her expression something was wrong. "Jack, you're dripping wet. Get out of that coat before you catch cold."

Great. Cordell was planning to seduce the woman he planned to propose to tonight, and all Maggie could come up with when she saw Jack was motherly concern.

Cordell snapped his fingers. A waitress instantly appeared at his side. "Yes, Mr. Cordell?"

"A brandy for the gentleman, please." Cordell glanced at the space beside him in the semicircular booth, then at Jack. "You will join us?"

"Don't mind if I do." Jack handed his rain-slickened coat to the cocktail waitress and took the seat next to Maggie. "Forget the brandy. Make it a beer. Anything local."

"And the check," the silver-haired president added. "Good to see you, Jack. We were beginning to wonder if you'd get back before we left."

Wait a minute. Before *they* left? What about Jack? He was included in the plastic celebration this evening or he never would have dressed in his monkey suit. Besides, with what he knew now, he had to go. To protect Maggie.

He looked to her to see if he had misinterpreted Cordell's statement. She widened her eyes with a look of panic that told him a whole heck of a lot was wrong. How much did she know?

"I'm never late," he told Cordell and lifted a finger in the direction of the champagne. "Celebrating your initiation into 'Lifestyles of the Rich and Famous?' "

"That and a few other things," Cordell said and gave Maggie a conspiratorial wink.

Jack could have gouged his eyes out. Beneath the table Maggie closed her hand over Jack's knee and gave him what felt like a squeeze of panic. Or was he reading things into her actions that didn't exist?

Cordell fussed priggishly with his rose boutonniere. "I want to thank you for helping make Maggie a celebrity." He beamed a smile Maggie's way, not even bothering to look at Jack as he expanded on his compliment. "You have women on several continents fantasizing they're our Cinderella Girl."

"That's what you're paying me for," Jack said and thrust his hand into his pocket to keep his fist out of trouble. His fingers closed over the velvet box. He'd planned the entire after-party evening, from telling Maggie about his nomination for a prestigious Ad Council award to cocktails to cuddling. The script didn't include Raleigh boy.

Is that what had Maggie upset? That Cordell was insinuating himself into the time she and Jack had looked forward to sharing in the privacy of her suite? God, he hoped so. He realized he'd have to be careful how he told her what Cordell had planned for her. If she knew everything, she'd be terrified. She had an important function to attend tonight.

And then it struck Jack. Cordell had probably choreographed the whole evening. After Maggie appeared with him on the "Lifestyles" show and on his arm at the watch party, he would probably make sure they were seen getting on his boat. What a stroke to the guy's ego to be linked in the gossip columns with the young, glamorous Cinderella Girl.

He heard the clearing of a throat. Beneath the table, Maggie dug her fingernails into Jack's thigh. He shook himself from his revelation to hear Cordell say, "Your work is so exceptional that Armand and I have decided you have a permanent position with us—if you don't mind traveling."

"I haven't minded so far," Jack said and slanted Maggie a private look.

"I imagine you haven't, traveling with this lovely lady. But I'm afraid we have something else for you to do now," Cordell said smoothly. "We're slipping in our large group bookings. Armand will be in touch with you tomorrow. Basically, we want you to cover several major conventions across the country."

"Conventions, huh?" Jack smelled a rat. A hotel rat. Someone had tipped off the big kahuna that Jack and Maggie were warming each other's feet at night. Instinct told Jack that Cordell was reassigning him to clear the field for himself.

"You'll find preliminary information in your room," Cordell told Jack. "I'm afraid it will keep you busy all evening. Now you'll have to excuse us." He stood and extended his hand to Maggie. "Maggie's leaving with me for Frankfurt tomorrow. We have a lot to talk about, don't we, my dear? Perhaps you'd like to say your good-byes to your friend while I make a call."

As soon as Cordell was out of sight, Jack pulled Maggie into the telephone alcove of the lobby. "You look like you swallowed green paint."

"What are we going to do, Jack?"

"I don't know. Give me a minute to think." Pacing the marbled corridor, he rubbed his forehead with his thumb and forefinger. "First, the party. Just before it's over, get a monstrous headache." He snapped his fingers. "Yeah, a migraine. Insist Raleigh bring you back to the hotel. I'll be waiting for you. We'll talk." He stopped and took Maggie's arms. "Promise me you'll do that. Promise!"

"I'll try, Jack, but Raleigh's already planned to give me a nighttime tour of Seattle after the party."

"You can't go."

Maggie looked at him strangely. "Is there something you're not telling me?"

"I said it before, I don't trust the guy. He doesn't fool me for a minute by reassigning me. He's trying to separate us."

"I'm afraid you're right. He told me people have been asking if we're involved. He said it wasn't good for my career. He sprang the news about your convention assignment only moments before you got here. How do you feel about it?"

Jack pulled Maggie into his arms. "How do you think I feel?"

She pulled back and looked at him. Her huge brown eyes were round and luminous. Moreover, they were trusting. Jack didn't want to see her confidence in people destroyed. That was one of the beautiful things about her. Her trusting, giving nature, although at times it got her in trouble. "Then you're going to turn down the job?" she asked him.

"I was going to save this until later, but it fits to tell you now. While you were in the beauty salon, I got a call from a friend of mine on the Ad Council. I've been nominated for a national award based on the work I've done on the Cinderella campaign. The award ceremony's in a month."

"Jack, that's fantastic!" Maggie said and threw her arms around his neck.

"My buddy has a friend who's the managing editor of *Affluence* magazine. When she heard I was up for the award, she said she might be interested in having me do some work for her, after I finish for the hotel."

"Jack, *Affluence* is *the* high-fashion magazine."

"How well I know. I also know any self-respecting managing editor would call Armand Foster for a verbal recommendation before she signed me to a contract. There are a lot of temperamental photographers out there who give these editors hell. If I play difficult with Grand Perimeter, Foster won't give me a good rec. While you're gone tonight, I'll look over what Foster's got in mind for me, then decide what I'm going to do. What about you and this Frankfurt trip?"

"I can't go. I've got to be at work on Monday."

Jack expelled a breath of relief. "Good. That's good. He'll have to understand that." He paused, knowing he needed to warn Maggie somehow. "Be careful tonight. Back there in the lounge, Cordell was looking at you like he hadn't eaten in weeks, and you were a thick, juicy steak."

Maggie patted Jack's cheek. "I love it when you get jealous, but your imagination is working overtime. Raleigh's like a father to me."

Jack rolled his eyes. "Even you can't be that naive."

"He's almost old enough to be my grandfather."

"You've never heard of May-December relationships?"

"Raleigh and me?" Maggie gave a little shudder. "That's sick."

"I tell you, Maggie. He wants you."

Maggie shot a furtive glance over Jack's shoulder. "Here he comes. We can talk about this when I get back. But I'll tell you something, Jack. I miss home. I miss Homer. I'm getting behind on my homework. I'm real close to having enough money to open my boutique."

"How close?"

"Another month ought to do it."

"Then what?"

She gave him that old Maggie grin. "I wouldn't mind my carriage turning into a pumpkin."

"You're sure you're ready to give all this up?" Jack asked.

"Positive."

Jack couldn't hope for anything more encouraging. The demands of celebrity life left her pitiful little time to relax. Friday afternoon, they'd rush to the airport and take off for a jam-packed weekend of appearances and social functions. Weekdays Maggie had to devote gobs of time to hair and nail appointments and wardrobe purchases. At Armand's insistence, she took speech and diction lessons to tone down her Texas twang. She stopped off at the gym to work out on her way home from work. Armand called nightly. Evenings Maggie spent boning up on important folks she'd meet during her next weekend's appearances and what she was expected to be able to discuss with them.

If she gave up her position as Cinderella Girl, she and Jack could live the life of a normal married couple. One more month. Jack could hardly wait. Still, the thought that they might not be working together anymore had him reaching for her.

Right there, in the lobby, in full view of the concierge, the harpist and the crafty president, Jack planted a hot, open-mouthed kiss on Maggie's lips that branded her his. "Think about that tonight," he told her, pleased by the heat in her returning kiss.

"I see you've said your good-byes," Cordell said coolly. "Maggie—the limousine?"

She gave her boss a hesitant smile, then turned to Jack. "I'll phone you when I get in so we can discuss—"

"You'll be awfully late, my dear. After the party, we have reservations for dinner. And don't forget the tour. Let the poor man get some sleep. You can call him from Frankfurt tomorrow evening."

Jack needn't have worried about Raleigh Cordell, Maggie thought, as the gallant gentlemen helped her from his sleek, silver limousine late that evening.

All night Raleigh had been the perfect gentleman. When she complained of a headache near the party's end, he ordered her a special drink guaranteed by the bartender to cure what ailed her. On the way back to the hotel, he sat a respectable distance from her while the driver gave them the tour of downtown Seattle. While she thought about Jack waiting for her, Raleigh regaled her with trivia about the Great Fire of 1889. He told her that historic Pioneer Square was rebuilt a full story atop the original downtown storefronts that were abandoned in 1907.

As what he called the *pièce de résistance,* he asked his driver to take them to Raleigh's boat for a nightcap so she could experience the lights on the water. Maggie didn't want any more to drink. She wanted to sit down with Jack and figure out what they were going to do about their future. So she smiled sweetly and begged off. Visibly disappointed, Cordell nonetheless reacted like the consummate gentleman. He respected her plea to return to the hotel.

Now, just before the stroke of midnight, he escorted her to the end of the carpeted hallway to her suite across from Jack's.

As soon as she opened the door, she would tell Raleigh she couldn't possibly go to Frankfurt. She had her job and her classes.

The work with the hotel chain, although lucrative, was detouring her from her priorities. She wouldn't have minded one weekend a month, or maybe the two she had originally agreed to. But every weekend? She'd had enough. One more month to finish stashing away the seed money for her design boutique, then she'd go into retirement as the Cinderella Girl. Do an occasional appearance to provide continuity in the promotional program, but concentrate on what was important. Jack. Her design career.

She couldn't remember the last time she had spent a Saturday in Austin, relaxing with him, giving Homer quality time. She also desperately needed to work on the orders her Aunt Barbara was getting for Maggie Kincaid Originals.

Raleigh couldn't possibly complain if Maggie opted to go home tomorrow, instead of to Frankfurt. If he did, he'd get over it. For once she was going to put her glass-slippered foot down.

Maggie stole a quick glance at Jack's door, hating that their plans for the evening had been ruined. She should have been with Jack, celebrating the success he so richly deserved. Helping him make his decision about his change in assignments for Grand Perimeter. Was he awake? Would he still be in the mood to come to her suite?

To make love?

Raleigh took Maggie's card key and inserted it into the horizontal slit in the brass plate of the door lock. The tiny round light flashed green. Raleigh handed her the card back, opened Maggie's door and followed her inside.

The clock on the credenza was chiming twelve when Maggie turned to him. "Thank you for a delightful evening, Raleigh. Before you leave, I'd like to discuss—"

"Twelve o'clock," Raleigh interrupted and, holding Maggie's gaze, pressed his lips to the back of her hand.

Something in Raleigh's gesture niggled at Maggie. The look in his eyes. The way he held her hand, her gaze a bit longer than proper decorum between a boss and his employee dictated. His breath all but slithered across her skin. Maggie's heart shifted into a warning rhythm. She cast around for a diversion to dilute the tension.

"We need to discuss this trip to Frankfurt you're talking about. But first, I really should check for messages." She reached for the phone on the credenza. The sick pooling in her stomach told her that Jack's concerns about her boss might not have been totally unfounded.

Raleigh caught her arm with an insistent hand. Stepping toward her, he eliminated all but the most personal of space between them. His breath bore the odor of the expensive brandy he had sipped in the limousine. Maggie remembered Raleigh insisting a glass of the amber liquid would ease her tension and enable her to sleep. Had sleep been on his mind, or something else?

"Fortunately, we won't depart for the airport until ten, my dear." He craned his neck and undid his bow tie. "If we leave a wake-up call for seven, we'll have time to order room service before we leave."

Panic swept up Maggie's arms, a flash of pinpricks that stung her disbelieving brain. Surely Raleigh didn't mean *we* in the Jack sense, as in one call to wake up both of them in the same bed.

The possibility Raleigh might be introducing sex into their relationship had Maggie's stomach clenching. Surely she was imagining things. Yes, that was it. Jack had put ridiculous thoughts into her head. She tamped down the swell of panic and squeaked, "We?"

Behind his back Raleigh twisted the knob that clicked the security bolt into place. "Now that Jack's out of the way, we'll be free to . . . get to know one another." His gaze did a slow perusal of her body. "You are an incredibly stunning woman."

I don't trust the guy.

Once you're in a guy's apartment, you're at his mercy.

Jack's warnings reverberated in Maggie's ears. Why hadn't she listened to him? She wasn't in Raleigh's apartment, but she might as well be. At the thought she was alone, truly at Raleigh's mercy, her mouth went dry.

Talk, she thought. *I'll try to talk my way out of this first. Don't damage the man's ego. Put him off. Yes, that might work.* "I'm pooped, Raleigh." She brought a hand to her hair and looked furtively in the mirror above the credenza. She gave a nervous laugh. "Goodness! My hair's a mess. I've got to wash it before I go to bed, or tomorrow I'll—"

Raleigh's face appeared beside hers in the oval mirror. He took a lock of her hair, closed his eyes and slid it between his fingers. "I was right. Your hair is the texture of silk." He opened his eyes. "Auburn—Armand truly is an expert when it comes to color."

"Armand?" Maggie sidestepped away from Raleigh and moved toward the door. So far all he had done was say a couple of things that she might have misinterpreted, and he'd touched her hair. She had to be careful what she said and did or she might insult the man without cause. If she was wrong, other people might get hurt.

Jack.

Panic climbed up the back of her throat. *Call, Jack. Now!*

Cordell leaned casually back against the credenza, bracing his hands on the gleaming cherry wood surface. Maggie exhaled a small sigh of relief. If Cordell had been making any moves on her, she had effectively distracted him. "The beautician thought blond was your color," he explained. "Armand insisted auburn."

"You mean she almost changed the color of my hair this morning without telling me?" Maggie asked incredulously.

"Not this morning. Let's see, when was it?" He glanced at the ceiling, as if he'd find the answer in the fractured glow of the light from the credenza's crystal lamp. He brought his head down and smiled. "August—yes. That's when you won your weekend, wasn't it?"

"Yes, but Armand wasn't there."

"Not in your room, but surely you know by now that Armand is obsessive about details. When he told the beauty coordinator to phone you, she had strict instructions on which—"

"Wait a minute," Maggie cut in. "Are you telling me my make over was Armand's idea?"

Raleigh looked at her blankly. "I thought you knew. Armand said he let it slip to Jack. Naturally we assumed . . ."

"I didn't know. And I don't appreciate it. Not a bit."

"You could hardly call yourself a victim. Look at you. You're exquisite. Before, you were, well . . ."

Maggie whirled on Raleigh, the reason for the deception suddenly clear. "Plain? Is that the word you were going to use? Was I too plain for your press conference? Did you summon your fairy godmothers so I wouldn't embarrass Grand Perimeter?"

Cordell caught Maggie's hand and brought it to his lips. "You were a lovely rosebud that merely needed assistance in blooming, my dear." He turned her toward the mirror. "Look at you. You're beautiful, glamorous—not at all like that poor little waif who walked into our Austin property."

This time Raleigh settled his hand at Maggie's waist. His thumb lifted to lightly stroke the underside of her breast.

An alarm tripped in Maggie's enraged mind, adding fear to the anger-charged adrenaline in her bloodstream. There could be no misunderstanding of motives now. With that one stroke of his thumb, her boss had crossed the line.

Her fury overpowered her fear and fueled an intensive physical reaction to the indignity she had suffered. She had trusted Raleigh like a father. He had betrayed that trust. Her heart thumped loudly in her chest, so strongly it almost robbed her of her breath.

Turning she shoved hard against Raleigh's chest. "Mr. Cordell, you're out of line. I want you to leave. Now."

Raleigh didn't budge. He raked her with a feral gleam in his eyes. "So, our Cinderella Girl is as fiery as her hair. I like that." His smile faded. His arm snaked out and pulled her to his chest.

Maggie flattened her hands against the slick satin of Raleigh's tuxedo lapels. Disgust swirled in her abdomen. "Let me go, Mr. Cordell."

"Now, Maggie, surely you knew sooner or later there would be a price to pay for . . ."

From the shadows a fist shot out and slammed into the president's jaw. Raleigh's head snapped back. Moaning, he grabbed his chin and staggered against the suite's entry door.

"She said let go of her, you asshole."

"Jack!"

He pulled Maggie into his arms. His pectorals were tensed, his arms hard as rocks. His eyes blazed with fury. "Are you okay, Mags?"

She was trembling so hard her teeth were chattering. "I'm f-fine. But you sh-shouldn't have done that. You're going to b-be in a lot of trouble."

"Smart lady."

Maggie turned to look at Raleigh. Blood trickled from a gash in one side of his mouth. His eyes were frosted over. His omnipresent rose boutonniere lay at his feet, the bud snapped at its base.

Raleigh dug in his pocket for a handkerchief and pressed it to his lips. "That was a most unfortunate mistake, Jack. You will, of course, pay for it."

"If anybody pays, it'll be you, you jerk." Jack yanked Raleigh away from the door, opened it and shoved him into the hallway. "Now get lost before I call the police."

"You're forgetting something, aren't you? This is my hotel. I'll call the police. When they come, you'll be the one they'll lock up in their patrol car."

"Is that so?" Jack acted like inspiration had struck. "Then perhaps we should call the media as well. I can hear the lead-in now: 'Hotel Prexy Tries to Jump Cinderella's Bones. Film at ten.'"

Jack drew back his fist. Cordell backed down the hall.

Jack scooped up the smashed boutonniere and pitched it at the president. "Now get the hell out of here before I give you an even fatter lip, you slimy bastard."

Sixteen

"You didn't have to slug him, Jack," Maggie lectured him sternly a short time later as he watched her wrap her beaded gown in white tissue paper. "I could have gotten Raleigh to leave."

Pretending his pillow was Cordell's pasty face, Jack punched it smartly, then stuffed it behind his back. "Before or after he molested you?"

"Raleigh was only making a pass at me. I was already putting him in his place when you let your macho male ego get the best of you."

Jack almost told Maggie about Cordell's breakfast arrangements on his boat but thought better of it. She'd undergone enough trauma for one night. "Maggie, my girl, face it. Cordell was trying to force himself on you."

She slipped into bed beside Jack, the white satin of her teddy slick against his bare skin. "Make love to me?" She blew a hot breath through the hair on his chest and tucked his arm into the valley between her breasts.

Jack drew her tight against his chest. Maybe she was right. Maybe he shouldn't have decked the bastard. When he had, he'd turned Maggie's coach into a pumpkin prematurely.

A little while longer and she would have been able to stash away the rest of the money she needed to open her design boutique. Now because of him, she'd have to continue to suck up to Caroline McCann and endure the taunts of the resentful seamstresses.

Oh, boy, the snippy bitches would have fun with this one, wouldn't they, when they read the news accounts? Cinderella Girl forfeits international spokesmodel career after getting caught sleeping with her soon-to-be, but not-yet-successful photographer.

At the thought of Cordell's sleazy insinuations, of the jerk's slimy thumb touching Maggie's breast, Jack's blood boiled. He sank a possessive hand into her hair, dipped his head and poured his frustrations into a kiss.

Maggie opened her mouth and her body to Jack. They made love fiercely, as if trying to hang on to the final thread of the idyllic existence they had shared the past few months. They came together and shattered in each other's arms, like a piece of Grand Perimeter signature crystal.

Their lovemaking left a clot wedged in Jack's throat. If Cordell hadn't gotten the hots for Maggie, right now she'd be wearing the ring he'd bought on his secret shopping trip that afternoon.

He thought of the velvet box he'd tucked away in the nightstand drawer, intending to give it to her when she returned from the party. He couldn't ask her to marry him now. Too much was uncertain. The mood was too somber. "I love you, Mags."

She traced the curve of his ear with her finger. Her breath feathered across his chest. "I love you, too, Jack."

"I'll find a way to patch things up for you with the hotel."

"Forget it," she murmured, already drifting off to sleep. "It isn't important."

"First thing in the morning I'll go see Cordell."

Maggie's head snapped up. "I don't think that'd be a very good idea."

"Don't worry. I won't deck him again. Not that it won't be tempting."

"What will you do?"

"Grovel," Jack said and stared across the room. Doing so would be hell, but he'd do it for Maggie. "Tell him to find somebody else for my job."

"Somehow, I think that's a given," Maggie murmured regretfully.

"I'll confess tonight was my fault. I'll reason with him. I'll tell him he'd be a fool to let you go. The magazine ads come out in less than a month. It's too late to reshoot with another model. Your pictures are on billboards across the country, on the backs of buses. The airline frequent-flyer programs have already mailed those hotel promotions with your pictures in them. If Cordell fires you, the entire Cinderella promotion is kaput. Over. History."

He paused, stroking his thumb over the softness of Maggie's cheek. "I just want to know one thing. Who's going to protect you when I'm not there?"

* * *

Dawn had not yet begun to creep around the closed drapes of the suite's window when Maggie crawled from bed.

Careful not to wake Jack, she pulled on her red jumpsuit and slipped noiselessly from the room. In another minute she was knocking on Raleigh's door.

The third round of knocks drew a muffled, "Who is it?"

"Maggie," she replied and hoped she wasn't making a terrible mistake going to his suite. But she had to talk to him before Jack.

Jack wasn't thinking straight. He thought Raleigh planned to fire her as well as him, and he planned to plead with the president for Maggie's job.

Raleigh couldn't afford to fire her. Jack had recounted the reasons himself. That gave Maggie power. She planned to use it.

It was because Jack had the backbone to defend Maggie's virtue that he would lose his job. Without him, she never would have become the Cinderella Girl, been able to save enough to open her own design boutique. Could she do anything less than stand up for him in return?

"Go away," Raleigh replied sourly.

Maggie knocked again. "Raleigh, please. We need to talk."

She waited. Presently the door opened. Raleigh was dressed in a silk smoking jacket in the official burgundy color that Maggie was tiring of. He held an ice pack to the corner of his mouth. Tiny red lines snaked across the whites of his eyes like farm-to-town dirt roads in Texas. He looked as if he'd combed his usually impeccable hair in the dark.

He turned his back on Maggie, strode across the sitting room of the suite and sank into an armchair. He gestured to the love seat across from him. "You may join me, if you like."

Resentment, hot and instant, flared in Maggie's mind at Raleigh's condescending attitude. Mindful of her purpose, though, she took the proffered seat and cleared her throat. "I'm truly sorry about last night, Raleigh."

"Not as sorry as you'll be after you hear from my attorneys."

"You've contacted them already?"

Raleigh checked his watch. Maggie knew it was 6:00 A.M. She also knew any attorneys he would call to help him file charges with the police would have to live in the state of Washington, because that's where Jack had struck Raleigh. She didn't know many attorneys who kept these early office hours.

"I'll call when they get in. Nine o'clock."

"Very well. Before you do, perhaps we should discuss the finer points of our dilemma."

"Your lover hit me, Maggie. He loosened three teeth and cut my lip. Those are the finer points of what you call 'our dilemma.' He has, of course, destroyed a promising career with Grand Perimeter. He'll be charged with assault and battery. I'll see to it that he goes to jail."

As she had suspected, Raleigh said nothing about her losing her job. She drew on the inspi-

ration that struck as she lay awake, wondering
how she could save Jack's job. Raleigh might be
the president, but he was elected by and served
at the whim of the board of directors. She had
overheard talk about the upcoming annual meeting at a cocktail party last month in Atlanta. "I
assume you've discussed the charges with the
board."

Raleigh arched a brow. "Not yet."

"I see. Your reelection is slated for next month's
board meeting, isn't it, Raleigh?"

The president's eyes iced over. "Yes," he replied curtly.

Maggie nodded and let him worry that thought
for a moment. "I don't suppose it would help you
if the board learned you made a pass at me in
my suite last night."

"You're the one who let me in."

"And that gave you the right to sexually harass
me?"

Raleigh's face blanched. "That term. You
wouldn't use it . . ."

"Oh, wouldn't I?" Maggie drummed her fingers on the arm of the love seat, delighted to have
two clamps to squeeze around Raleigh's neck. "If
you charge Jack with assault and battery, you'll
find out."

The president's cosmopolitan facade broke.
"Five months ago I never would have believed
you capable of blackmail."

"I'm merely pointing out your options." She
launched into clamp number two. "When I signed
your contract, I had no intention of spending this

much time working for the hotel. Being the Cinderella Girl is wearing me out. I have plans and dreams of my own. I want to get back to them. I'm resigning."

"You can't," Raleigh protested. "You've got a contract."

"I read it over last night when I couldn't fall asleep. It seems there's an interesting clause. Since I'm not officially a hotel employee, and I'm being paid by the job, I have the right to refuse to go on these weekend junkets. So, if I can't resign, I'll accomplish the same thing by refusing to go on any more trips."

"If you do, all the groundwork we've laid will be wasted. The *Affluence* and *Leisure Travel* ads will appear next month. We have appearances scheduled for you. Press conferences! We're even thinking about doing a Cinderella Girl doll."

"Pity," Maggie said and shook her head. "Of course, there's one thing you could do to persuade me to honor my contract for a couple more months."

"Don't tell me. You want me to forget about pressing charges against Jack."

"You'll do that anyway if you don't want to be brought up for sexual harassment charges. If you want me to stay on, you're going to have to keep Jack as the campaign's director of photography."

"You're crazy if you think—"

A knock sounded at the door.

"Room service?" Maggie asked.

"I didn't order anything," Raleigh grumbled and went to the door. "Who is it?"

"Jack Lewis."

"Oh, great!" Raleigh sneered. "Just what I need. Your prize fighter."

Jack banged on the door again. His voice boomed into the suite. "Cordell, I'm not going away until you talk to me."

"I'll handle this," Maggie said and waved Raleigh into the sitting room. "First, do we, or do we not have a deal?"

"You'll stay on six more months."

"Two."

"Four."

"Deal," Maggie said with a sigh. "Now sit down and keep your mouth shut."

"I beg your pardon."

Maggie yanked open the door. Jack stood in the hallway, freshly shaven and dressed in a suit and tie. "I figured it was you. Come on in."

"Maggie?" he blustered disbelievingly.

"Hush or you'll wake up the whole floor." She took Jack's arm and pulled him into the room. "Sit down," she told him and gestured to the chair farthest from Raleigh.

"Do you mind telling me what's going on?"

She slanted him a warning look. "If you sit down and listen, Raleigh will tell you."

Jack glared at his adversary. "Leave us alone, Mags. Cordell and I need to talk."

"Not on your life."

Jack stuck a finger between his starched shirt collar and his Adam's apple and craned his neck. He looked like he'd deck Raleigh again if Maggie turned her back. Instead, he cleared his throat. "How's your mouth, sir?"

"Cut, bleeding."

"I'll pay for any doctor's bills."

"As I'm sure you know, I can well afford to pay for my medical treatment."

"I want to apologize for hitting you last night."

"Good Lord, am I hearing things? Jack Lewis, acting halfway civilized? Well, I'm waiting."

Jack cleared his throat. "I'm sorry."

"Maggie put you up to this, didn't she?"

Maggie opened her mouth to speak, but Jack held up a silencing hand. "No, Princess, I've got to do this." He took the chair Maggie had indicated, hiked his pants and linked his fingers in the space between his knees. "What happened last night was my fault. I shouldn't have lost my temper. I should have let Maggie speak for herself."

"Is there a point to this?" Raleigh asked dryly.

"What I'm trying to say is, don't penalize her for what I've done. I'll get out of your hair. When I get home, I'll call Foster and tell him I don't want the convention job. All I ask in return is you keep Maggie on. It'd be a shame to see all our work go down the drain when it's beginning to come together."

"Your chivalry is touching," Cordell commented with a satisfied look, "as is your concern for Grand Perimeter, not that I believe for a minute it's sincere."

"If you're thinking of filing charges, maybe I should point out if the media learn what happened last night, you and Foster could have one hell of a scandal on your hands. Women are sick of violence. They constantly fear for their personal safety. Two men fighting over the Cinderella Girl at one of the hotels you're promoting for an idyllic weekend destroys the fantasy, don't you think?"

If Maggie could have done so without threatening the tentative truce, she would have flung her arms around her prince's neck and given him a resounding kiss. "Gentlemen, I'm pleased to see we can still work together."

"Gentleman? Him?" Raleigh threw back his head and laughed, then winced at the stretching of skin around his mouth. "Forgive me, but including Jack in that category makes for an all-time low in the history of civilization. The man only knows how to communicate with his fists."

"At least I don't use my position to take advantage of a lady," Jack barked.

Maggie rolled her eyes. "Raleigh, zip it. Jack, stuff a sock in it."

The two men sat glaring at each other, the tension as thick as tire rubber.

"There, that's more like it," Maggie said and stood to address both of them. "Jack, I came down this morning to discuss my feelings about my job with Raleigh. Isn't that right, Raleigh?"

"That and—"

Maggie gave the president an icy look that silenced him. "Raleigh has come to the conclusion that, while last night was most unfortunate, he can't afford to let either of us go, Jack. For some of the reasons you mentioned."

Jack looked at both of them as though they'd lost their minds. "You want to run that one by me again?"

"Basically, nothing's changed. Right, Raleigh?"

Raleigh said nothing. He merely sat there and scowled at Maggie.

"Except," she told Jack, "that you're staying on as the Cinderella Girl director of photography."

"What did you do to get him to agree to that?" Jack asked. "Drug his coffee?"

"I merely pointed out the value of both of us staying on. He agreed on one condition. You've got to promise not to slug anybody else. If you do, you're fired."

"If anybody else makes a pass at you—"

"I'll handle it," Maggie said with a lift of her chin. "I *am* capable. Gentlemen, do we have an agreement?"

President and photographer exchanged killing looks.

"I'm sorry. I couldn't hear either of you," Maggie said. "Raleigh?"

"Okay, it's a deal. Now get out of here—both of you."

"Jack?"

"Yeah, yeah. Come on," Jack said and pulled Maggie to the door of the suite. "The company in here gives me the creeps."

"Oh, Raleigh," Maggie called over her shoulder. "You'd better cancel that trip to Frankfurt. I don't think any of us is up to it."

* * *

While Jack packed, he caught a recounting of the "Lifestyles" segment on Maggie and Cordell on a cable news entertainment channel. He resisted the urge to put his foot through the screen.

Downstairs, waiting for Maggie in the lobby cafe, he nursed a cup of coffee and glanced through the Sunday paper. Good old Armand had covered the local print media as well. The pictures Jack had taken of Maggie and Cordell in their "Lifestyles" duds made the women's section.

Maggie joined him at nine, in time for a quick breakfast before they took the limo to the airport. Still perpetuating the just-buddies myth until Maggie told him otherwise, Jack refrained from hauling her into his arms as he had last night in the lobby. She sat across the table from him, unusually quiet and pensive. Well, hell, Jack mused. He could hardly blame her after what she'd been through.

She was taking the first bite of her muffin when the first autograph seekers, three teeny-boppers from Cedar Rapids, Iowa, meekly approached their table. Maggie graciously signed her picture in the morning paper for the three girls and took time to answer their questions. Thirty minutes later Jack had to drag her away from her fans, so they could leave on time for the airport.

Finally alone with Maggie in the limousine, Jack slanted a look over his shoulder at the hotel's tenth floor. He could hardly wait to put the weekend behind them, to get her home and propose to her. "I don't know what you told Cordell," he thought out loud, "but if looks could kill, I'd have been a dead duck up there."

"We merely had a civilized discussion. Without fists," Maggie added pointedly and opened the newspaper to her picture. "Really, Jack. You must learn to control yourself."

"Level with me. What did you have to promise Cordell to get him to keep both of us on?"

"Well . . . I pointed out the key roles we play in a campaign the hotel has spent a sizeable fortune on."

"And?"

"He agreed."

"He didn't look agreeable when I walked in. Are you sure you didn't say anything else?" Jack asked suspiciously. "Promise him your firstborn perhaps?"

"Let's see, I emphasized the hotel needs us, as you said. Oh, yes, and I mentioned in passing that if he fired us, I'd tell the hotel's board of directors he sexually harassed me."

Jack's mouth fell open. "You blackmailed Cordell?"

Maggie stuffed the newspaper in her attaché case. "I wouldn't exactly call it blackmail."

"Mags, you're a genius. Now you can call the shots. Work until you've got the money you need, then quit. Just think, one more month, and we'll have our weekends free."

"Well . . ."

"The timing's perfect. The Ad Council's awards ceremony is in a month. If I win, I won't need a good rec from Foster. I'm sure Cordell's already filled him in on last night, so I can kiss off high praise from the PR guru. If I don't win, well, I'll have a month to figure out a way to get by without Foster's recommendation."

What Jack wanted to add was, in just one more month he and Maggie would have time to plan their wedding. He'd decided to wait, though, until they got home and put the weekend's hellish events behind them before he popped the question.

"Is there any bottled water in that bar?" Maggie asked. "I need a couple of aspirin. I've got a monster headache."

Jack found some of Cordell's favorite water imported from France. Reluctantly, he splashed a few ounces in a hotel tumbler and gave it to Maggie. She washed down two tablets and handed him the glass. Jack lifted it to his mouth, to drain the balance of the water.

"I've been thinking," Maggie said and glanced out her side window, "maybe I'll stay on with the hotel a little while longer."

Jack nearly choked on the water sliding down his throat. "I knew we shouldn't have drunk this stuff. Either you're not thinking straight, or I'm hearing things. Last night you couldn't wait to quit. One month, you said. That's all you needed. Did you change your plans overnight for the boutique? Do you want a bigger place?"

"Not really."

"Then it isn't the money."

"No. Well, in a way it is. Plus some other reasons."

An uneasy feeling gnawed at Jack's stomach. "How much longer do you figure it'll be? Weeks? Months?"

"Months."

"How many months?"

"A few.

"How many is a few? Three, ten, a dozen?"

"We'll see," Maggie answered and, leaning her head back on the plush gray upholstery, closed her eyes. "Four. Maybe five. It depends."

Jack recalled how Maggie's face had lit up when her fans approached her back there in the hotel. She had gotten a kick out of meeting her fans, there's been no doubt. Was that why she'd changed her mind about quitting? After growing up in the shadows of her sisters, was she reluctant to give up her place in the limelight?

Also, for several years Maggie had endured the ridicule of her sister seamstresses. The ugly stepsisters, Jack thought wryly. Now Maggie's glamorous face was plastered everywhere. Fans were beginning to seek her autograph, wanting her attention, not ignoring her. Did this make her happy?

"This is what you want?" Jack sought to clarify. "To go on like we have been?"

"For a while," Maggie replied and glanced away again.

Why was she avoiding his eyes when she answered him? Jack caught her chin in his hand and turned her face toward him. Apprehension over her vague answer stirred in his chest. "Do you still want to open your own design boutique back home?"

"Of course," she answered him and again averted her gaze.

"You do realize, the longer you work for the

hotel, the longer it'll be until you have the time to devote to your new business?" To him and their future together, Jack thought, but that ought to be obvious.

"Jack, I've made up my mind." She lifted her chin, determination sparking in her tired eyes. "I'm staying on. Let's just drop it for now, all right?" She moved her gaze to the window. "Would you look at this traffic? I hope we make our flight in time."

Who was this woman next to him? She wasn't acting like the Maggie he knew and had fallen in love with. "Just tell me this much," he persisted. He figured if he understood her reasons for changing her mind, he might be able to accept it. "I'm not arguing your decision now. But I'd sure like to know. What was it that made you change your mind? Was it the fans?"

"Truthfully?" She hesitated. "They're part of it."

"What else?"

"I have other reasons," she answered, a sharp edge to her voice that cut and hurt.

"And they're none of my business. That's what you're saying."

"No, I'm not."

"Then explain."

"You don't have to know every thought that goes through my mind," Maggie snapped and shut her eyes.

She might as well have slapped him. She had told him her reasons for changing her mind were none of his damned business. "I'm the guy who loves you, remember? I'd like to know your reasons, when they affect our future."

"Future?" Maggie's eyes flew open. She turned to him. "What future?"

"Forget it," Jack muttered and looked away, because for the first time in months, he was beginning to question a future with Maggie. If she stayed on the celebrity circuit, the chances of their making it as a couple were about as good as Buck's and his ex-wife's—lousy. Jack wanted a marriage like Wilson and Polly's. Two individuals who had their own dreams and aspirations but shared them, for the most part, in the same house, in the same city. If Mags had hooked into the adulation of fans and other celebrity perks, she might never settle for the kind of life he thought they both wanted.

His gaze fell to the camera bag at his feet. Tucked into one of his lens cases was the ring he'd bought yesterday for Maggie. If Cordell's hands hadn't wandered last night, Jack would have asked Maggie to marry him. Now she was hinting that she might be a career globetrotter. What kind of a mother would that make for a kid? What kind of a wife for a man who needed a woman to hold, to make love to, to share his everyday life with?

Old insecurities crept from the dusty cubbyholes of his mind and haunted him. Memories of nights after his mom had left. Unwanted recollections of lying awake in his bed, just a little fella, alone in the dark. Holding his purple Easter bunny tight to his chest and sniffing deeply of its shaggy plush in hopes a bit of his mother's scent lingered there. If he could smell her, maybe he could recall the comfort of being held in her arms. Of having his hand held while they walked outside. Of seeing her smile at him and murmur a mother's "I love you, Son."

After his mother had left, he'd heard his dad cry late at night when Jack was supposed to be asleep. How lonely his dad must have been, and with a needy kid to care for when his own heart was breaking.

Jack watched Maggie drift off to sleep. The brief fluttering of her long, thick eyelashes was a tormenting reminder of how they brushed his chest when she lay cradled in his arms.

Still, no matter how much he needed Maggie by his side, her happiness was more important to him than his needs. He wanted her to know that.

He kissed the tip of her nose. "Hey, sleepy-head."

Her eyes drifted open. Seeing him, she gave him one of her smoky smiles that reminded him painfully of hot nights and tangled sheets. "Hmm?"

"I want you to know something."

"What is it, Jack?"

"If staying on as the Cinderella Girl will make you happy, that's what I want, too."

"Oh, Jack." She drew the corner of her lower lip between her teeth. Her eyes filled with tears. "You are such a dear, sweet man."

"When you're eighty, I don't want you looking back and wishing you hadn't walked away from this. So go for it, kid." Ignoring the ache in his chest, he added, "I'm behind you all of the way."

Seventeen

Four days later Maggie sat at her machine, frantically tearing out a crookedly sewn seam in a Valentine's ball gown of red taffeta.

Tomorrow she and Jack would fly to Aspen for the grand opening of another new Grand Perimeter. The thought of getting on another plane, smiling at all those people she didn't know, answering the same questions posed by the media, stressed her more than the pressure to finish the gown.

There was something comforting about the whir of sewing machines and the pervasive smell of new fabric dye at Miss Caroline's. Even the smell of break-time coffee warming on the burner gave her a sense of the dependable and familiar.

She shifted an afghan over her lap to ward off the February chill in the drafty old house and wondered if she was destined to marry. Instead of cocktail parties and press conferences and autograph-seeking fans, what she wanted was to snuggle up to Jack on his couch. Devour a bowl of popcorn together. Bury her nose in his chest and draw in the stimulating blend of his cologne and clean, male scent.

Since their cab ride home from the airport

Sunday evening, though, she hadn't gotten close enough to Jack to indulge herself in that pleasure. As soon as they got home, Jack helped her with her bags. Then he gave her a peck on the cheek and darted downstairs to check his answering machine. He was back in a flash with the news that the word of his Ad Council nomination had spread. He had bites for a couple of lucrative assignments.

Since then, updating his portfolio had consumed his time—and his energy. He'd worked day and night developing, printing, organizing presentation materials.

The fact that his career was taking off gave Maggie a measure of satisfaction. Still, she couldn't risk reneging on her agreement with Raleigh. Jack might be getting more assignments, but they didn't compare with the potential job at *Affluence* magazine. She'd learned, during her tenure as the Cinderella Girl, that businessmen in positions of authority and power maintained a communications network that rivaled the military's best. If she didn't honor her four-month commitment, Raleigh could neutralize the threat of sexual harassment she held over him. He could ruin Jack's career.

It killed her that she had to let Jack think she'd succumbed to the lure of fans, of glamour dust. Maggie couldn't tell him the truth, though, or he wouldn't let her make the sacrifice of several more months at the celebrity grind for him.

But for Jack's gift as a photographer, her name might not be bandied about by the likes of "En-

tertainment Tonight" hosts. One day soon that
name recognition would build a demand for her
original fashion designs. She owed Jack, plain and
simple, and she would deliver.

An intentional throat-clearing broke through
her thoughts. Glancing up, she found Kayla standing before her, her expression reverent, her smile
hesitant.

"Could you use some help with what?" Kayla
asked and gestured awkwardly at the dress. "I'm
all caught up."

"I can manage by myself," Maggie replied, knowing she was behind in her work because she'd had
to field a host of phone calls from the media since
her return. Expecting the other girls to pick up the
slack would be unfair. "But thanks for the offer."

"We—that is Desiree, Juliana, and I—were
thinking if you could get away, we'd like you to join
us for lunch. There's this trendy new restaurant on
Sixth Street that was reviewed in yesterday's paper.
It's supposed to be the watering hole for all the
lobbyists. We thought it might be a great place to
meet guys."

Funny. Several months ago Maggie had dreamed
of such an offer. Now it and her attendant suspi-
cions had her fingers tightening around her seam
ripper. "Why?"

"Why?" Kayla repeated blankly.

"I mean, why now?" Maggie replied directly.
"You've never asked me before."

The workroom fell quiet. No whirring of machines, no snip-snipping of scissors broke the awkward silence. A pink flush creeping up her cheeks,

Kayla slanted Desiree a pleading, bail-me-out glance. In her peripheral vision Maggie caught Desiree shrugging her shoulders.

"Well . . ." Kayla finally answered with a nervous laugh, "I guess until now we didn't think you'd want to go."

How naive do you think I am, Kayla? Of course I wanted you to ask. I would have died for an invitation. Now?

Maggie let her gaze drift to the window. Outside, the barren branches of the live oak clattered in the raw February breeze. "Another day maybe. I have a fitting at noon," she replied, then realized with hot resentment that Kayla knew that. The fitting was included in the day's schedule posted on the back wall.

Kayla turned toward her work station, then hesitated. "Maggie?"

"Yes, what is it?"

"You think there's a chance we could get on at the hotel?"

Why hadn't Maggie guessed! Kayla and the others wanted her to pull strings to get them jobs with Grand Perimeter. How dare they even hint that she should help them! "I guess you won't know until you apply," Maggie responded coolly.

"Could you put in a good word for us?"

The old Maggie would have agreed to call the Austin property's personnel manager to recommend her sister seamstresses, because doing things for people gave her pleasure. But in the past few months she'd grown wiser. She now knew her friendship was something to value. She wasn't obligated to extend her good will and her heart to everybody.

Kayla, Desiree, and Juliana were people users. Not only did Maggie not owe them an entree to the hotel personnel manager, she wouldn't recommend them as employees. Why should she wish their condescending attitude on a staff that worked as a cohesive, companionable unit?

"Tell you what," Maggie replied by way of compromise. "If you're serious, I'll let them know you'll be applying. But you'll have to sell yourselves. I'm not sure how much longer I'll be working for the chain anyway."

Kayla shot Maggie a frosty glance. "Thanks. For nothing."

"You're welcome," she replied. "For roughly the same."

Miss Caroline poked her heard around the doorway to her office. "Maggie, phone for you."

Maggie's hands stilled on the taffeta. Was it Jack? "Who is it?"

"Sandi Johnston."

Sandi was the morning talk show host and noon news anchor for the local ABC-TV affiliate.

"Tell her I'll have to get back to her," Maggie said and slipped the tapered sleeve of the red gown under the pressure foot.

"She insists on speaking with you now. She wants to interview you on the noon news."

"I'm sorry," Maggie said without looking up. "Tell her I can't right now. I've got a fitting for this dress at noon, and I still have to set in the sleeves, line the bodice, and put in the zipper."

"Kayla could finish it for you," Miss Caroline offered.

By now Kayla was back at her work station. She was taking out her pique at Maggie's refusal, by stomping on the power fabric feed. She was sewing so fast, her machine's motor was transforming the lubricating oil into acrid-smelling smoke. At Miss Caroline's offer, her back stiffened visibly. Her machine fell silent.

Oh, no, Kayla wasn't going to finish this dress. In her current mood, she might sew the sleeve of Maggie's garment closed. "I'm not in the mood to be interviewed anyway," Maggie explained to her boss. "Tell Sandi I'll call her this afternoon."

"Don't forget to mention the Couturier during your interview," Miss Caroline admonished her, "and I won't dock you for the time you miss."

"Thanks," Maggie grumbled and wished she could tell Miss Caroline what to do with her time card.

On the flight home from Seattle, though, Maggie had taken a critical look at her situation. Sure Raleigh had agreed to keep her and Jack on under the terms Maggie had dictated. But once he discussed their verbal contract with Armand, the two crafty hotel execs might figure out the truth. She'd been bluffing about threatening to file sexual harassment charges against Raleigh.

She would never file those charges. Even though she had done nothing to encourage Raleigh's advances, in the attendant publicity he no doubt would make her look as if she had used him to climb the celebrity ladder. She didn't want or need the sensational character assassination that would be played out in the media with Armand's slick assistance.

There would be no winners in the mud-slinging, least of all Jack. He needed a dependable reputation if he wanted to land that job with *Affluence* magazine.

All Maggie wanted was Jack's faith in her, his proposal for marriage. The promise of a future together, nurturing the children their union and passion for each other would produce. That and her own design boutique.

So Miss Caroline's was her safety net. If Grand Perimeter dumped her before she earned another month's appearance fees, her steady seamstress salary would pay her bills. She could sell a few designs through her aunt and eventually accumulate what she needed to open her boutique.

Since she'd shared her dream of several years with Jack, she felt like he was part of it. But would he ever be?

The thought of a future without him was as bleak as the steel gray sky outside the window.

"Jack? Jack? Are you there? If you are, will you please pick up the damned phone. I've got to talk to you about the Aspen specs."

Jack lay in his bed, his hands crossed behind his head, gaining buckets of satisfaction from the irritation in Armand Foster's voice.

Aspen tomorrow, with Maggie. Jack had managed to avoid her all week, but now they'd be thrown together for three days—and nights. How could he ignore the need to lay claim to her body that had made him grouchy all week?

"I'll FAX you the specs this afternoon. And by the way, you and Maggie'd better get some après-ski boots. They've had a foot of snow since last night. The tickets will be waiting for you at the airport, same as usual. If you have any questions, give me a call."

Maggie could wear her Doc Martens, if she wanted to, Jack thought. Wouldn't that be a laugh. Cinderella Girl in combat boots.

The vision of Maggie in her comfy old boots gave Jack an unexpected rush of pleasure. What a fool he'd been not to see past her uninspiring attire to the lovely, passionate woman she was. Now, mostly because of him, she was caught up in appearances—pretentiousness that just didn't fit the Maggie he knew.

The logic behind that thinking prompted questions that had haunted him since Sunday in the limousine. What if he had misinterpreted her reasons for staying on with the hotel indefinitely? Her change of mind had been mysteriously abrupt. Was it possible she was hiding something from him? Did she want what he wanted—to tell the hotel to stick their Cinderella Girl promotions sideways so she and Jack could get back to the business of really living?

As before, he arrived at no startling revelations. But the wondering was driving him crazy. If Maggie wasn't the one for him, he had to know now. If she was going to gradually slip away from him, he might as well suffer a broken heart now and get the fracturing process behind him.

But how to pose the question so he could make himself perfectly clear?

His first smile in days toyed with the corners of his mouth. He yanked on his sweat pants and grabbed the key to Maggie's apartment.

When he walked in, Homer leapt off the couch back and trotted straight to Jack, his tail held high. Jack scooped him up and tucked Homer's head under his chin. "Hey, boy, miss me?"

Homer's purr motor kicked into high gear. He lifted his head and gave Jack's chin a sandpapery swipe.

"Yeah, me, too. Listen, I got to have your help. If we're successful, one day soon you can sleep with both Maggie and me. Well, some nights anyway."

Eighteen

For all these months Jack had avoided entering the lair of womanhood called Miss Caroline's.

For one thing, he figured he'd run into a bunch of snotty society shrews who would remind him of his mother. He'd also been sure he couldn't trust himself to behave civilly if he walked in and found Maggie's sister seamstresses cutting into her again.

Now that he was there, he knew he'd been smart to trust his instincts and stay away. The damned carpet was pink. Pink! The cloying scent of rose oil hung over the stuffy reception area like a putrid, wet quilt. The morning sun streamed through panels of lace with cutesy hearts and porky cherubs and splayed on the floral wallpaper in squiggly, distorted blotches.

Everywhere Jack looked he saw horizontal shelf crud—pictures in gilt frames, dead flowers in fancy glass bowls—Maggie called it potpourri—and antique lamps whose shades were dripping with beaded fringe.

No wonder Miss Caroline's seamstresses were always at each other.

Jack cleared his throat and waited for some-one—Maggie maybe?—to acknowledge the tinkle of the stupid bell he'd tripped when he walked in the front door.

From what appeared to be a workroom in the back filtered a montage of female voices. Figuring he might as well scope out the joint before he walked in, Jack edged closer to a lace curtain that partitioned off the reception area. He discovered a lively conversation in progress.

"I can't believe she won't help us get jobs at the hotel. I mean, what's it to her?"

"Maybe we should have asked her to lunch before this. It was kind of obvious, doing it on the same day we wanted her to put in a good word for us at the hotel."

"I think we can forget getting any help from her. Did you see the look on her face when you asked her? I didn't think Maggie had it in her."

"Where is she anyway?"

"Still upstairs, with her fitting."

"If she doesn't hurry and get down here, she won't have a prayer of finishing that gown by tomorrow. She's leaving at noon to catch a flight. You know what that means."

"Overtime," the three women moaned in unison.

"It must be a real comedown to be on 'Lifestyles of the Rich and Famous,' then have to sew ball gowns for people like that chunk she's fitting upstairs."

"That chunk's worth several million."

"I don't care how much she's worth, she's fifty pounds overweight."

Jack cleared his throat and drew the lace-paneled

partition aside. Three women—Kayla, Desiree, and Juliana, he was betting—jumped as if they'd been caught loafing on the job. The redhead—Kayla?—folded a newspaper and handed it to the other two. "May we help you, Mr. . . . ?"

"Lewis. Jack Lewis. I'm here to see Maggie. You must be Kayla."

"You know my name?" Kayla purred.

"Yeah. Maggie's told me about all of you."

"How nice," the ultra bitch responded.

That's what you think, sister.

From behind Jack came a rustle of fabric. The light floral scent Jack would know anywhere wafted over his shoulder. Clutching the brown grocery sack tightly in his fist, Jack turned around.

It was Maggie all right. The sight of her had his pulse leaping. "How you doing, Mags?"

"Okay," she said with a shrug he figured she meant to be casual. But the high color in her cheeks, the flash of warmth in her eyes betrayed her. "You'd better come back. I can't talk right now. I'm awfully busy."

Despite the tone of her reception, hope flickered in Jack's tight chest. When Maggie got that look in her eyes, she couldn't hide what was in her heart.

She skirted past him and took a seat at a sewing machine.

"I only need a minute," Jack insisted, following her.

She cast a furtive glance at the back of the room. Jack noticed an office there and figured it to be the boss lady's den.

"If it's really urgent, all right," Maggie replied and motioned him forward with her hand. "Sorry, though. I'll have to sew while you talk. My client's upstairs, waiting for this alteration."

Jack thought about leaving, but dismissed the idea. He wanted an answer, and he wanted it now while he had his courage screwed to speak his mind.

He moved to stand in front of her. She slid what looked like a bright red tent on her machine's cabinet and flipped a lever, pulled on a thread.

She didn't even look up at him. Jack almost said to hell with it and walked out. But he couldn't go on wondering if God had blessed him with Maggie, or cursed him with hope. He dug into his sack and pulled out her boot. "I'm looking for the woman this shoe fits."

Maggie's eyes slanted the briefest of gazes to her ugly black boot. Frowning, she looked up at Jack. "That isn't a shoe. It's a boot. It's mine. Where did you find it? I thought I left it in my closet."

"Maybe you'd better try it on to be sure."

"For Pete's sake, Jack. I told you. I'm busy." She inclined her head at the dragon lady's office. "I'm on the time clock."

"So get wild and crazy and clock out for a couple of minutes." All too aware that the other three women weren't even trying to disguise their curiosity, Jack gave them something to gawk at. He lowered one knee to the floor and turned Maggie's boot around so she could slip her foot into it. "Upsy-daisy."

"Jack, I don't have time to play games. Miss

Caroline will have a fit if she walks in and finds me talking to you when a client is waiting for me upstairs."

"Screw Miss Caroline."

"Excuse me?"

"The boot?"

Maggie threw her hands up. "Okay, okay. If it'll get you to leave, I'll drop what I'm doing. Whatever's on your mind must be more important than anything I could possibly be responsible for."

She swung her body around, slipped off her high heel and reached for the boot.

"Oh, no, let me," Jack insisted, holding the boot in his hand. "I think I should rephrase my earlier statement. I'm not looking for the woman this boot fits. I'm looking for the woman who fits this boot."

"Jack, maybe you ought to go back home and go to bed. You're not making much sense." She slipped her slender foot into the boot. "See, I told you. It's mine."

"You're sure."

"I told you I was. You'll excuse me now?"

"Maggie, dammit, you're missing the point."

"The point is, you're about to get me fired."

"I sincerely doubt that. This is the point you're missing." Jack reached into his pocket, pulled out the black velvet ring box and snapped it open. "Or about one hundred points to be more accurate."

The morning light slanting through the window struck the marquise diamond and sent rainbow-colored flecks dancing about the room.

What little pretense of work that was being perpetuated halted abruptly. Murmurs of rhapsodic female appreciation betrayed the eavesdropping seamstresses.

Maggie's boot clumped to the floor. Her mouth fell open. Her eyes misted over. "Jack?"

He swallowed hard. Twice. "Maggie Kincaid, this is a clunky boot. It hides your great ankles. It makes me think of John Wayne and Army movies. But it represents something else."

"What, Jack? What does it represent?"

"The woman I fell in love with. She's sweet and she's down to earth. She's got her feet—sorry, her boots—rooted in Texas soil. She wants a home and a family like I do. I'm asking that woman to marry me. I want her to be my wife and have my kids. I want her to watch football with me and help me keep black, fuzzy things out of my refrigerator. In return, I promise to love, honor, and sometimes obey her. I promise to forsake all others, except my buddies for poker twice a month, and if she insists, I'll cut back to once. I promise to encourage her and help her realize her dreams. What I've got to know is . . ."

"Yes, Jack, go on," Maggie said, moving to the edge of her chair. "I'm listening."

She was smiling. Her eyes were sparkling. She'd let the red tent dress slide from her fingers to the floor. She slipped her hand beneath Jack's and joined it with his. The touch of her soft skin against his palm broke through his stubborn resistance. They had made mind-boggling love in a dozen cities. But the way he felt when they joined hands told Jack more eloquently than whispered words of passion that his love knew no conditions.

Maggie's smile was so tender Jack knew all she'd have to do is say yes, and he'd learn to live with Maggie, the celebrity, Maggie the designer, Maggie whatever-the-hell-she-wanted-to be.

"Jack, you were saying?"

"Too damned much, as usual. Well? Are you willing to become Mrs. Jack Lewis?" He held up one hand. "Before you answer that, I want you to know I see nothing wrong with you calling your designs Maggie Kincaid Originals."

"Oh, Jack, I was wondering if you'd ever ask me. Yes!" she squealed and flung her arms around his neck.

Jack planted one hell of a kiss on her lips, thinking what fun he would have making her a momma. Hardly able to contain his desire to make love to her right there, he slipped the ring on her finger.

Maggie curled her fingers around his, positively glowing. "I'd like you to finish your sentence. The one that began, 'What I want to know is . . .' "

"Forget it. It isn't important anymore. Come on, let's get out of here and celebrate."

"If I'm going to be your wife, I need to know what's bothering you, Jack Lewis. Especially if you have any reservations about us getting married."

"Ah, Maggie . . ."

"Jack," she insisted stubbornly.

"Okay, if you must know, I was going to say, I

want to know if you're still the woman I fell in love with. The woman who wore that boot."

"No, I'm not, Jack. That woman couldn't speak her mind. She let people run over her. The new me knows what she wants, and she's going for it. You do want that woman, don't you?" she asked guardedly.

"Hell, yes. I'm proud of you for learning how to stand up for yourself. What I meant was, I'm not too hot on the idea of you flitting around the country every weekend. The way I see it, a celebrity mom could be hard on kids—not to mention her husband. But, hell, Maggie, I love you so much, the truth is, I'll learn to live with it, if that's what makes you happy."

Maggie wanted to tell Jack she only extended her term as the Cinderella Girl to help him. But, as her mother had advised her in a phone call late Sunday evening, while she advocated honesty between husband and wife, there were some things a woman shouldn't tell a man.

Jack deserved to think the hotel decided to keep him on because of his extraordinary talent. Raleigh wouldn't have thought of firing him if he hadn't let his desire for a young woman cloud his thinking. Maggie was so proud of Jack, so much in love with him, her heart was bursting with joy.

"I guess you won't be too unhappy with me, then, when I tell you I'm retiring as the Cinderella Girl in four months."

"Four?" Jack's face lit up. "That's all?"

"I still plan to do an occasional appearance. I'd like to persuade Grand Perimeter to let me design the clothes for the Cinderella Doll." She bent to whisper in his ear. "Of course, I still want to open my own design boutique."

"That reminds me." Jack dug into his hip pocket and pulled out a folded envelope. "I got this fat check from the hotel this morning. I'm two months ahead on my bills. I've put some money aside. I'm getting more work than I can shake a stick at." He put the check in her hand. "Here. Keep this. It ought to be enough so you can open your shop right away and quit this joint."

"Does he have any brothers?" Desiree interjected from behind them.

Caroline McCann ventured out of her office. "Oh, hello, Mr. Lewis. Maggie, I just had a call from one of your clients. She saw you on 'Lifestyles' last weekend and absolutely adored the gown you were wearing. So much so that she called the producer, and the hotel office in Seattle. She got one of the secretaries to remember you'd told her you'd designed and made the gown. She was wondering if you could make it for her in her size."

"Tell her if she's a size seven, she's welcome to it," Maggie replied. "Tell her it's a Maggie Kincaid Original, and my price is a thousand dollars. If she wears a seven narrow shoe, I'll throw in a pair of glass slippers."

"*Your* price?" Maggie's boss asked stiffly.

"That's right. I designed the gown and sewed it on my own time."

"From fabric *I* gave you."

"I earned that fabric. It was part of my pay for modeling in the fashion show."

"I'm afraid we'll have to discuss this. Please, step into my office."

"There's nothing to discuss," Maggie replied, and mumbled under her breath, "Boy, this is going to be fun." She lifted her chin and spoke loudly, confidently. "Caroline, I'm tired of designing clothes and letting you take credit for them. I'm tired of working hours I don't get paid for. I'm going out on my own."

"You—you're what?"

"I'm quitting."

"You can't walk out of here, not now. There's work to do. Deadlines to meet."

Jack stuck his foot in the fray. "And a lady upstairs who's probably getting tired of waiting." He scooped Maggie into his arms. "So you'd better get somebody on this red dress quick. We're out of here."

"Jack, put me down," Maggie told him, wriggling in his arms. "I need to get my things."

"Uh-uh. No way." He tightened his hold on her and headed for the front door. "You can get them later."

"Where are we going?"

He gave her a shuttered look. "Can't you guess?"

A warm, honeyed feeling filled Maggie's abdomen. She wrapped her arms around Jack's neck and didn't look back as her Prince Charming carried her into their future.

Outside she stuck her foot out and angled it.

"I always did love these boots," she said and gave Jack a loud smooch on his cheek. "How do you think they'll look with maternity dresses?"

Dear Reader,

As a child, I loved the Saturday movies, where we were blessed with good-triumphs-over-evil serials and full-length movies. When the downtrodden hero finally got his fill, thrust out his chin, and said, "No more!" the audience cheered out loud. Although I yelled as loud as anybody, my enthusiasm was tempered by one disturbing realization. Too few of the protagonists who took control of their lives were women.

Cinderella bugged me especially. Why did she depend on her fairy godmother to free her from her stepmother's cruel grasp? Raised by nurturing parents to believe I could do anything that burned in my heart, I wanted to pull Cindy aside and give her a good lesson in self-determination. Thanks to Denise Little's enthusiasm for *Glass Slippers,* I can finally set Cindy straight.

When plotting Maggie Kincaid's story, I immediately decided Texas would be her home state. Lone Star women, whether natives or transplants, open their hearts and their homes with warmth and Southern hospitality. But, like my Dallas daughter, Lisa Baker, they tackle their '90s lives with fierce grit and determination that is the legacy of the state's pioneer women forebears. Some just need a gentle shove in the direction of fulfillment. Like Maggie Kincaid. I hope you've enjoyed her story.

**If you liked this book, be sure to look for others
in the *Denise Little Presents* line:**